The Adventures of SUPER DIAPER BABY

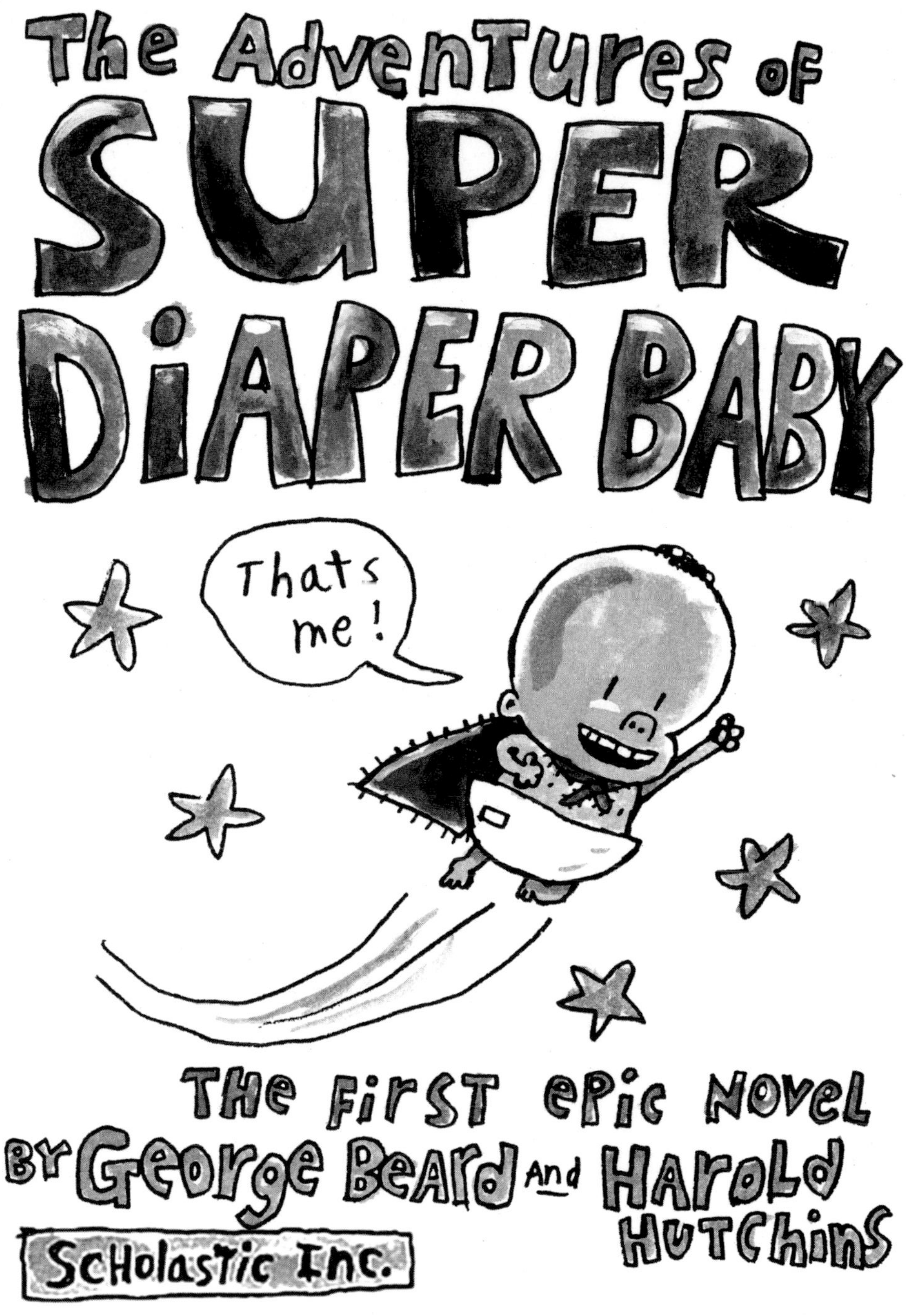
Thats me!

THE FIRST EPIC NOVEL

BY George Beard And Harold Hutchins

Scholastic Inc.

For my mom and Dad
— G.R.B.
To mom and Heidi
— H.M.H.

For information regarding permission, please write to:
Permissions Department, Scholastic Inc.,
557 Broadway, New York, NY 10012.

Be sure to check out
Dav Pilkey's Extra-Crunchy Web Site O' Fun at
www.pilkey.com.

Library of Congress Control Number: 2001043899
ISBN 978-0-545-66544-5
10 9   17 18

Printed in the United States of America   23
This edition first printing, July 2014

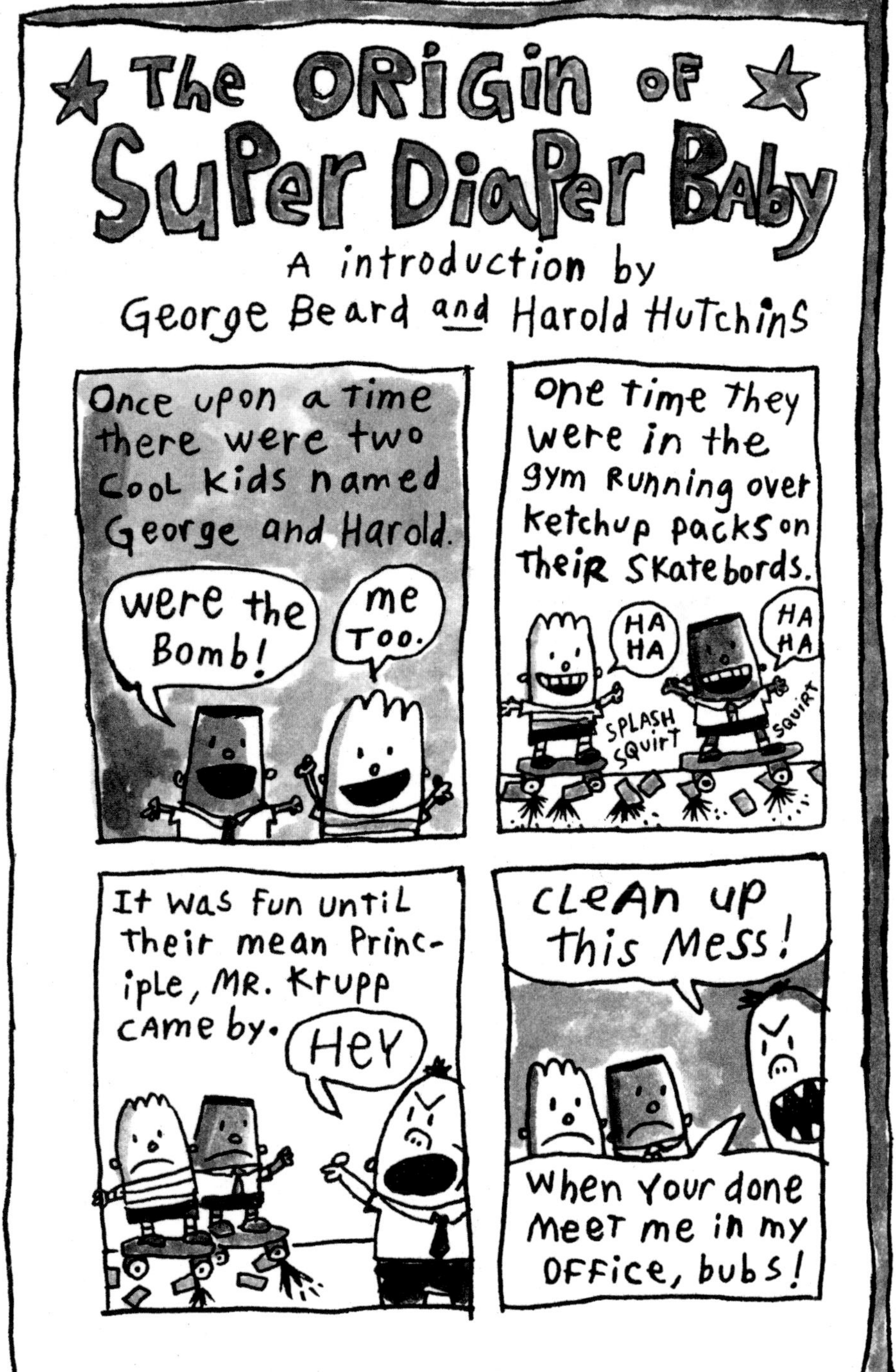
The ORIGIN of
Super Diaper Baby
A introduction by
George Beard and Harold Hutchins
Once upon a time there were two Cool kids named George and Harold.
were the Bomb!
me Too.
one time they were in the gym Running over ketchup packs on their Skatebords.
HA HA
HA HA
SPLASH
SQUIRT
SQUIRT
It was fun until their mean Princ-iple, MR. Krupp came by.
HEY
CLEAN up this Mess!
When Your done Meet me in my OFFice, bubs!

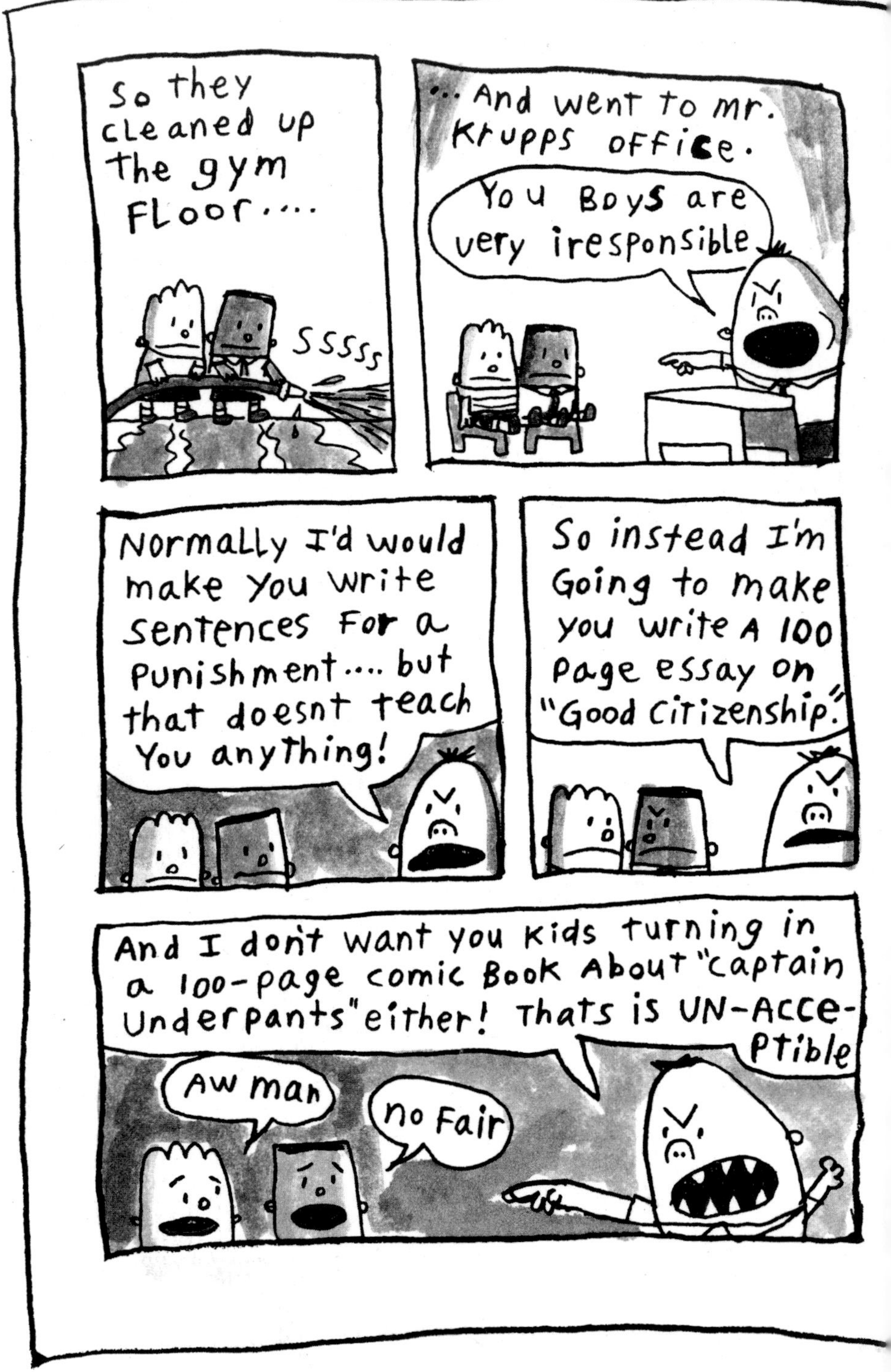
So they cleaned up the gym Floor....
SSSSS
...And went to mr. Krupps office.
You Boys are very iresponsible
Normally I'd would make You write sentences For a punishment.... but that doesnt teach You anything!
So instead I'm Going to make you write A 100 page essay on "Good Citizenship."
And I don't want you kids turning in a 100-page comic Book About "captain Underpants" either! Thats is UN-ACCE-ptible
Aw man
no Fair

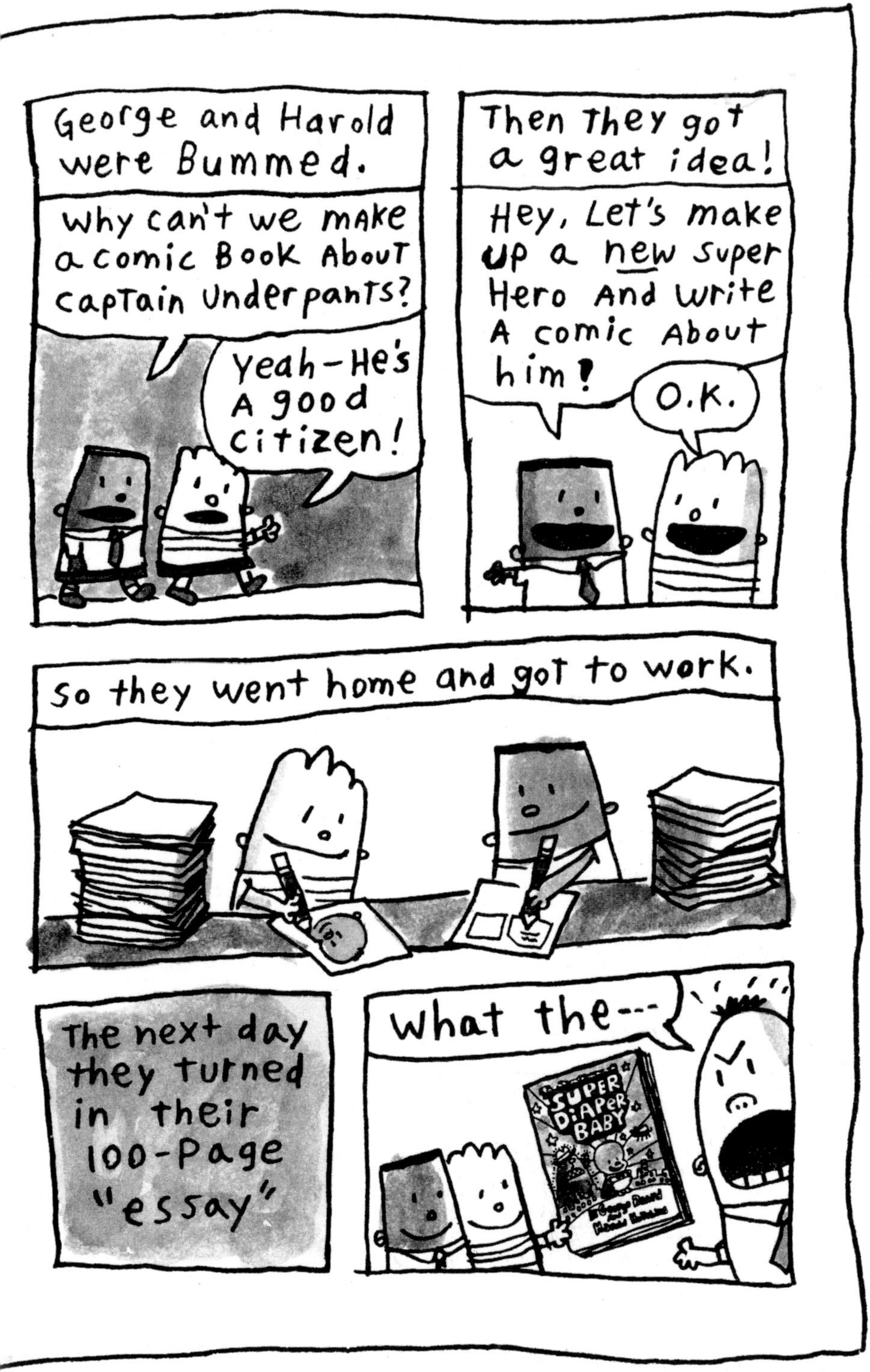
George and Harold were Bummed.
Why can't we make a comic Book About captain Underpants?
Yeah—He's A good citizen!
Then They got a great idea!
Hey, Let's make up a new Super Hero And Write A comic About him!
O.K.
So they went home and got to work.
The next day they turned in their 100-Page "essay"
What the---
SUPER DIAPER BABY

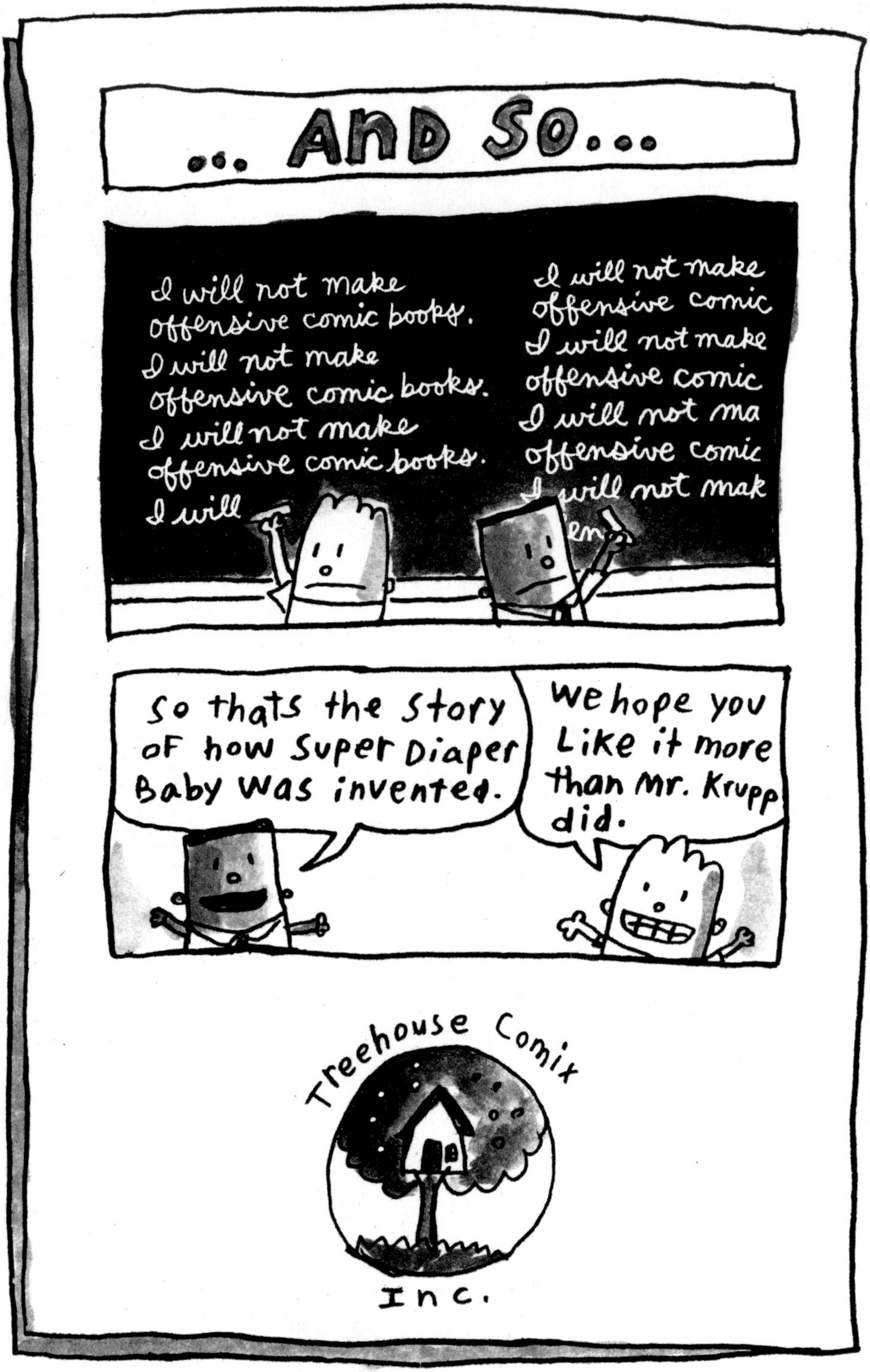
... AND SO...
I will not make offensive comic books. I will not make offensive comic books. I will not make offensive comic books. I will
I will not make offensive comic I will not make offensive comic I will not ma offensive comic I will not mak
So thats the story of how Super Diaper Baby was invented.
We hope you Like it more than Mr. Krupp did.
Treehouse Comix Inc.

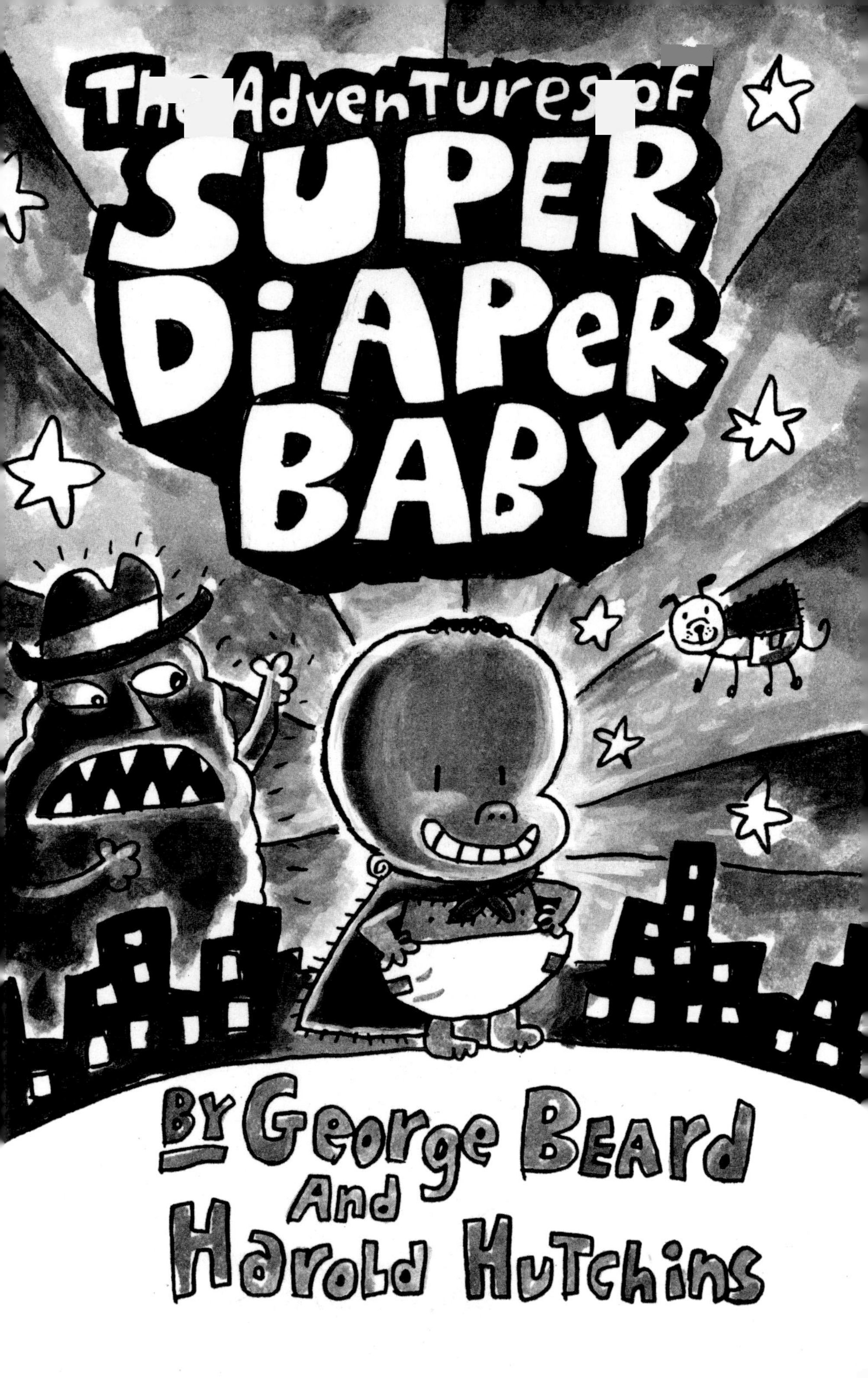
The Adventures of
SUPER DiAPER BABY
By George Beard
And
Harold Hutchins

Chapters

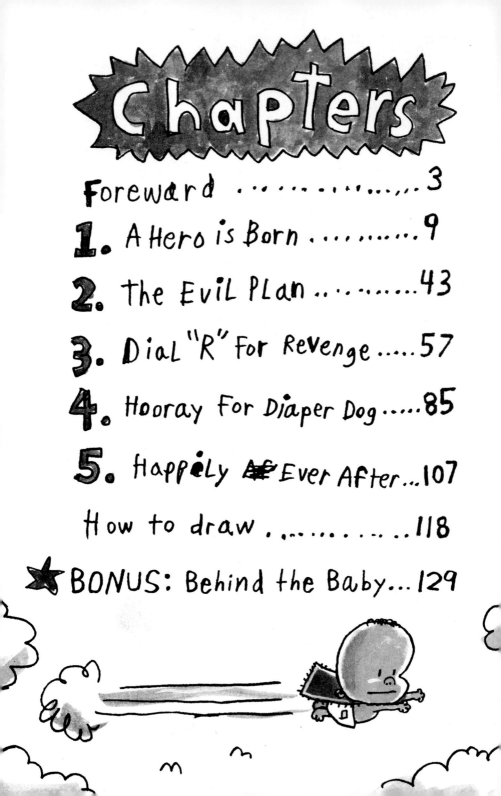

The Advenchers of ☆SUPER☆ DiAPer BABY

CHAPTER 1
"A Hero is Born"

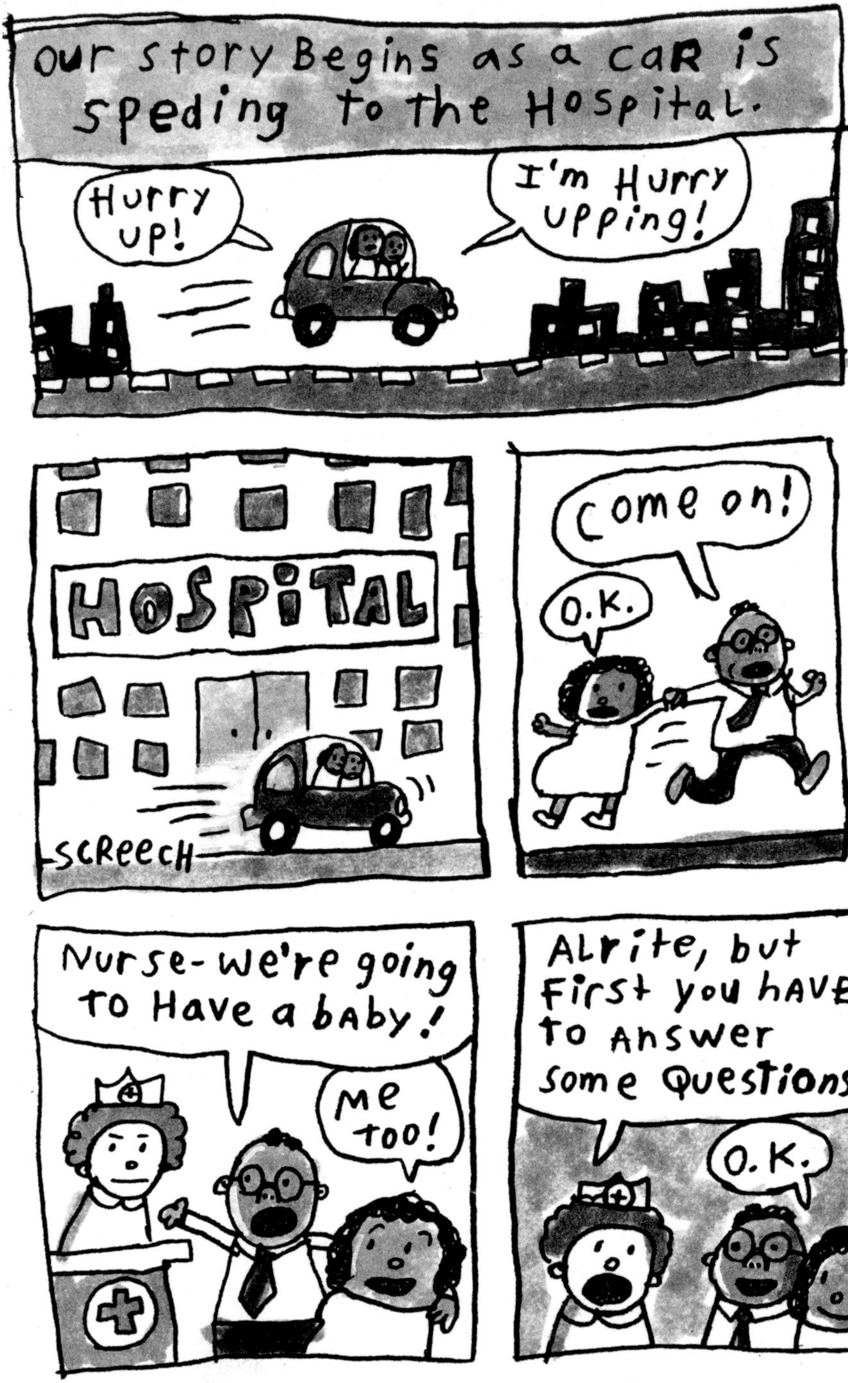
Our story Begins as a caR is speding to the Hospital.
Hurry up!
I'm Hurry upping!
HOSPITAL
SCREECH
Come on!
O.K.
Nurse- we're going to Have a baby!
Me too!
Alrite, but first you HAVE to Answer some Questions
O.K.

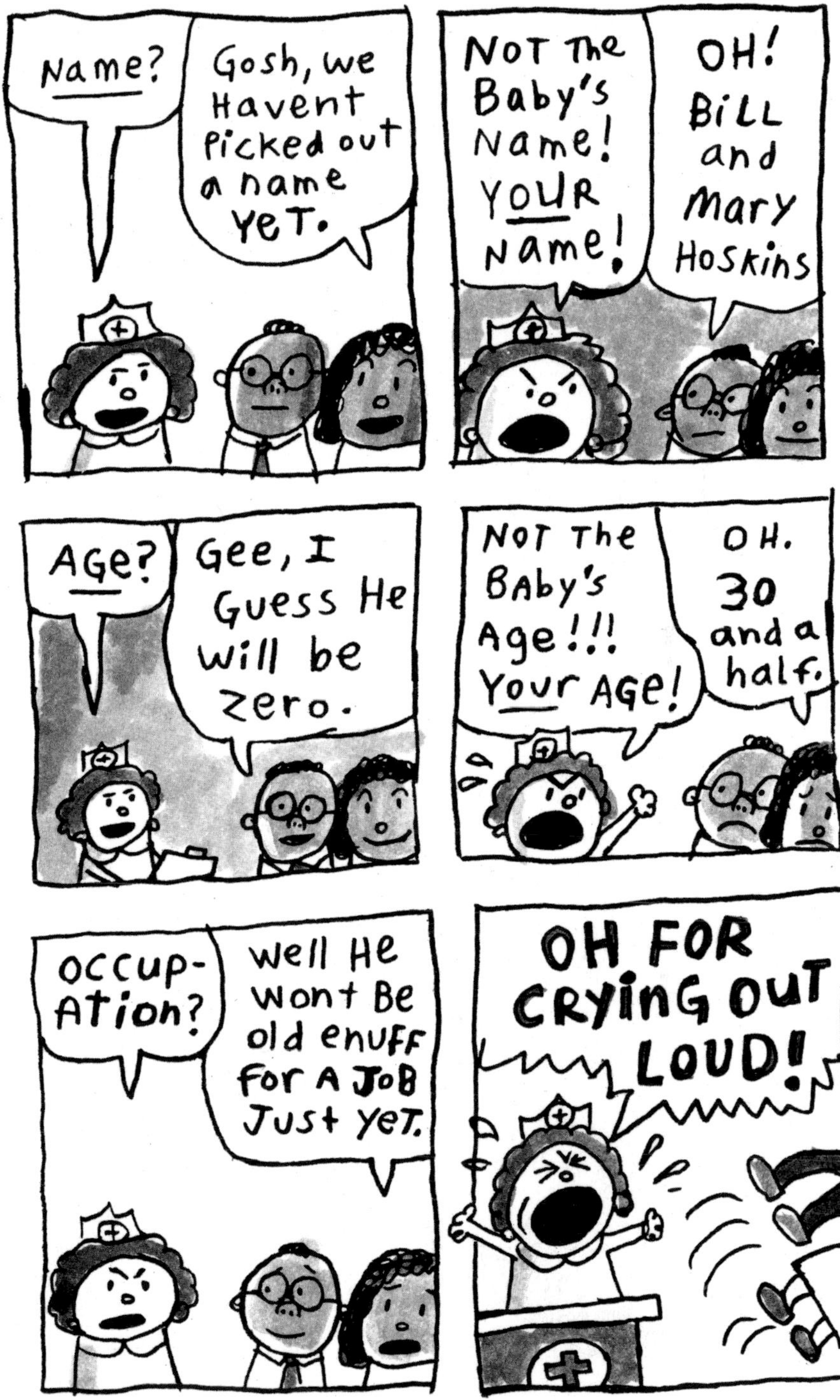
Name?
Gosh, we Havent Picked out a name yet.
Not the Baby's Name! YOUR Name!
OH! Bill and Mary Hoskins
AGE?
Gee, I Guess He will be zero.
Not the Baby's Age!!! Your AGE!
OH. 30 and a half.
Occup-Ation?
Well He wont Be old enuff for A Job Just yet.
OH FOR CRYING OUT LOUD!

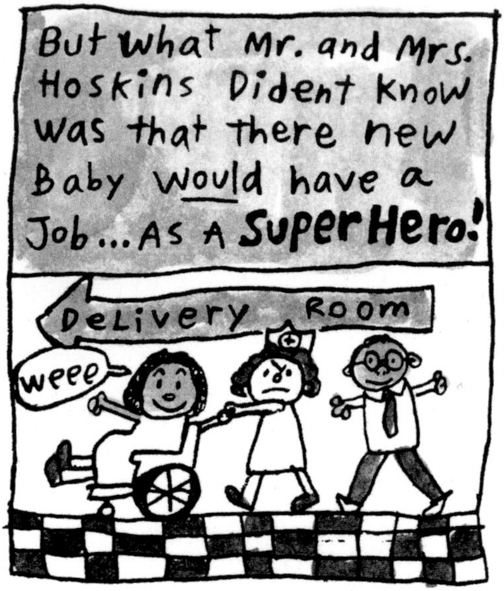
But what Mr. and Mrs. Hoskins Dident know was that there new Baby would have a Job... As a SuperHero!
DeLivery Room
weee

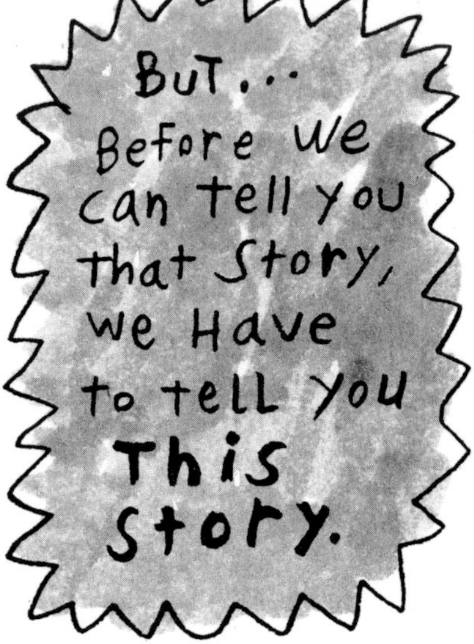
BuT...
Before we can tell you that Story, we Have to tell you This Story.

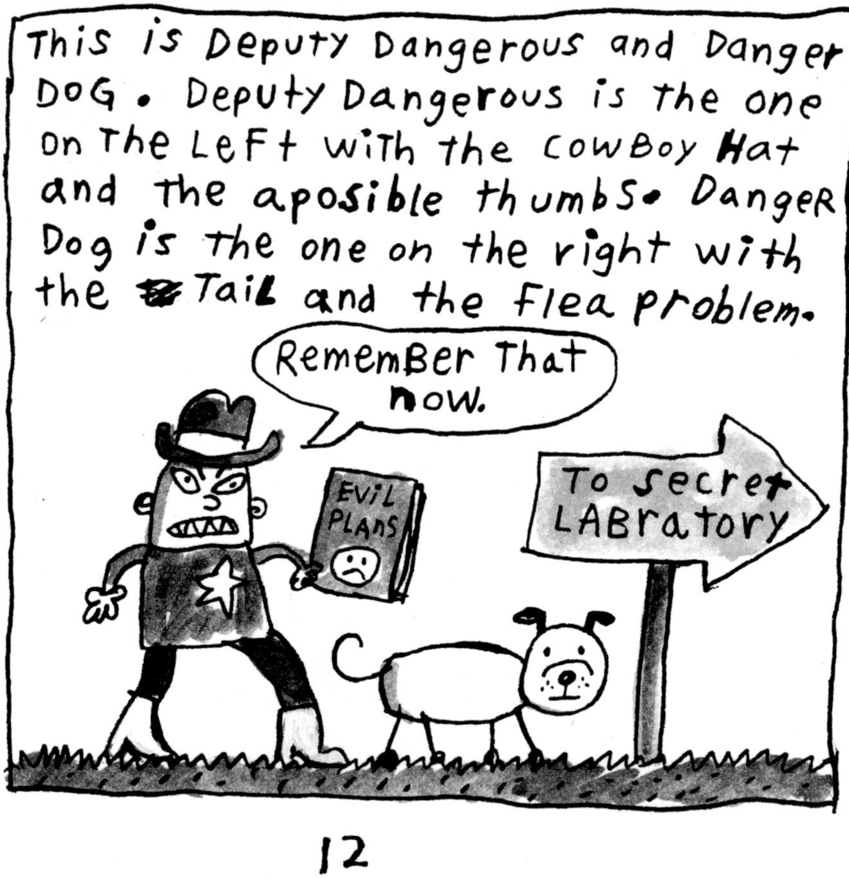
This is Deputy Dangerous and Danger DoG. Deputy Dangerous is the one on The LeFt with the cowBoy Hat and the aposible thumbs. Danger Dog is the one on the right with the Tail and the Flea problem.
RememBer That now.
EviL PLANS
To secret LABratory

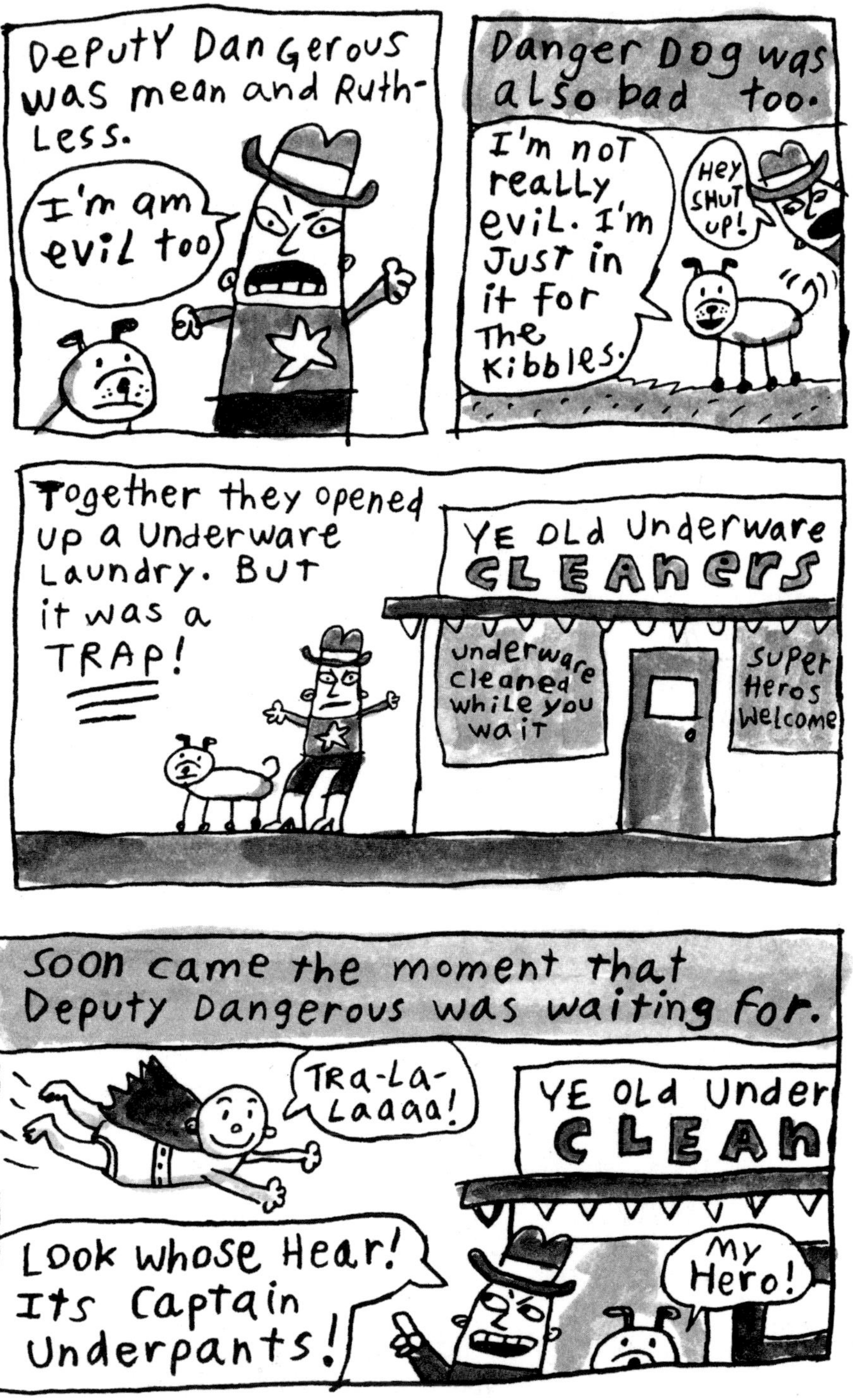
Deputy Dangerous was mean and Ruth-Less.
I'm am evil too
Danger Dog was also bad too.
I'm not really evil. I'm Just in it for The Kibbles.
Hey SHUT up!
Together they opened up a Underware Laundry. BUT it was a TRAP!
YE OLd Underware CLEAners
underware cleaned while you wait
Super Heros Welcome
Soon came the moment that Deputy Dangerous was waiting for.
Tra-La-Laaaa!
YE OLd Under
CLEAn
Look whose Hear! Its Captain Underpants!
My Hero!

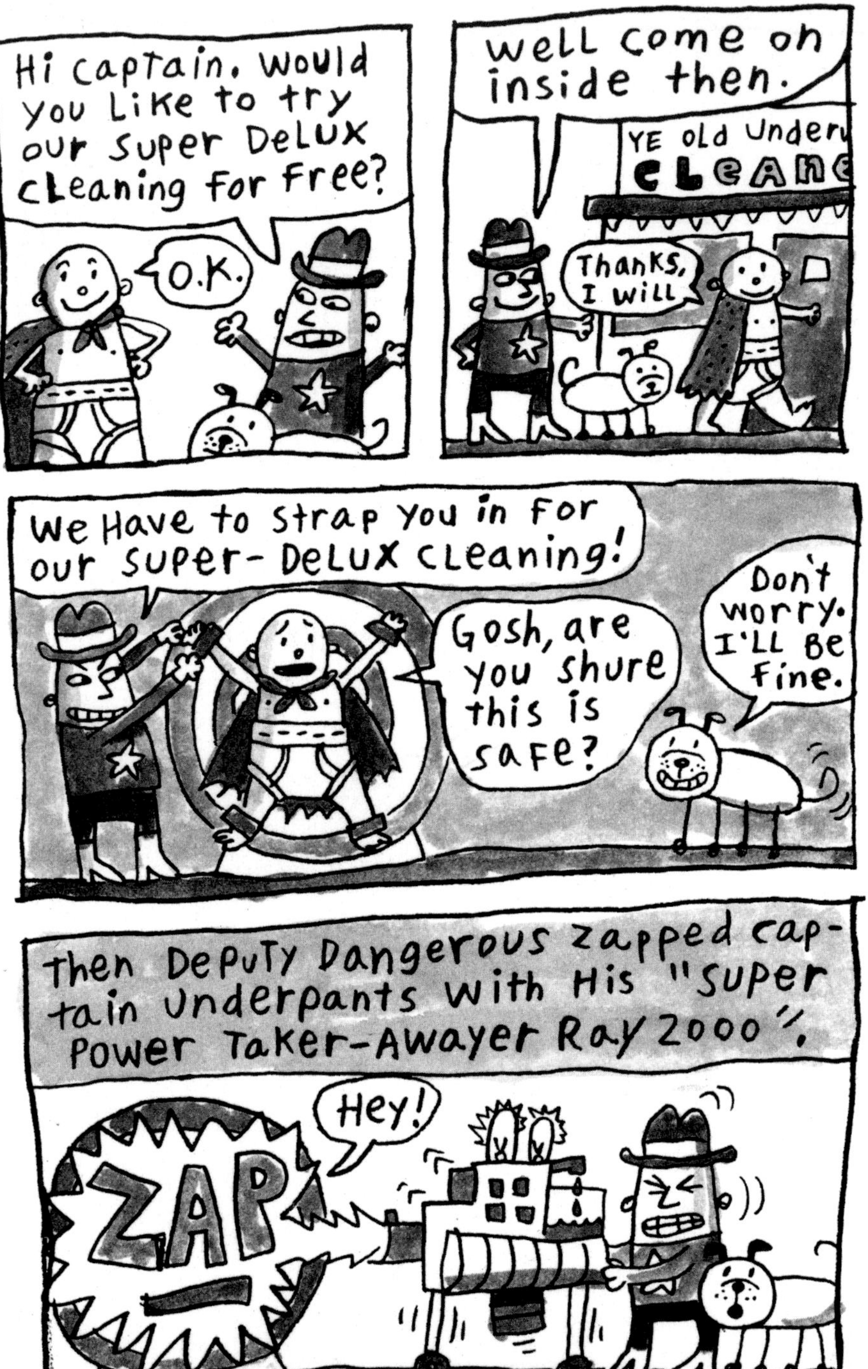
Hi captain. Would you Like to try our Super DeLux cLeaning for free?
O.K.
Well come on inside then.
YE old Underw
CLEANE
Thanks, I will
We Have to strap you in for our super-DeLux cLeaning!
Gosh, are you shure this is safe?
Don't worry. I'LL Be fine.
Then Deputy Dangerous zapped captain Underpants with His "Super Power Taker-Awayer Ray 2000".
Hey!
ZAP

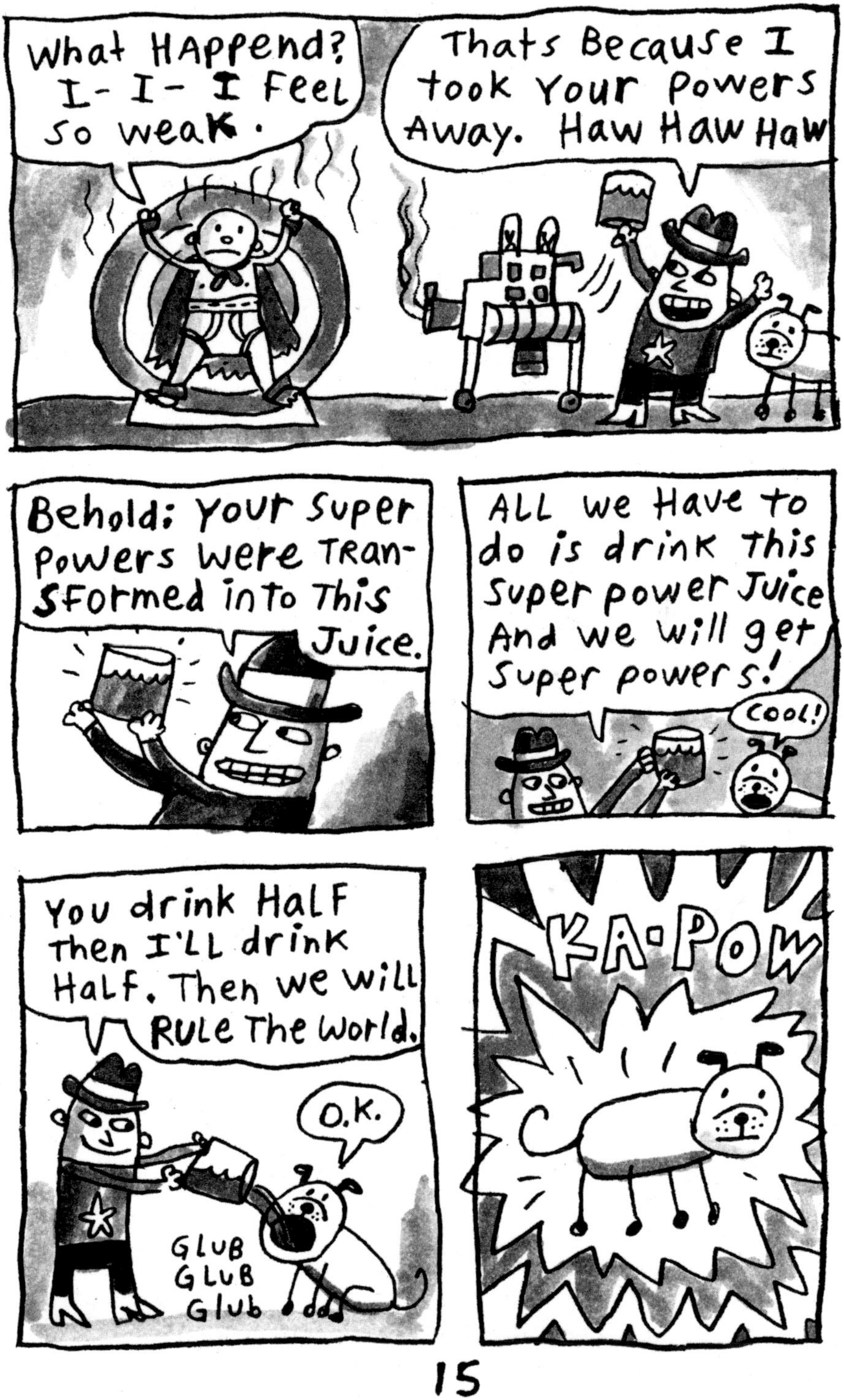
What HAppend? I- I- I Feel so weak.
Thats Because I took Your Powers Away. Haw Haw Haw
Behold: Your Super Powers were Transformed into This Juice.
ALL we Have to do is drink This Super power Juice And we will get Super powers!
COOL!
You drink HalF then I'LL drink HaLF. Then we will RULE The World.
O.K.
GLUB GLUB Glub
KA-POW

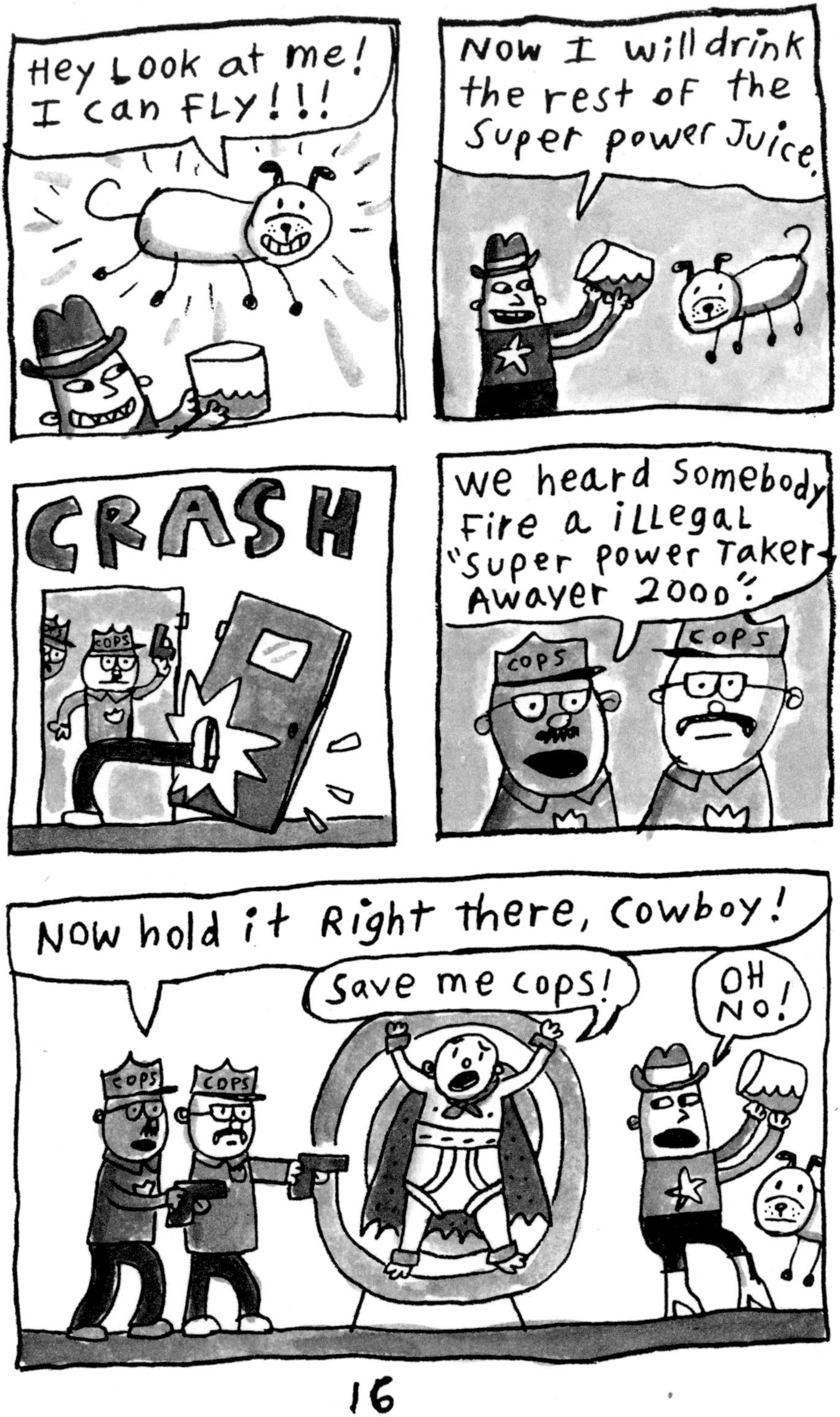
Hey Look at me! I can FLY!!!
Now I will drink the rest of the Super power Juice.
CRASH
COPS
We heard Somebody Fire a iLLegal "Super power Taker-Awayer 2000".
COPS
COPS
Now hold it Right there, Cowboy!
Save me cops!
OH NO!
COPS
COPS

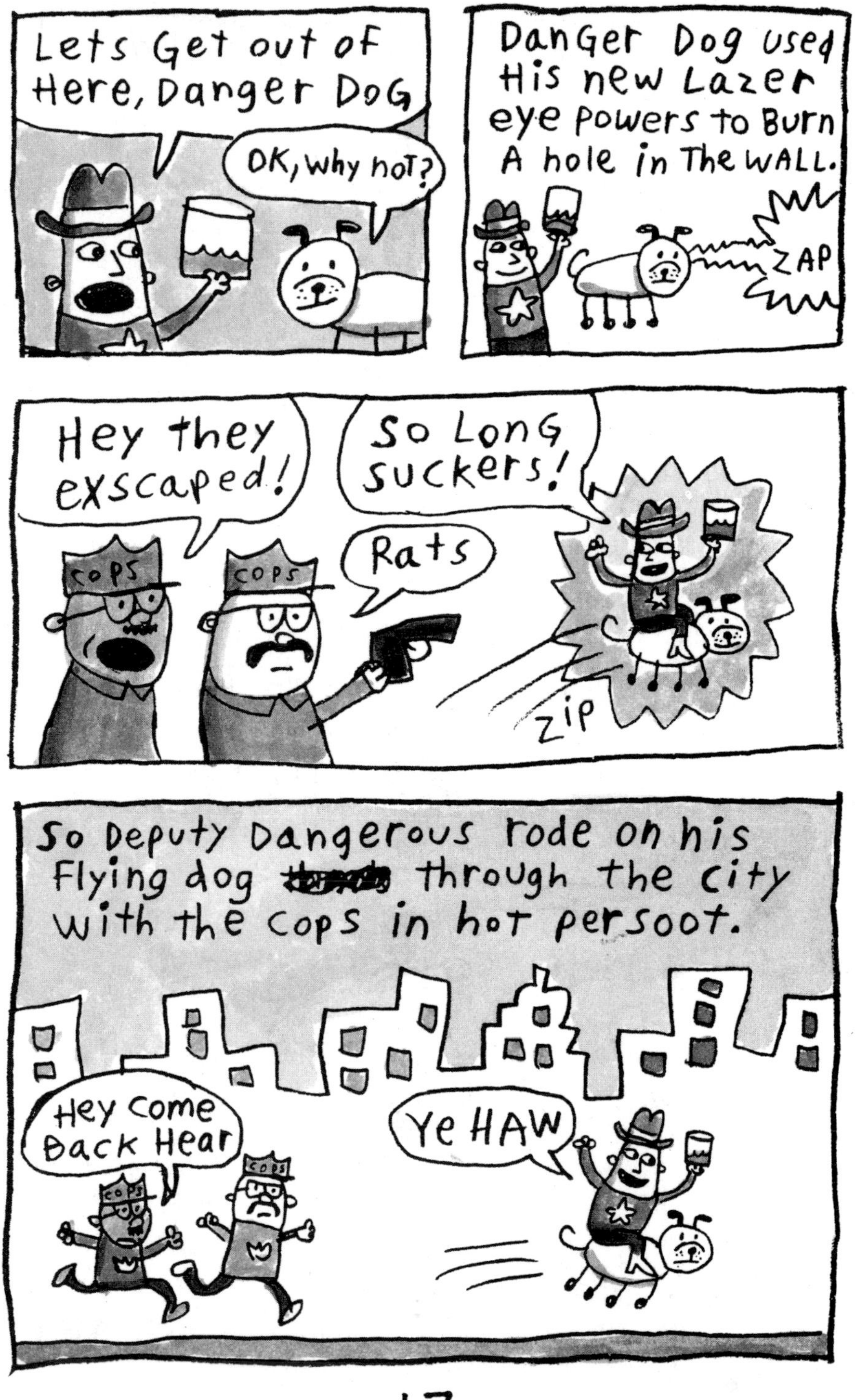
Lets Get out of Here, Danger DoG
OK, Why not?
Danger Dog used His new Lazer eye powers to Burn A hole in The WALL.
ZAP
Hey they exscaped!
So Long suckers!
Rats
COPS
COPS
ZIP
So Deputy Dangerous rode on his Flying dog through the city with the cops in hot persoot.
Hey Come Back Hear
Ye HAW
COPS
COPS

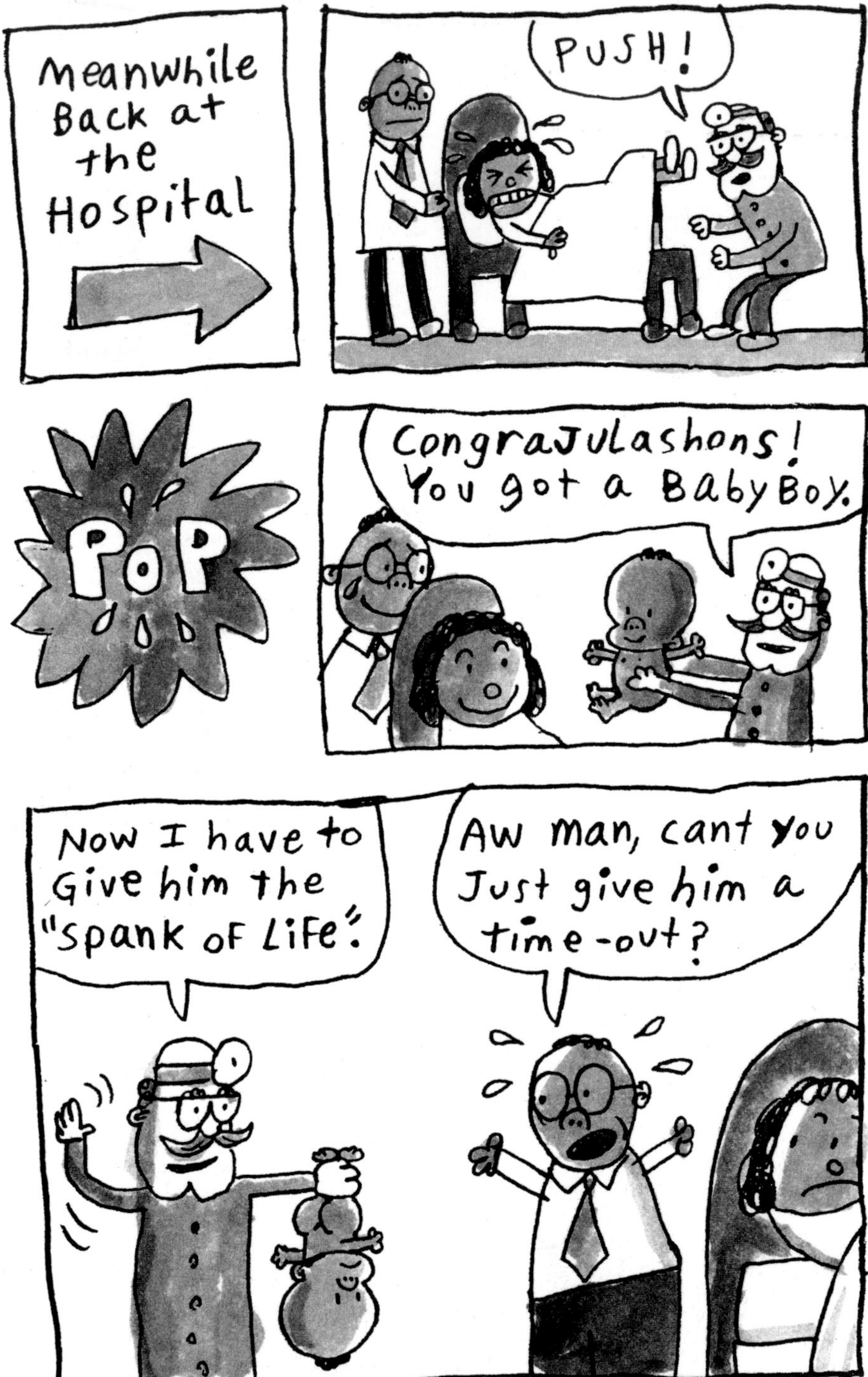
Meanwhile Back at the Hospital
PUSH!
POP
CongraJULashons! You got a BabyBoy.
Now I have to Give him the "spank of Life".
Aw man, cant you Just give him a time-out?

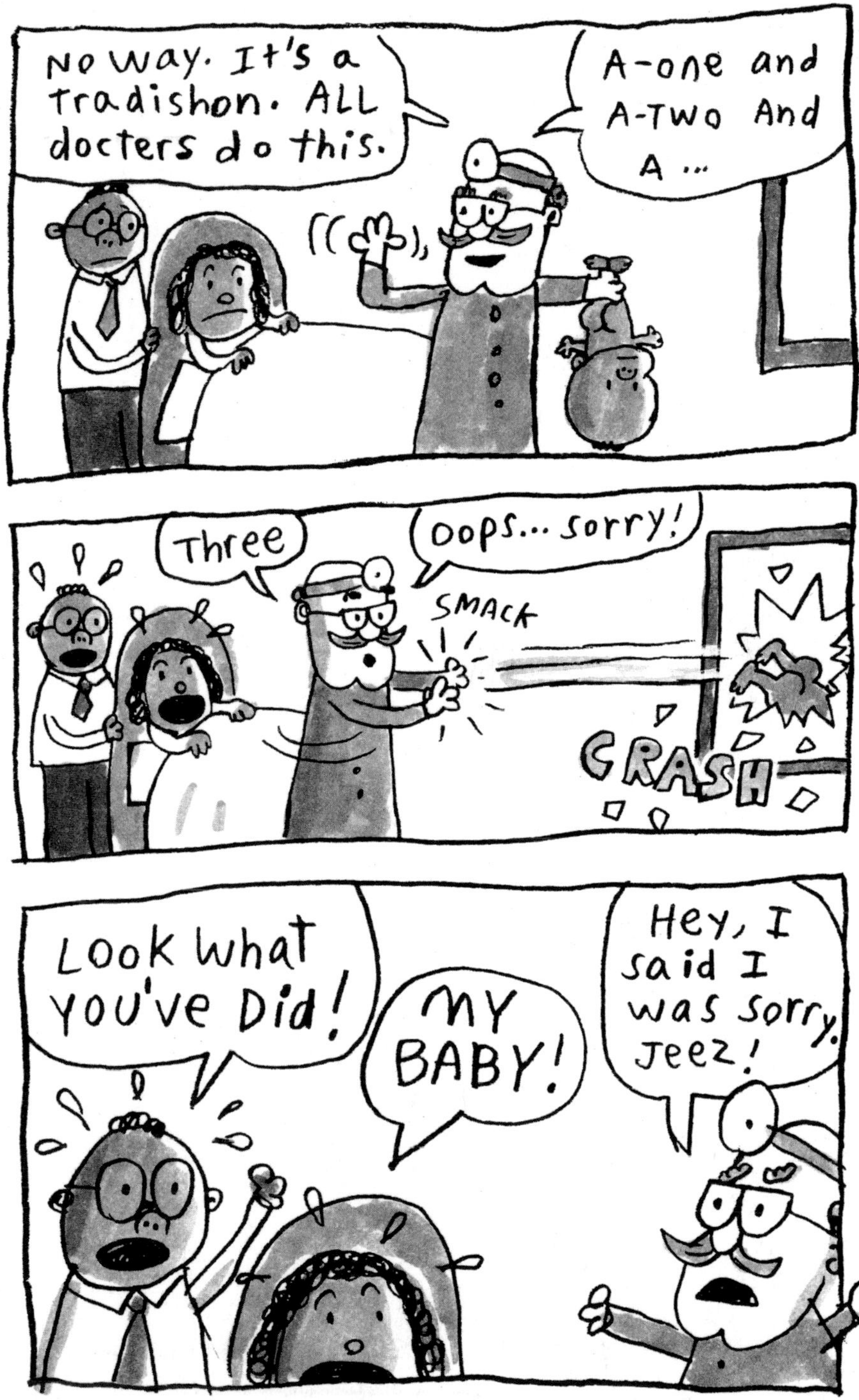
No way. It's a tradishon. ALL docters do this.
A-one and A-TWO And A ...
Three
OOPS... sorry!
SMACK
CRASH
LOOK what you've Did!
MY BABY!
Hey, I said I was sorry. Jeez!

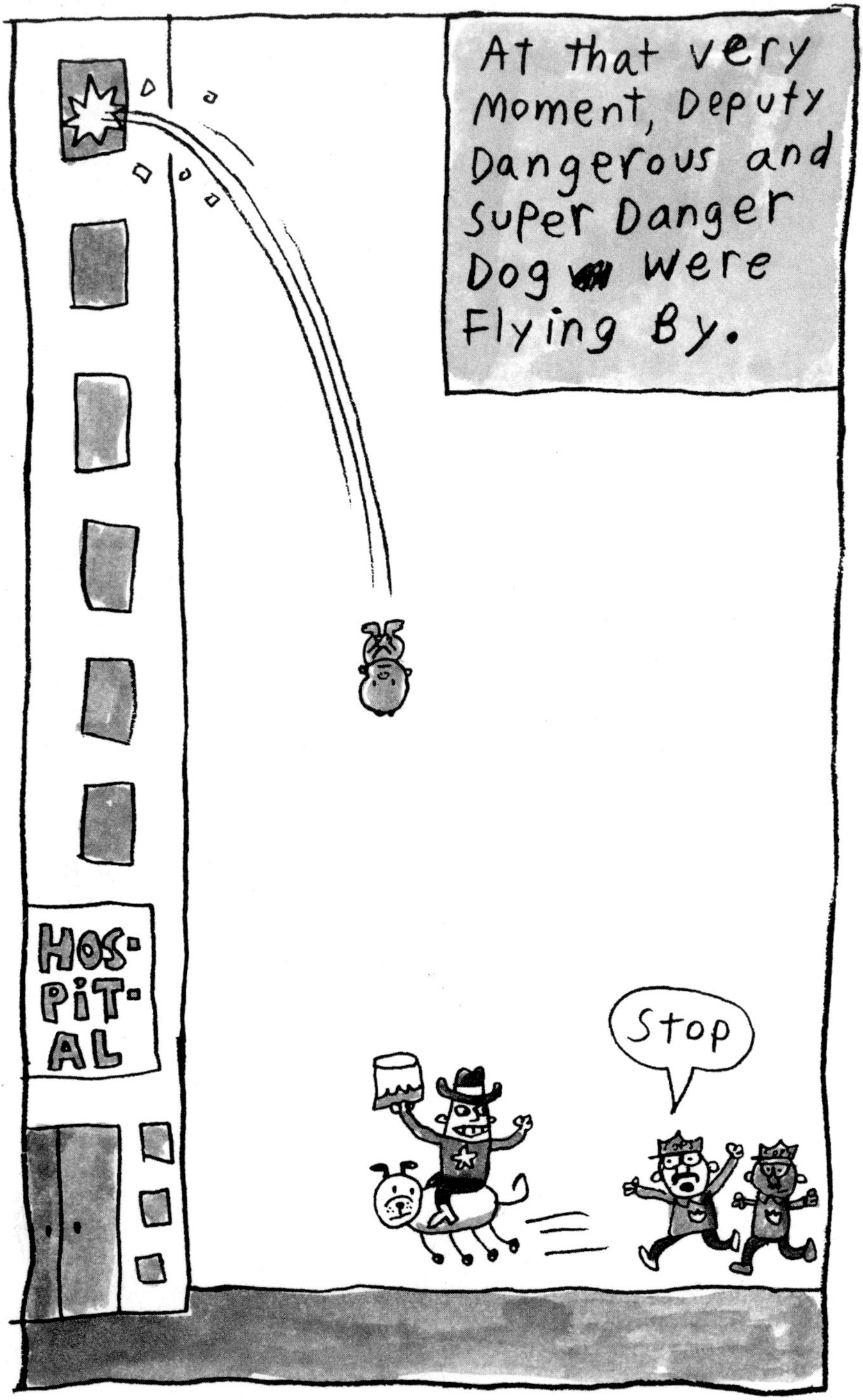
At that very Moment, Deputy Dangerous and Super Danger Dog were Flying By.
HOS-PIT-AL
Stop

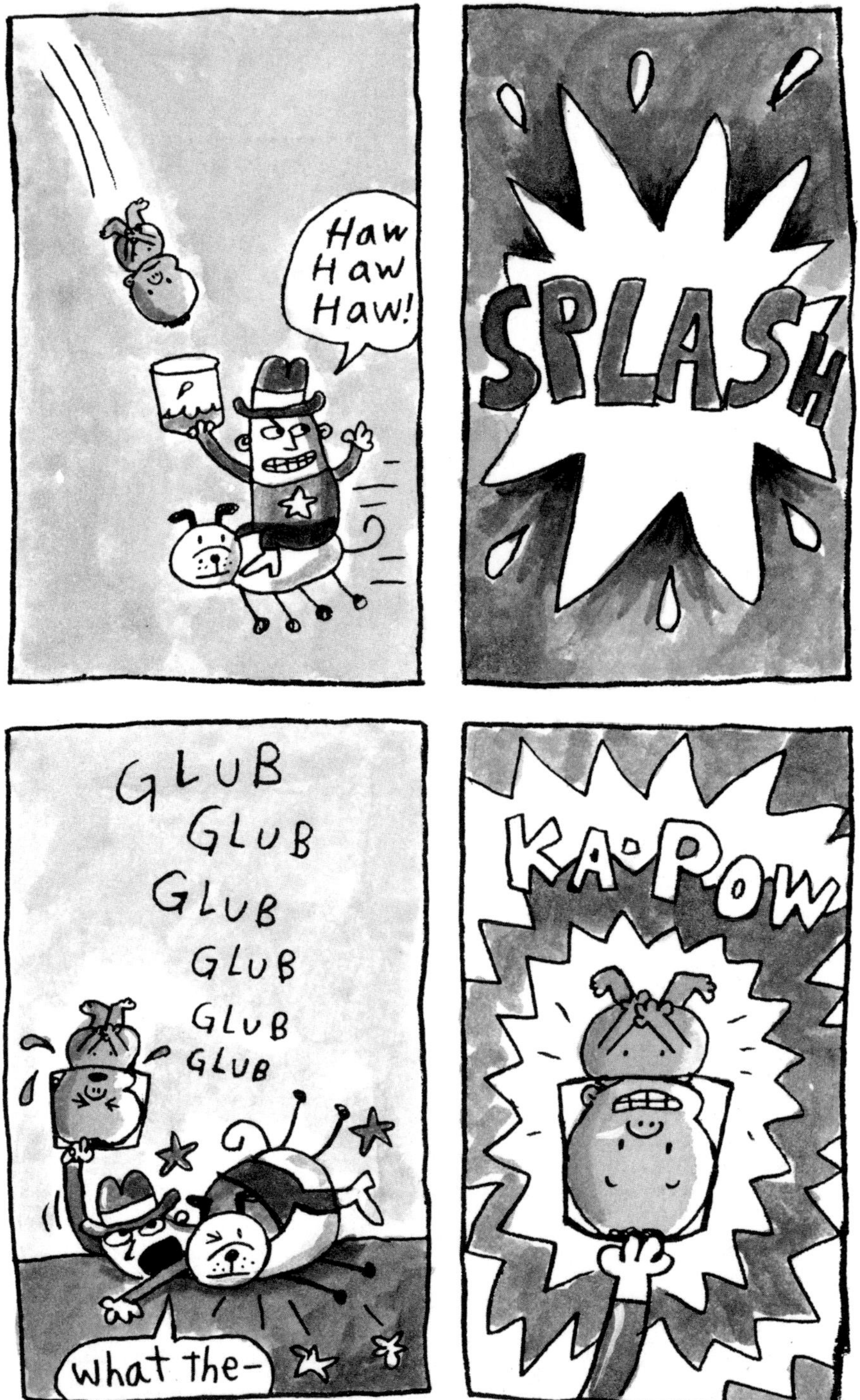
Haw Haw Haw!
SPLASH
GLUB
GLUB
GLUB
GLUB
GLUB
GLUB
What the-
KA·POW

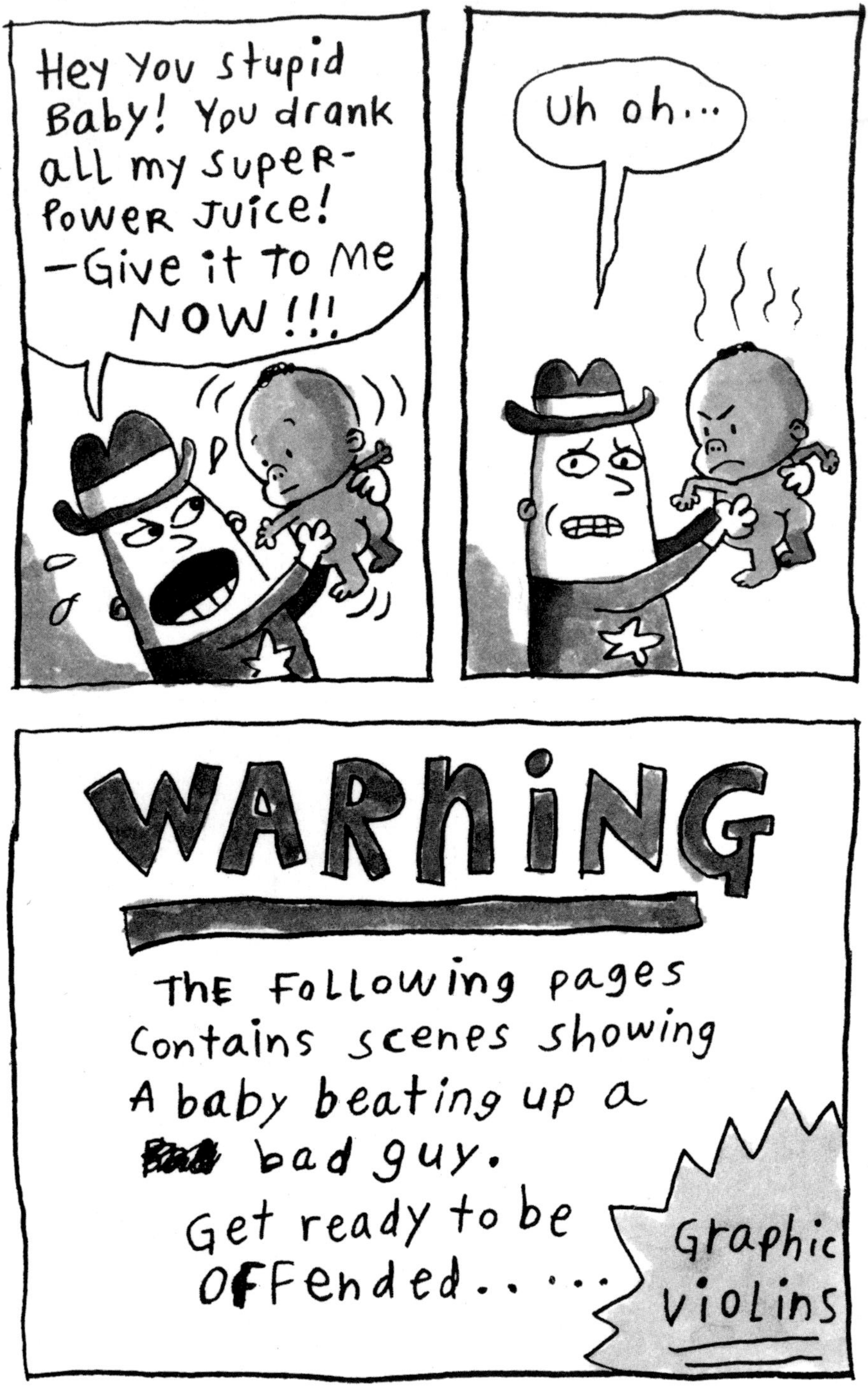
Hey You stupid Baby! You drank all my super-power Juice! -Give it to Me NOW!!!
Uh oh...
WARNING
THE Following pages contains scenes showing A baby beating up a [redacted] bad guy.
Get ready to be OFFended.....
Graphic violins

FLIP-O-RAMA

Here's How it Works!!!!

Step 1
Plase your Left Hand inside the dotted Lines marked "Left Hand Here." Hold the Book open FLAT.

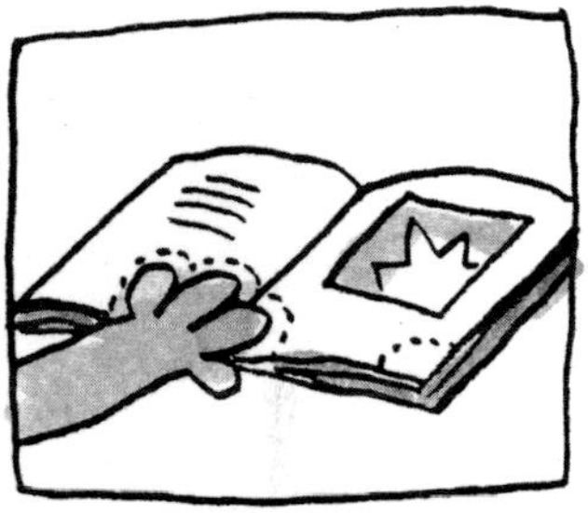

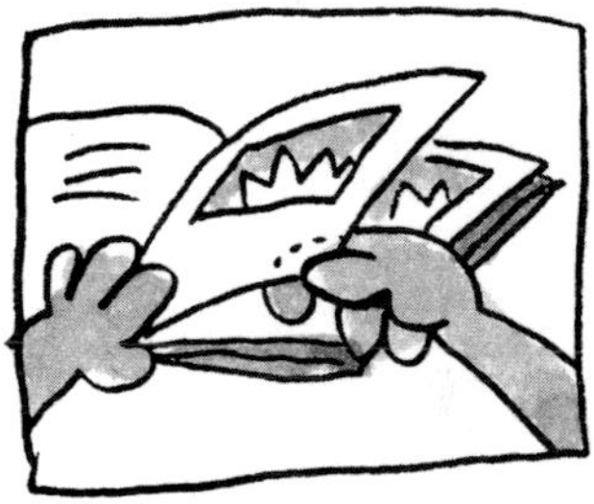

Step 2
Grasp the Right-hand Page with your Right thumb and index Finger (inside the dotted Lines marked "Right Thumb Here").

Step 3
Now Quickly Flip the Right-hand page back and Fourth until the Pitcher appears to Be Animated!

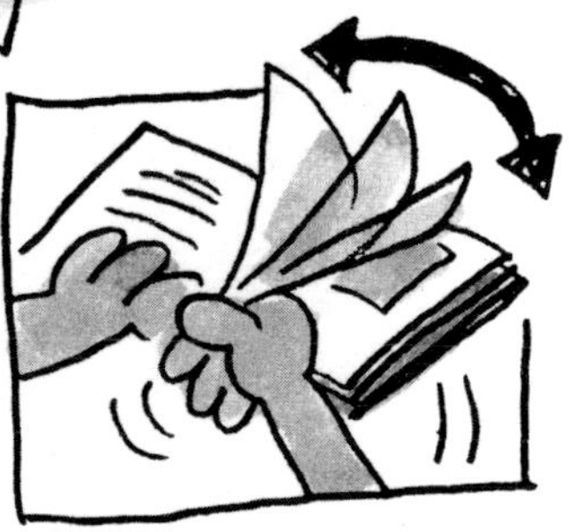

(for extra fun, try adding your own Sound-Afecks)

FLIP-O-RAMA # 1

(Pages 25 and 27)

Remember, flip <u>only</u> Page 25. while you are fliping, be shure you can see the Pitcher on Page 25 <u>And</u> the one on Page 27.

IF you flip Quickly, the two pitchers will Start to Look Like <u>one</u> Animated pitcher.

Don't forget to add your own Sound Affecks

Left Hand Here

take this!

25

right
Thumb
Here

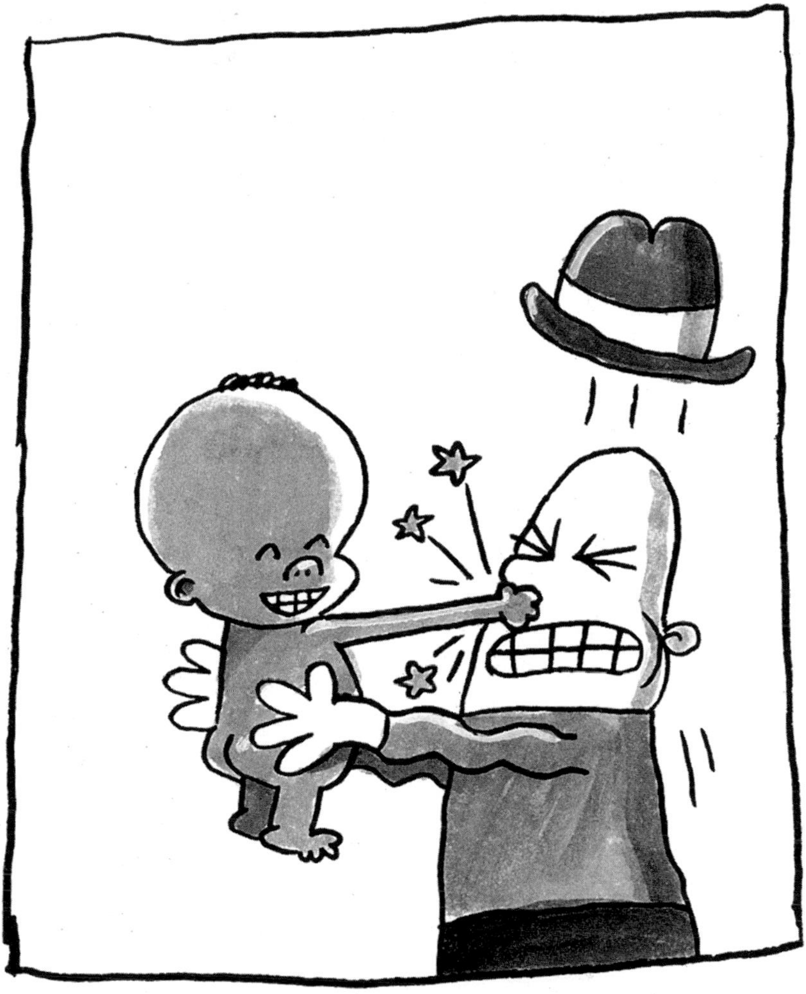

Take this!

FLIP·O·RAMA # 2

(pages **29** and **31**)

Remember, flip <u>only</u> page 29.
while you are fliping, be shure
you can see the pitcher on
page 29 <u>And</u> the one on
page 31.

   If you FLIP Quickly,
the two pitchers will
start to look like <u>one</u>
Animated pitcher.

Don't forget to
add your own
Sound Affecks

Left Hand
Here

... And that!

Right
thumB
Here

... And that!

FLIP-O-RAMA #3

(pages **33** and **35.**)

Remember, Flip only page 33. While you are Fliping, be shure you can see the pitcher on page 33 and ~~both~~ page 35.

IF you Flip Quickly, the two pitchers will start to Look Like yadda yadda yadda.

Don't forget to skip these pages without reading them.

Left Hand Here

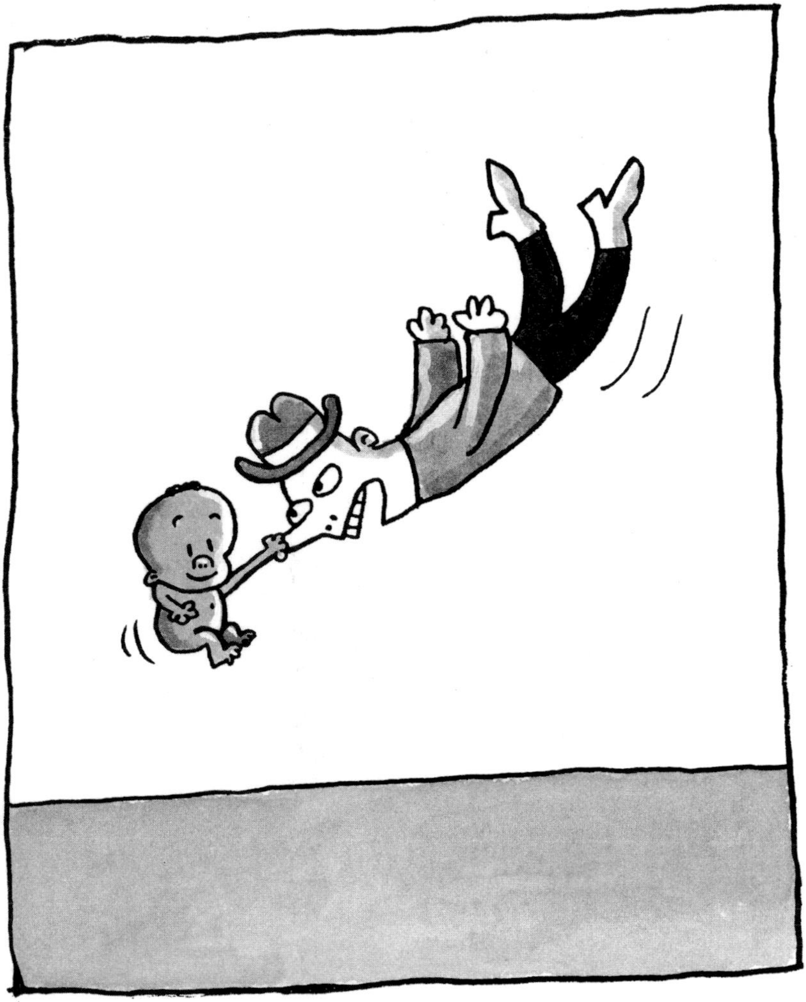

... And some of these!

Right Thumb Here

...And some of these!

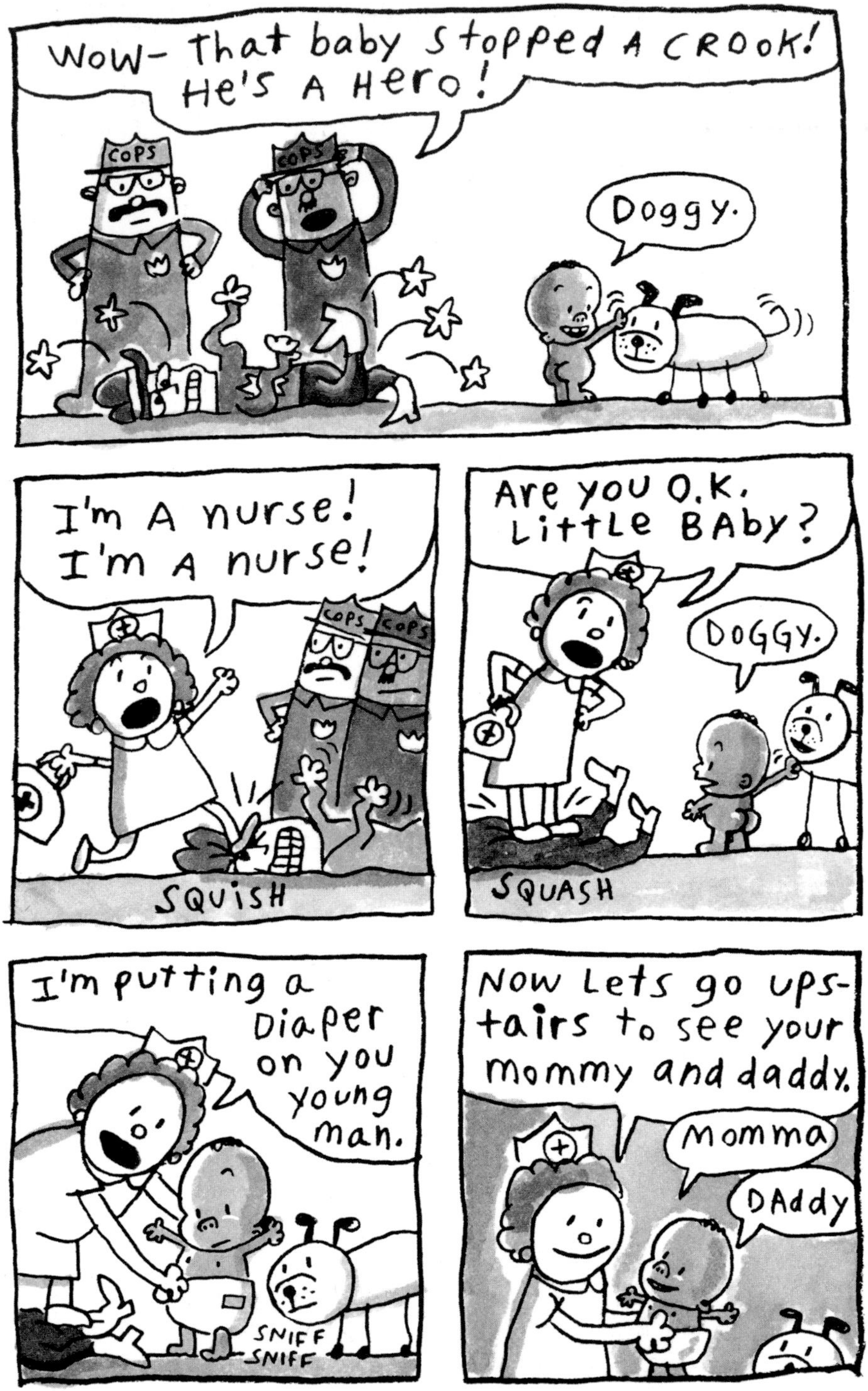
WOW- That baby stopped A CROOK! He's A Hero!
COPS
COPS
Doggy.
I'm A nurse! I'm A nurse!
COPS
COPS
SQUISH
Are you O.K. Little BAby?
DOGGY.
SQUASH
I'm putting a Diaper on you young man.
SNIFF SNIFF
Now Lets go ups-tairs to see your mommy and daddy.
Momma
DAddy

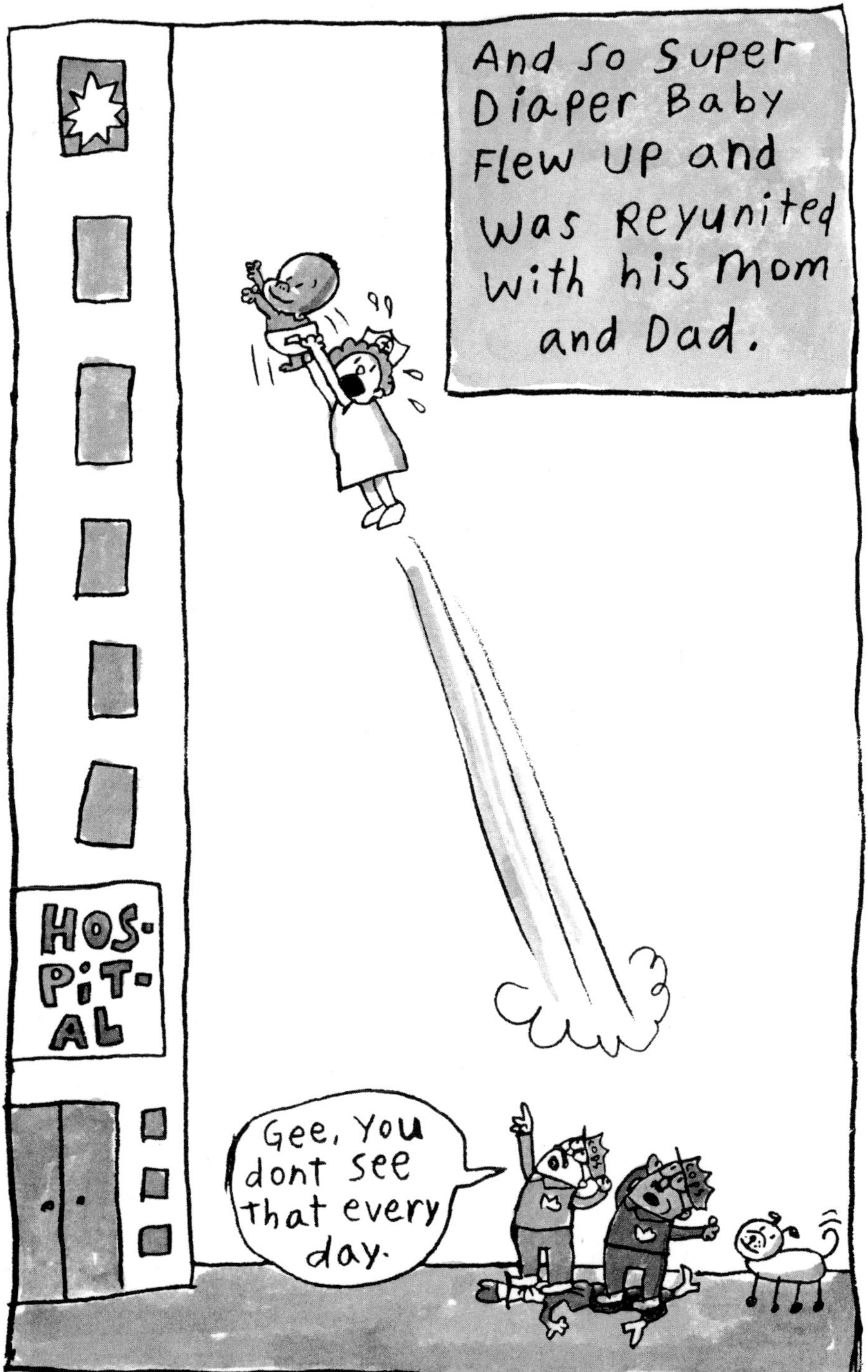
And so Super Diaper Baby Flew UP and was Reyunited with his Mom and Dad.
HOS-PiT-AL
Gee, You dont see that every day.

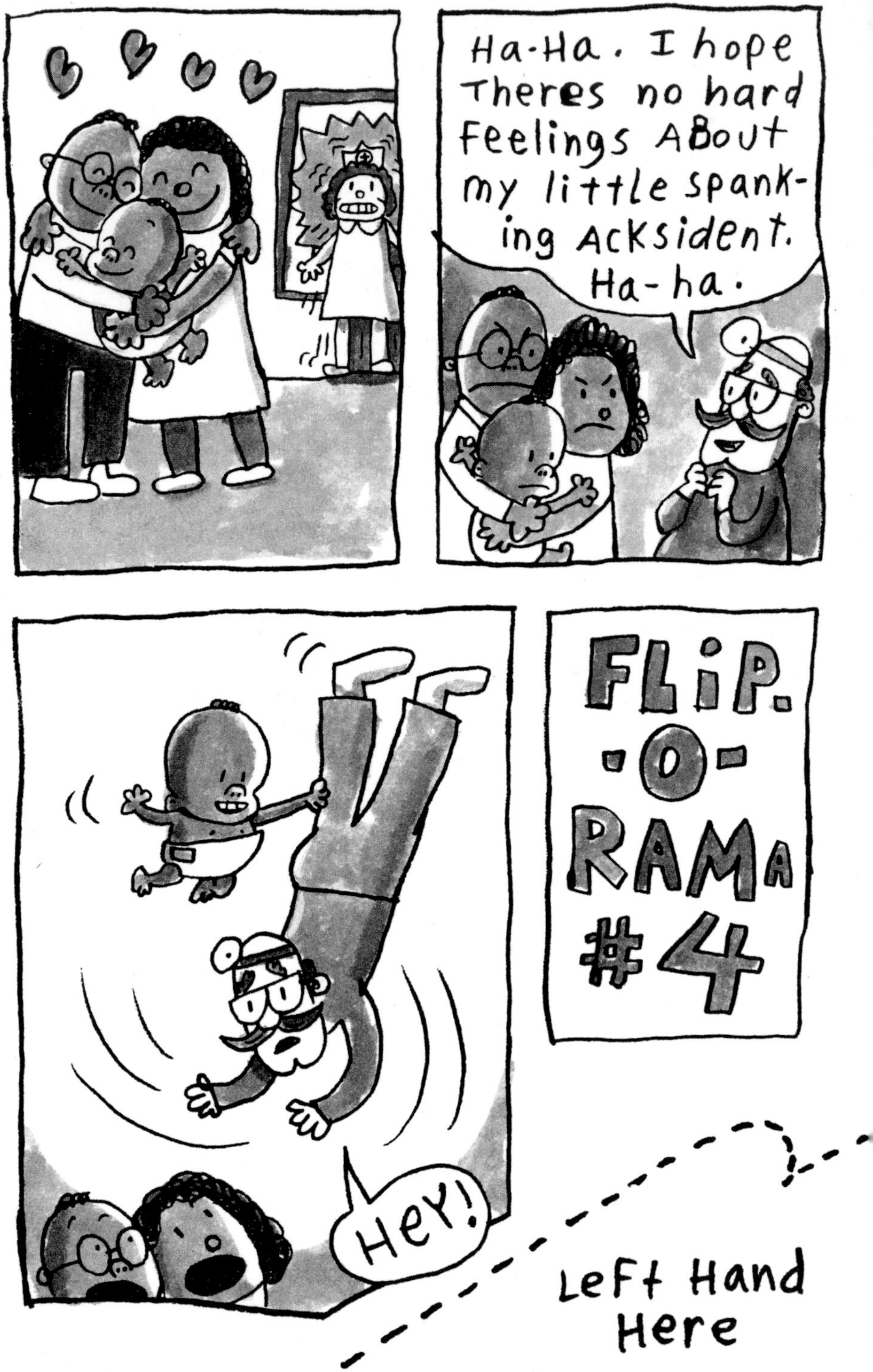
Ha-Ha. I hope Theres no hard Feelings ABout my little spanking Acksident. Ha-ha.
HEY!
FLIP-O-RAMA #4
Left Hand Here

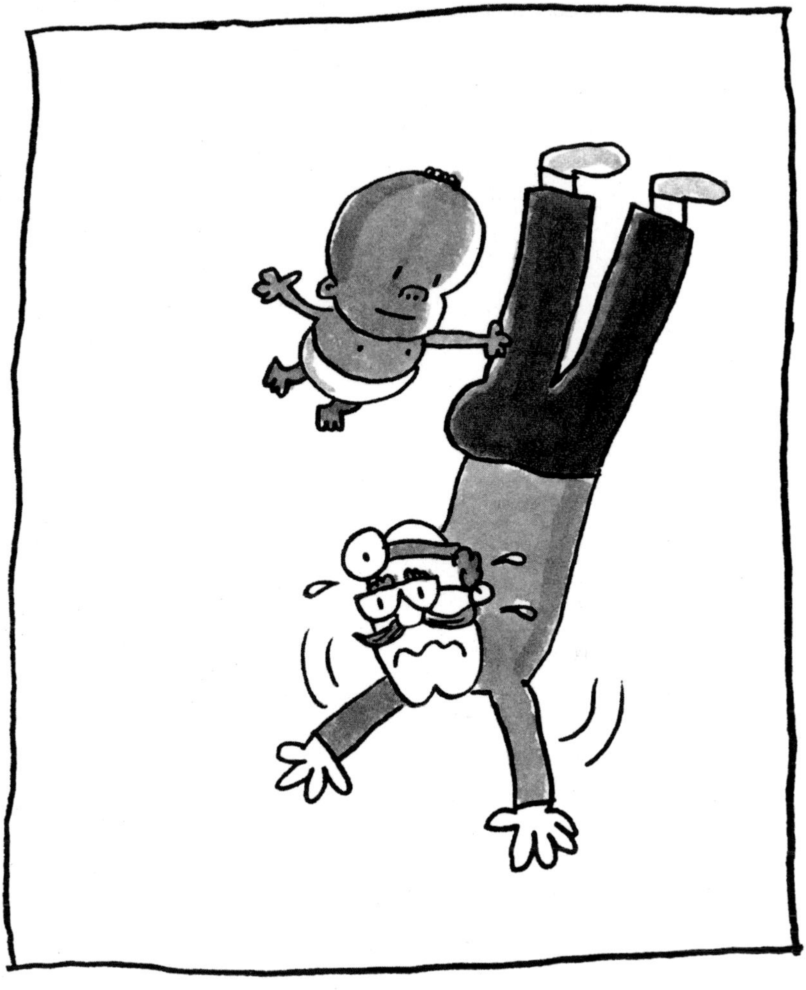

ALL is Forgiven

RiGhT ThumB Here

ALL is Forgiven

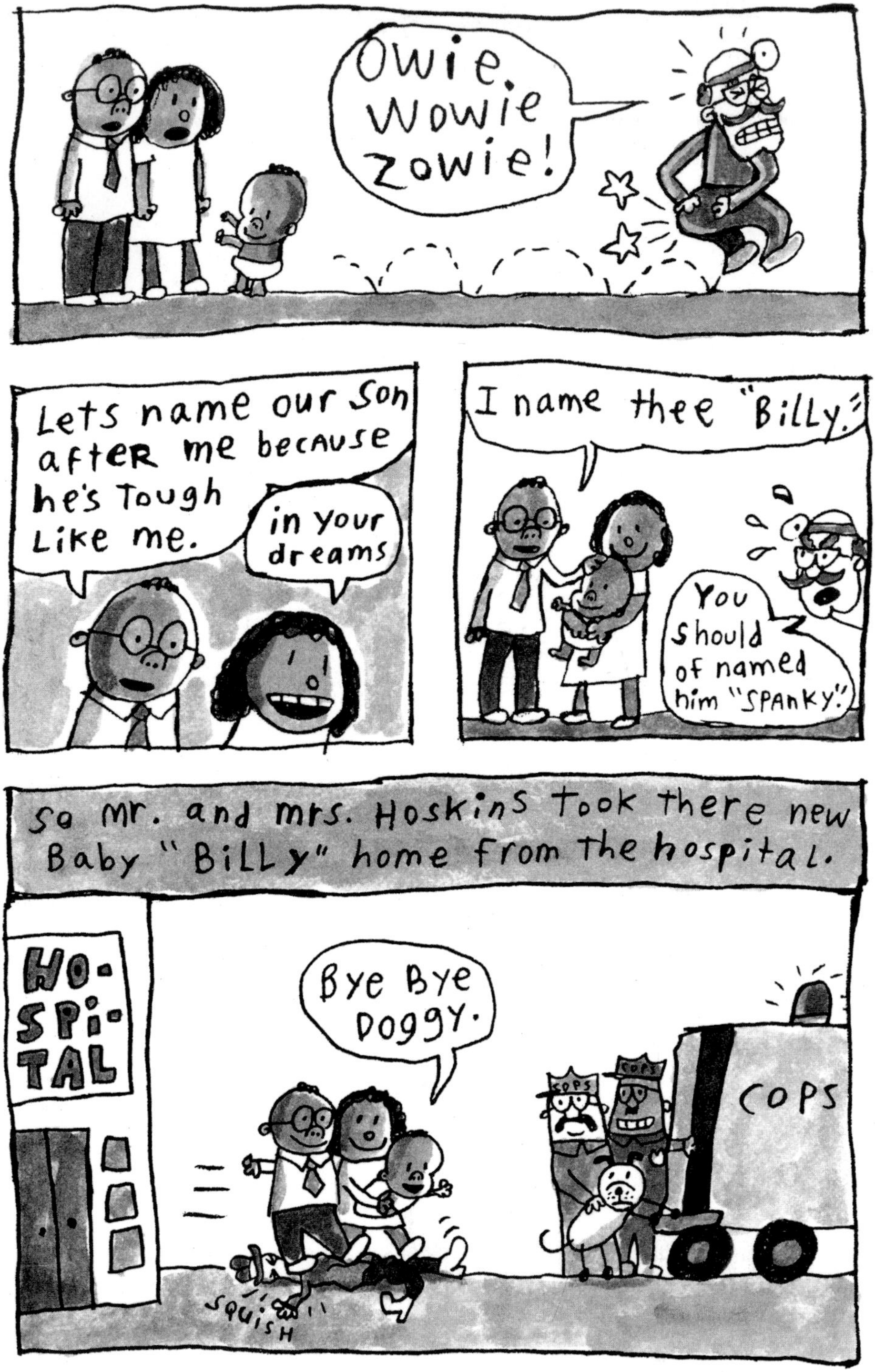
Owie. Wowie Zowie!
Lets name our Son after me because he's Tough Like me.
in your dreams
I name thee "BiLLy."
You should of named him "SPANKY."
So mr. and mrs. Hoskins took there new Baby "BiLLy" home from the hospital.
HO-SPI-TAL
Bye Bye Doggy.
COPS
COPS
COPS
SQUISH

SUPER DI-APER BABY

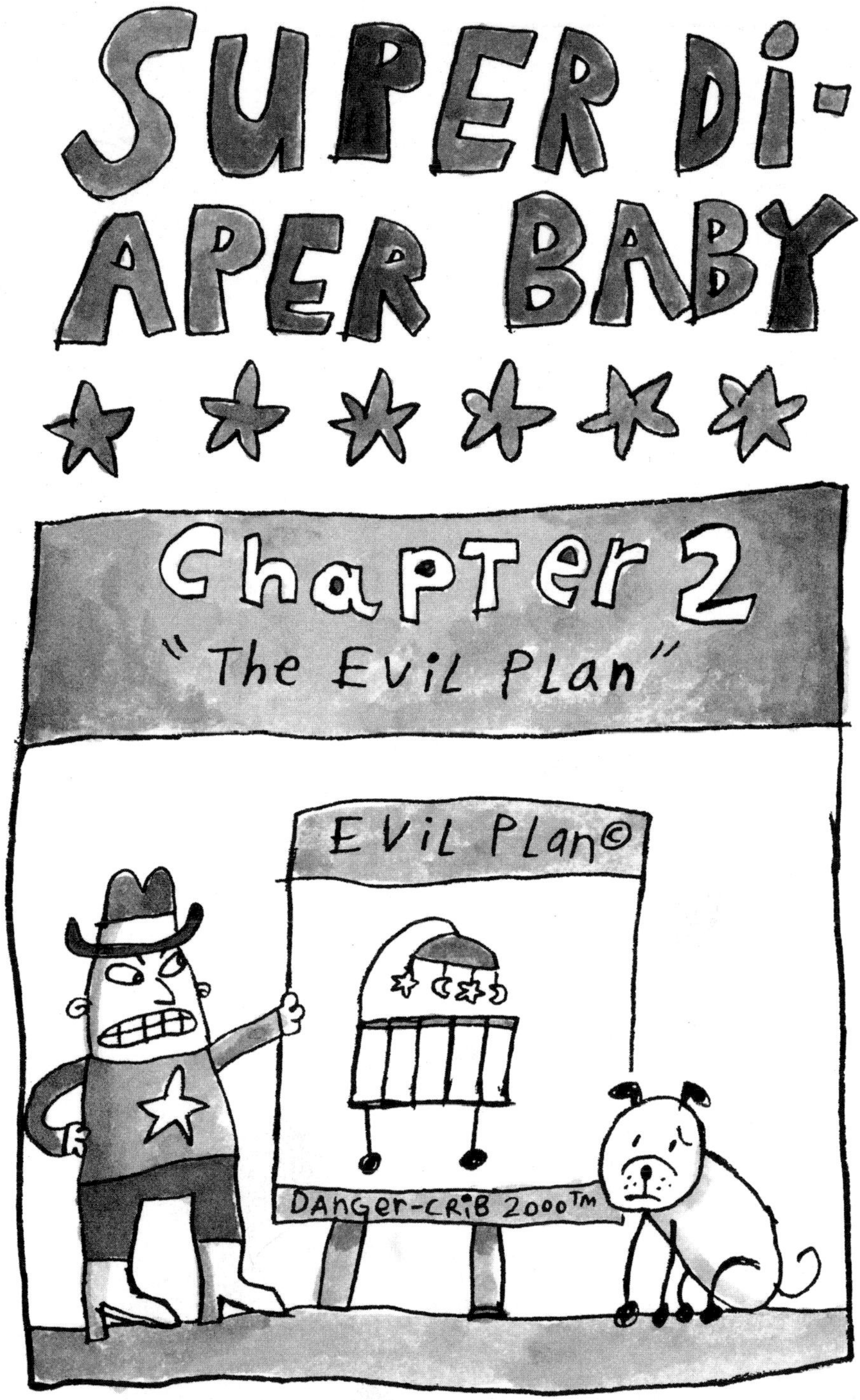

Chapter 2
"The Evil Plan"
Evil Plan©
Danger-crib 2000™

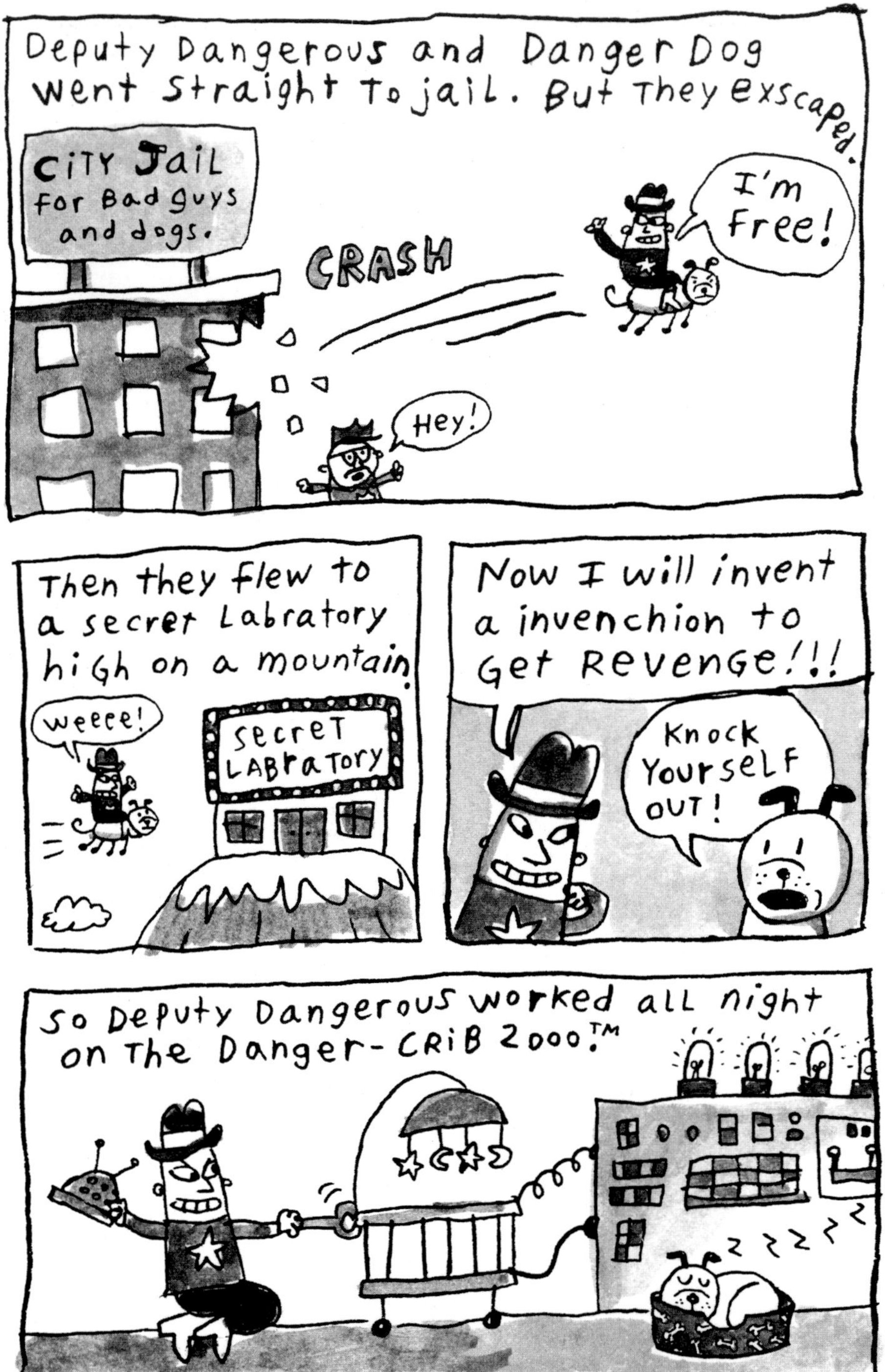
Deputy Dangerous and Danger Dog went straight to jail. But they exscaped.
CITY JAIL for Bad guys and dogs.
CRASH
I'm Free!
Hey!
Then they flew to a secret Labratory high on a mountain!
weeee!
SECRET LABRATORY
Now I will invent a invenchion to Get REVENGE!!!
Knock Yourself OUT!
So Deputy Dangerous worked all night on the Danger-CRIB 2000™
z z z z z

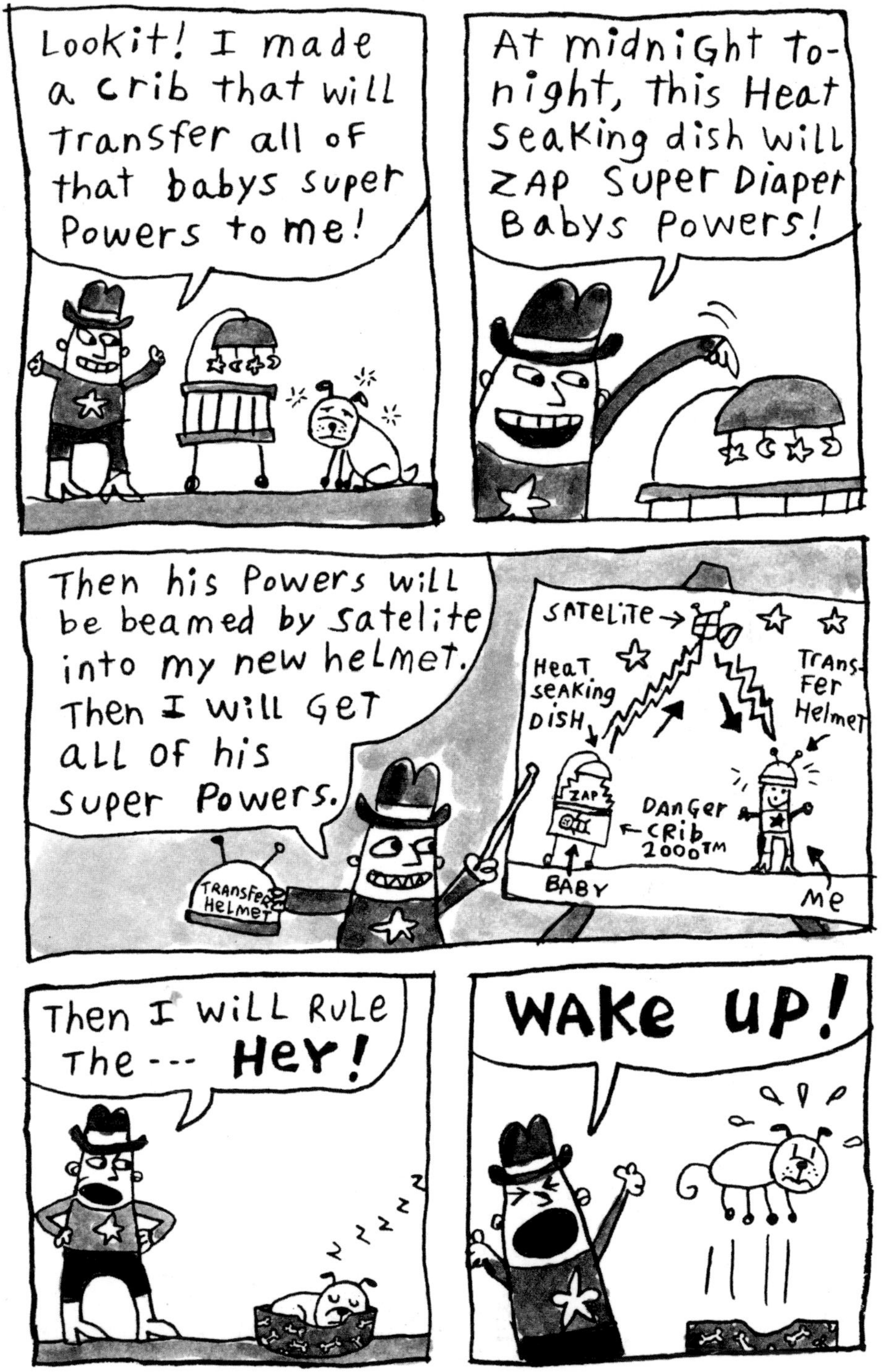
Lookit! I made a crib that will transfer all of that babys super powers to me!
At midnight to-night, this Heat seaking dish will ZAP Super Diaper Babys Powers!
Then his Powers will be beamed by satelite into my new helmet. Then I will get all of his super Powers.
SATELITE
HEAT SEAKING DISH
TRANS-FER Helmet
ZAP
DANGER CRIB 2000TM
BABY
ME
TRANSFER HELMET
Then I will Rule The --- HEY!
Z Z Z Z Z Z
WAKE UP!

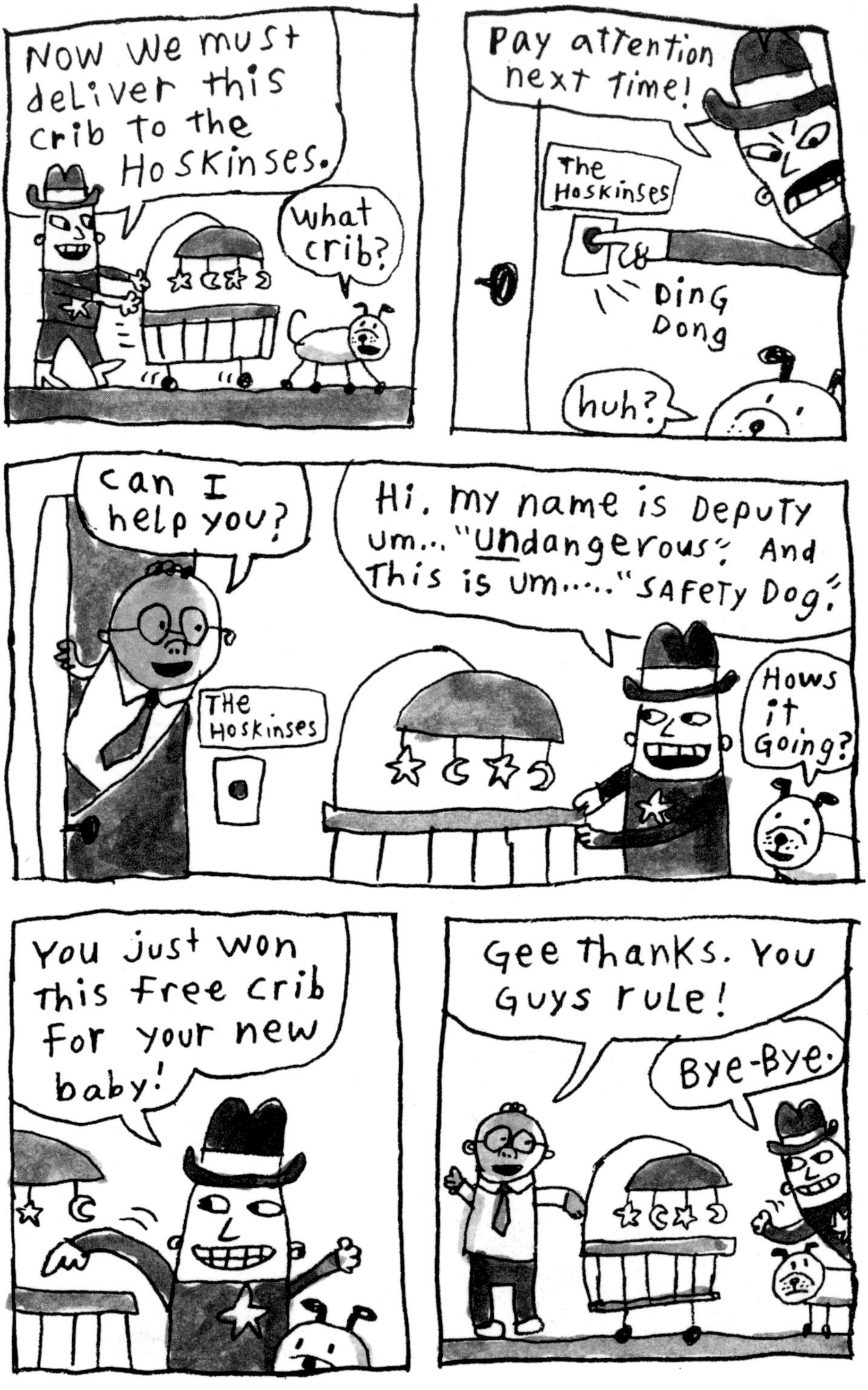

Now we must deliver this crib to the Hoskinses.
What crib?
Pay attention next time!
The Hoskinses
Ding Dong
huh?
Can I help you?
Hi. My name is Deputy um... "Undangerous." And This is um....."Safety Dog."
THE Hoskinses
Hows it Going?
You just won this free crib for your new baby!
Gee thanks. You Guys rule!
Bye-Bye.

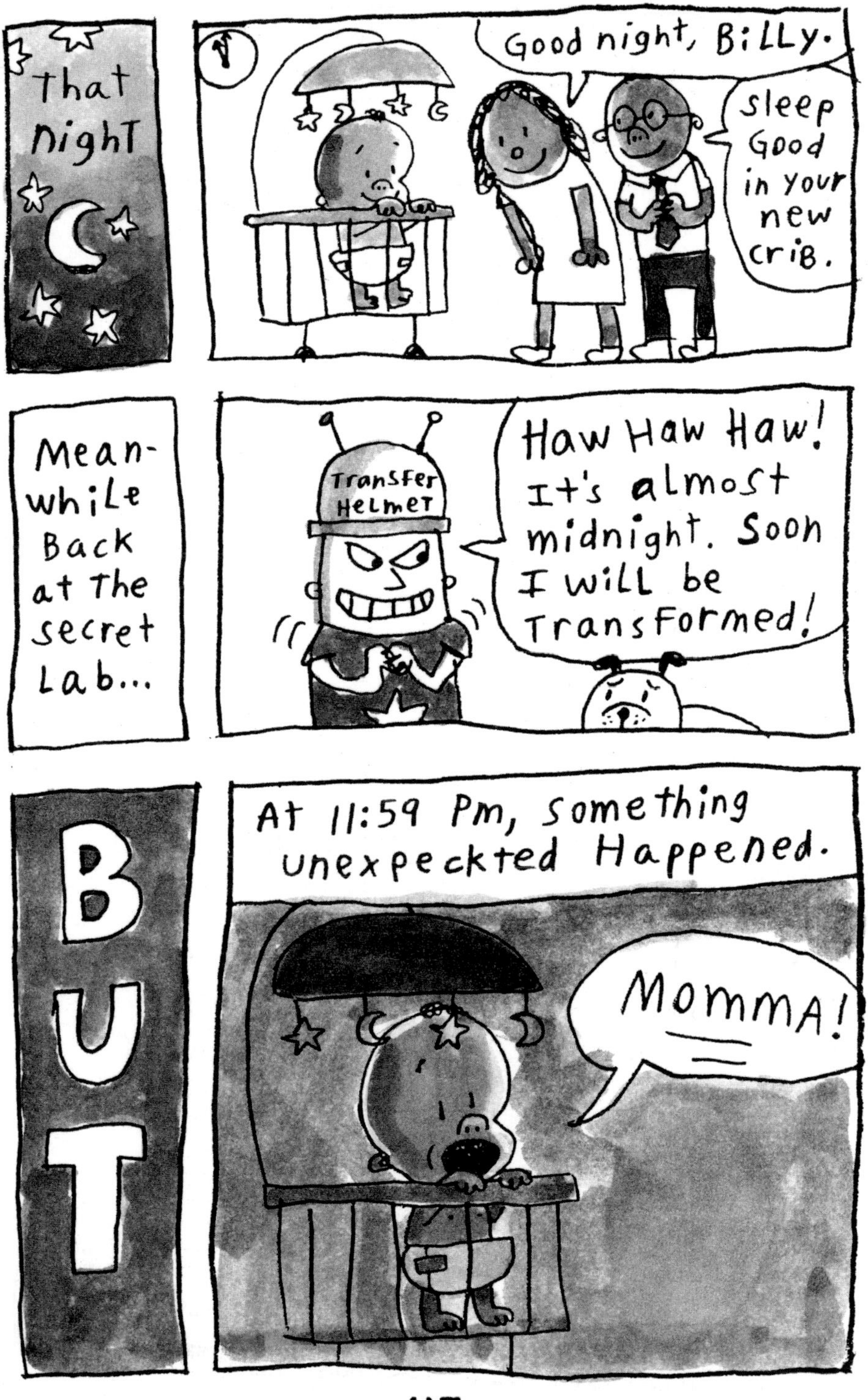
That night
Good night, Billy.
Sleep good in your new crib.
Meanwhile back at the secret lab...
Transfer Helmet
Haw Haw Haw! It's almost midnight. Soon I will be transformed!
BUT
At 11:59 pm, something unexpeckted happened.
MOMMA!

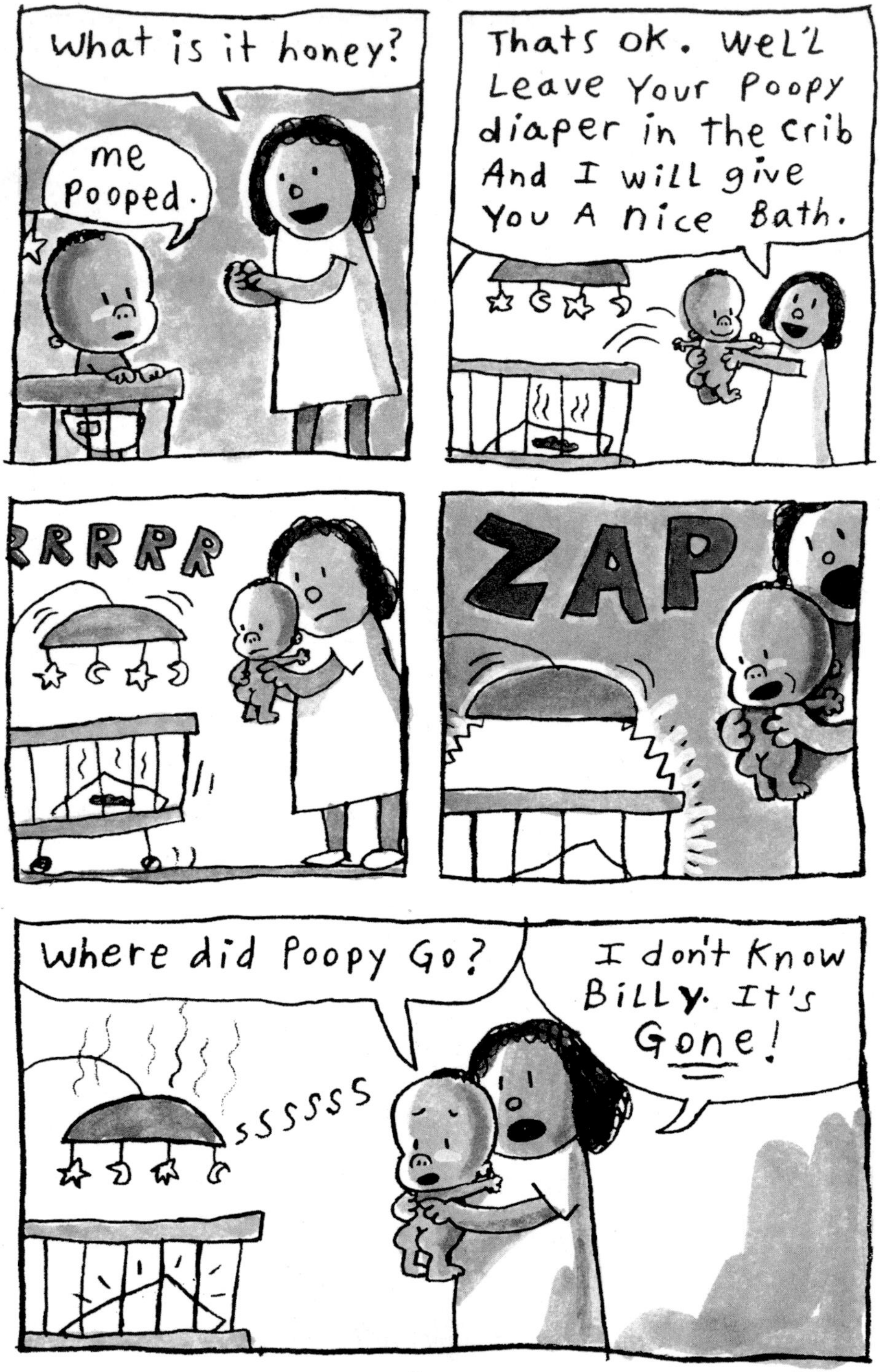
What is it honey?
me Pooped.
Thats ok. WeL'L Leave Your Poopy diaper in the crib And I will give You A nice Bath.
RRRRR
ZAP
Where did Poopy Go?
I don't Know BiLLy. It's Gone!
sSSSSS

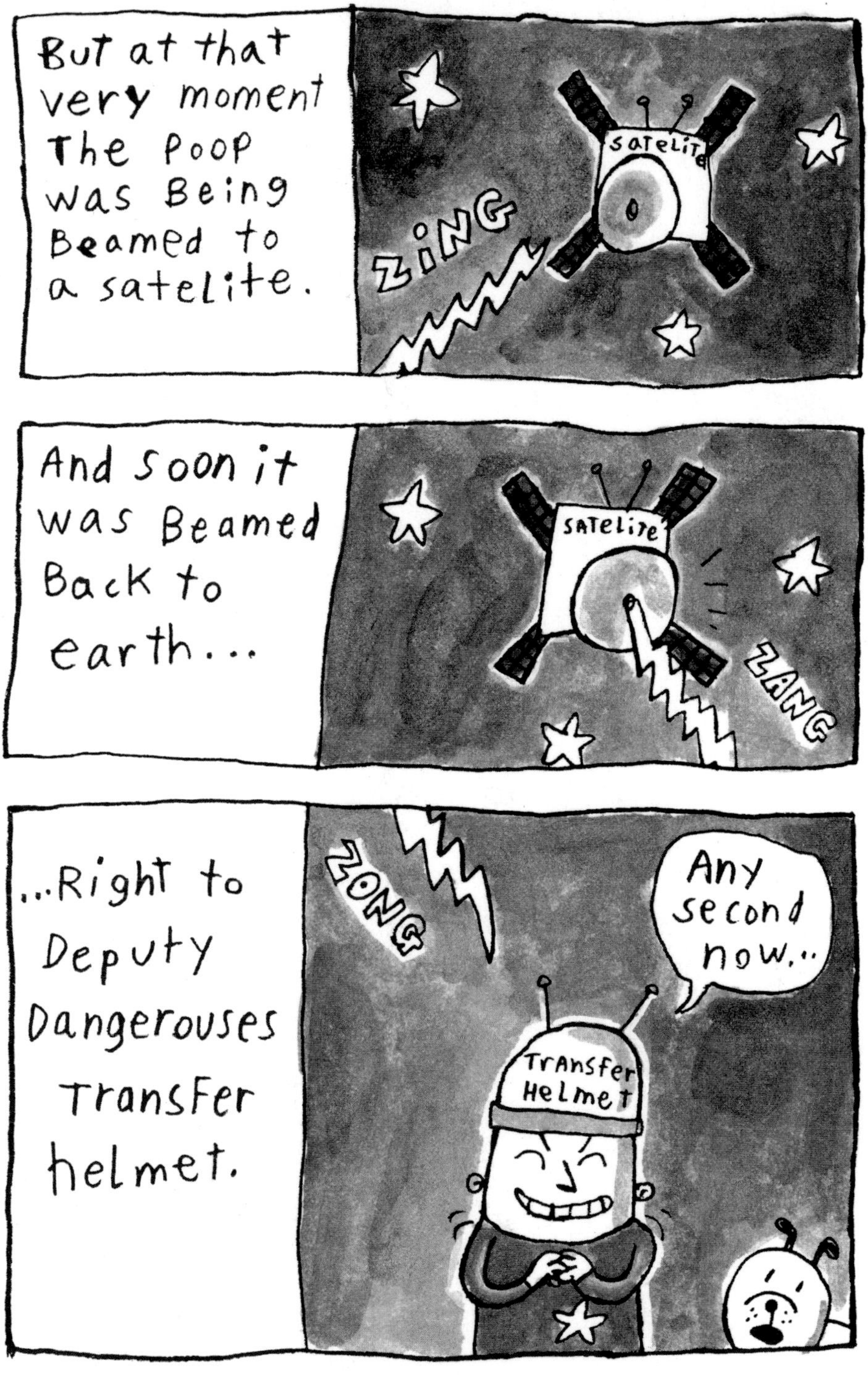
But at that very moment The poop was Being Beamed to a satelite.
ZING
SATELITE
And soon it was Beamed Back to earth...
SATELITE
ZANG
...Right to Deputy Dangerouses Transfer helmet.
ZONG
Any second now...
Transfer Helmet

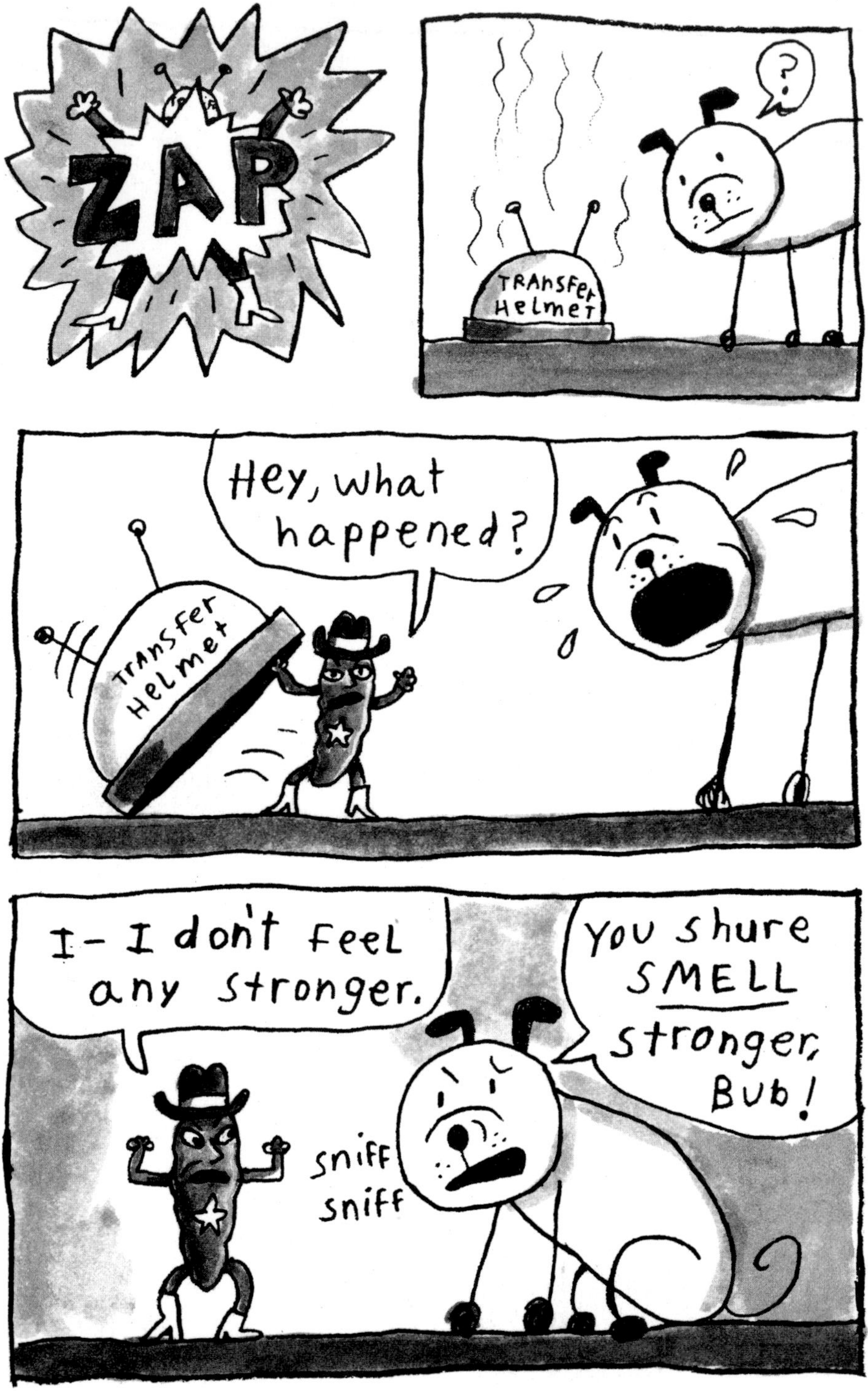
ZAP
TRANSFER Helmet
?
Hey, what happened?
TRANSFER Helmet
I- I don't feeL any stronger.
You shure SMELL stronger, Bub!
sniff sniff

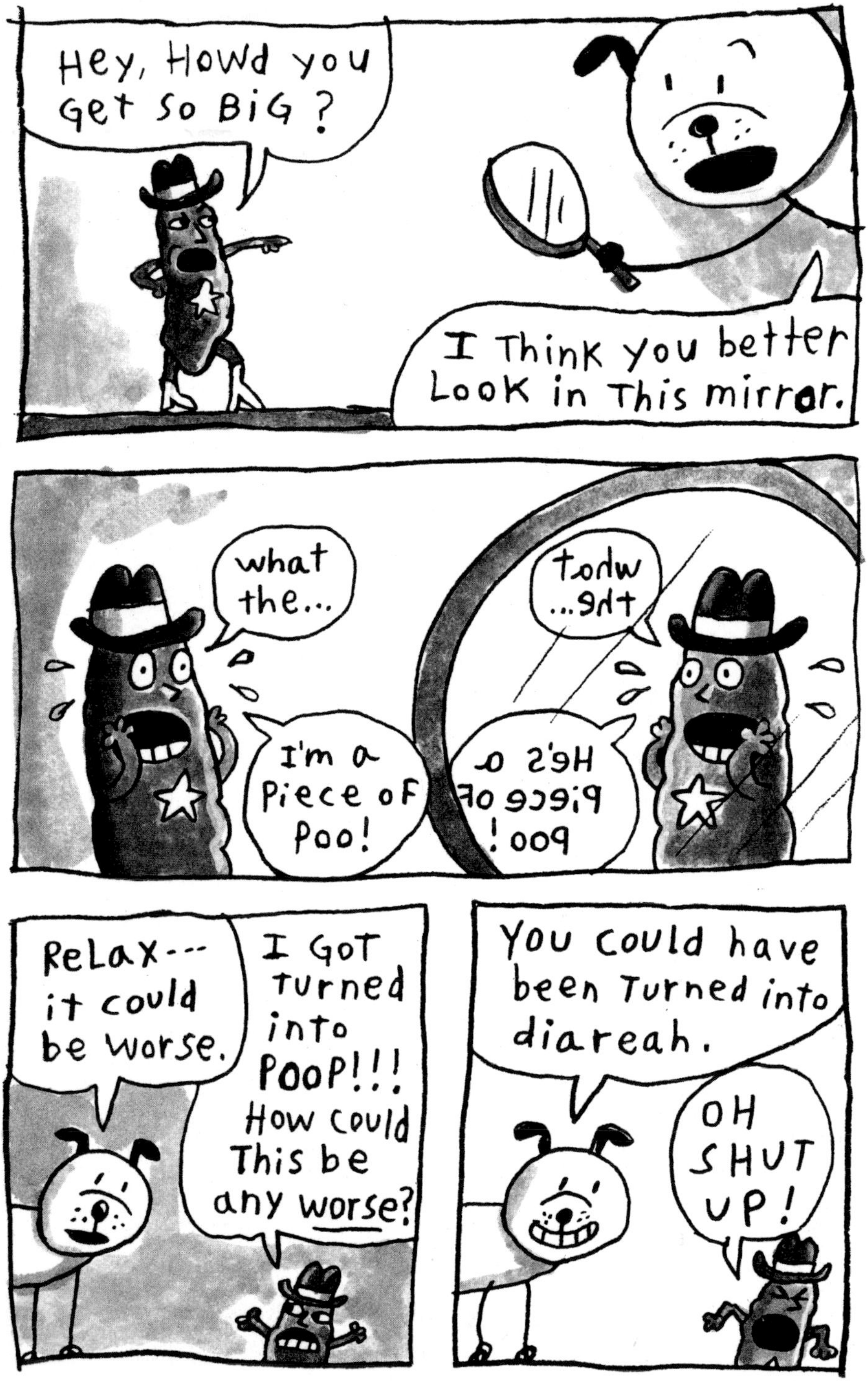
Hey, Howd you get so BiG?
I Think you better Look in This mirror.
what the...
I'm a Piece of Poo!
what the...
He's a Piece of Poo!
Relax--- it could be worse.
I GoT Turned into POOP!!! How could This be any worse?
You could have been Turned into diareah.
OH SHUT UP!

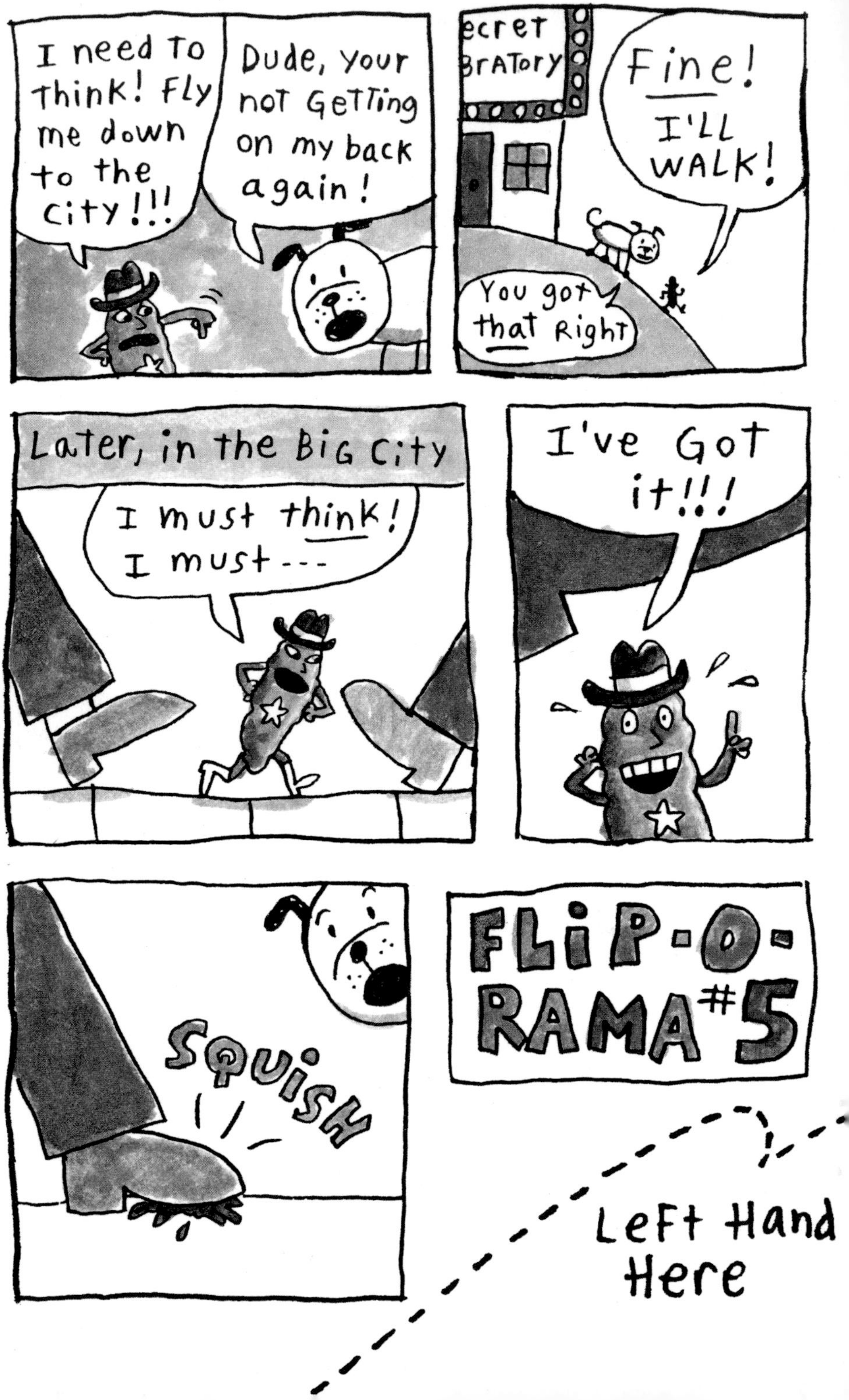
I need to think! Fly me down to the city!!!
Dude, your not GetTing on my back again!
ecret
BrATory
Fine! I'LL WALK!
You got that Right
Later, in the Big City
I must think! I must---
I've Got it!!!
SQUISH
FLiP-O-RAMA #5
Left Hand Here

---Aw Maaaaan!!!

Right
thumB
Here

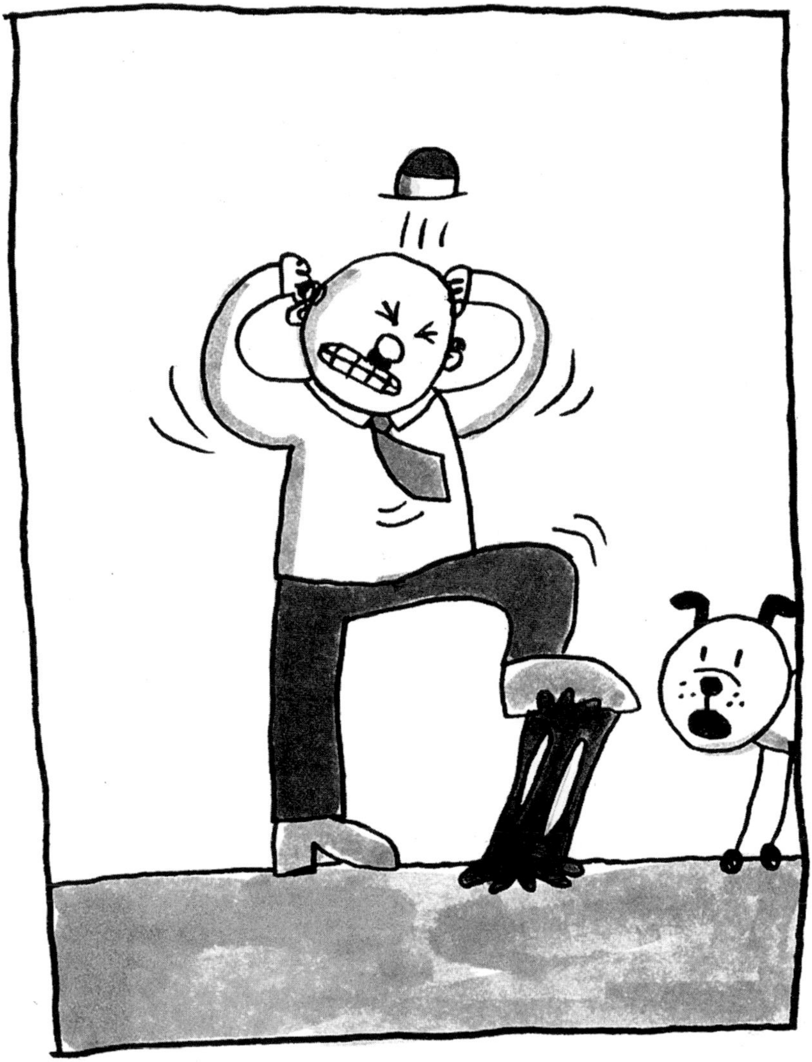

---Aw Maaaaaan!!!

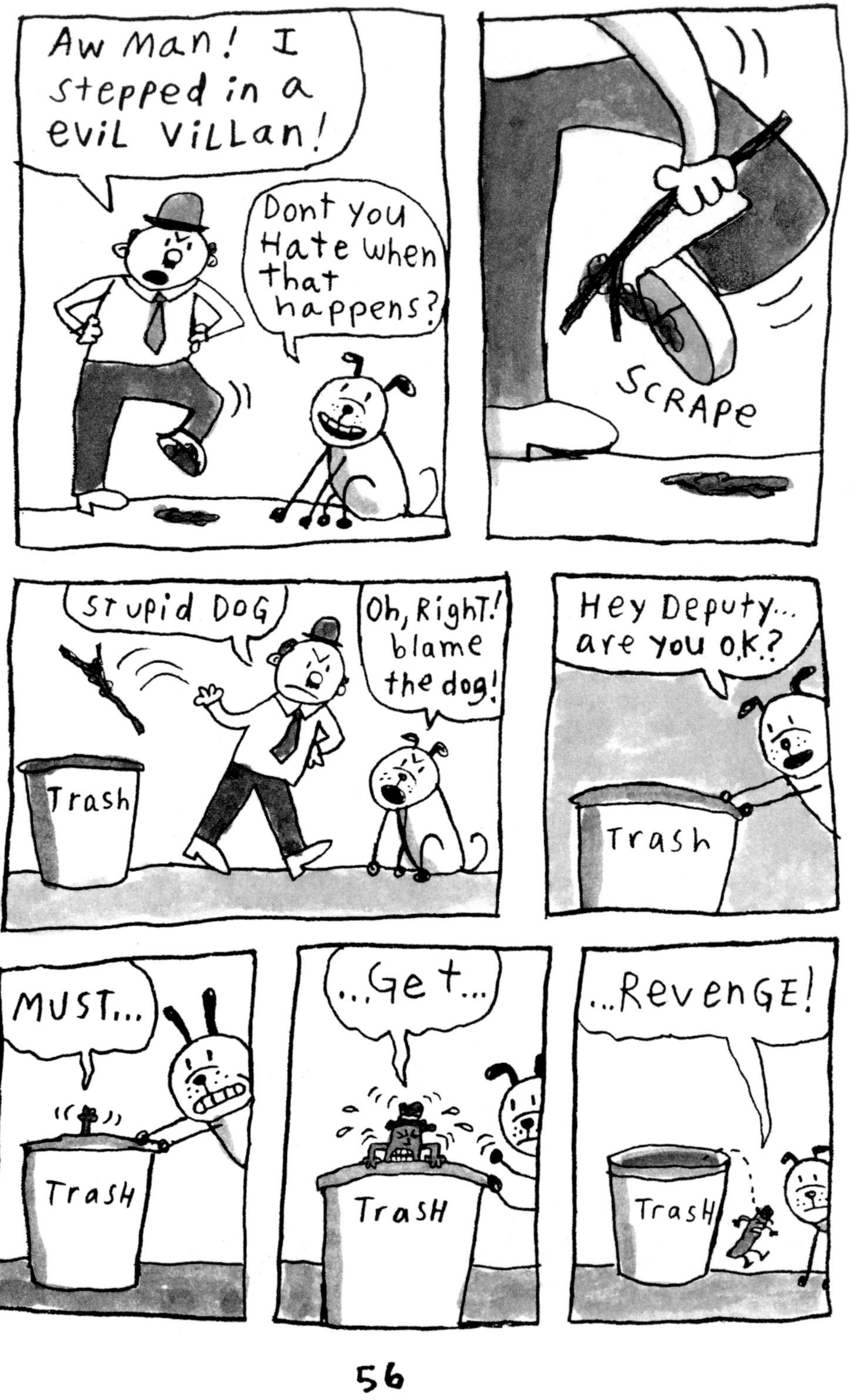
Aw Man! I stepped in a evil villan!
Dont you Hate when that happens?
SCRAPE
STUPID DOG
Oh, RighT! blame the dog!
Hey Deputy... are you O.K.?
Trash
MUST...
Trash
...Get...
Trash
...RevenGE!
Trash

SUPER DIAPER BABY

CHAPTER 3

Dial "R" for "Revenge."

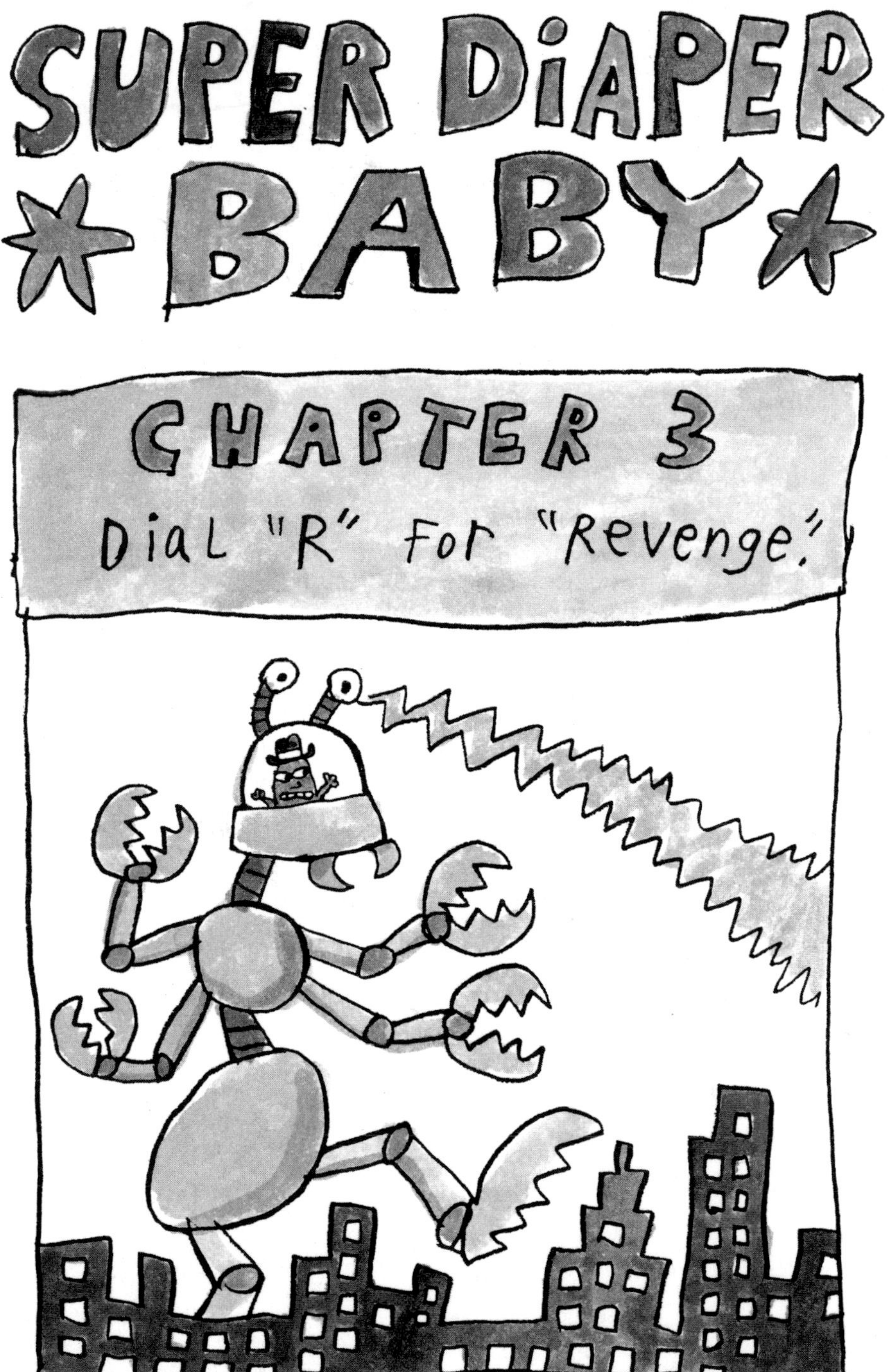

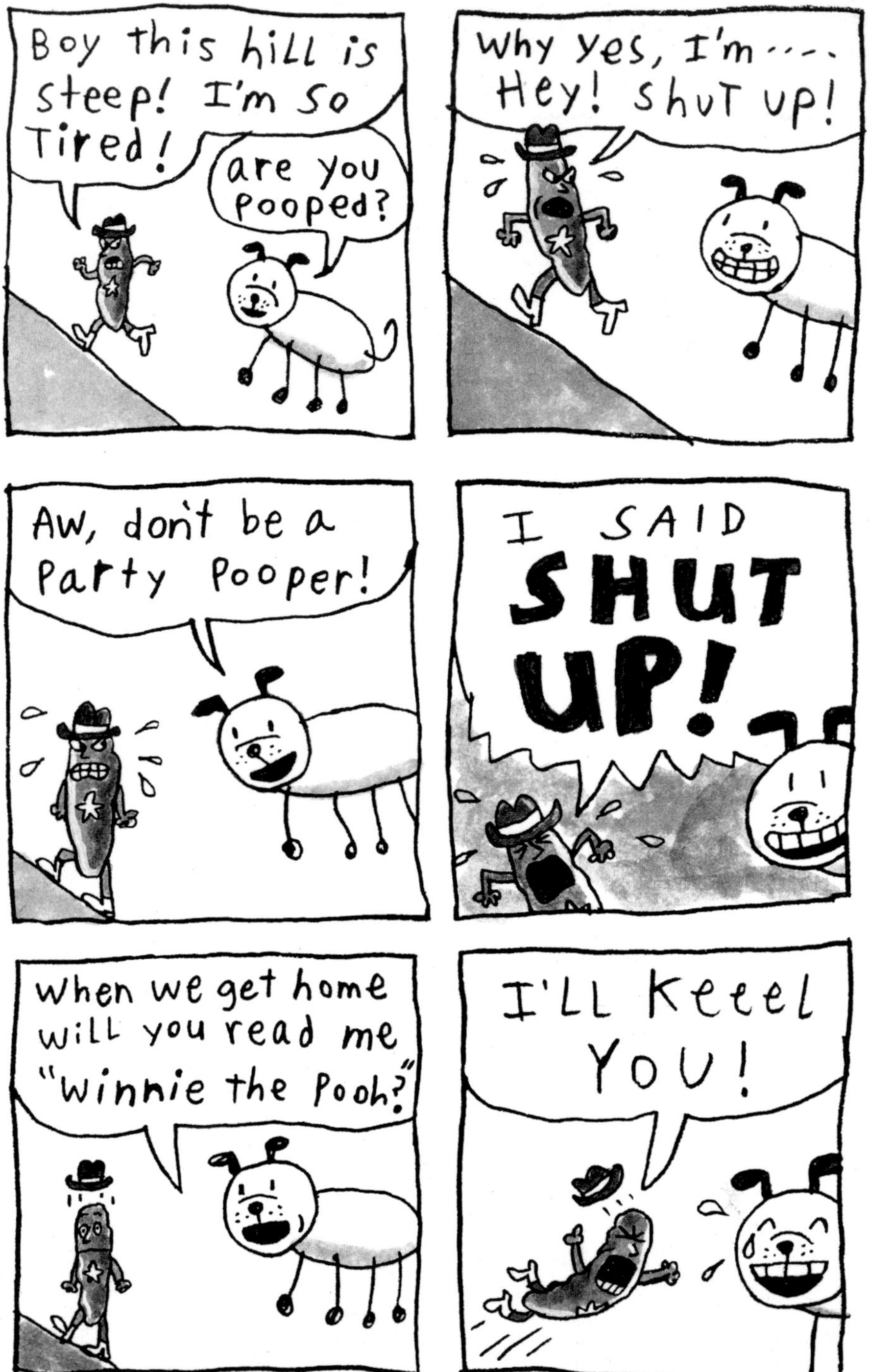
Boy this hill is steep! I'm so Tired!
are you pooped?
Why yes, I'm....
Hey! ShuT up!
Aw, don't be a Party Pooper!
I SAID SHUT UP!
When we get home will you read me "Winnie the Pooh?"
I'LL Keeel YOU!

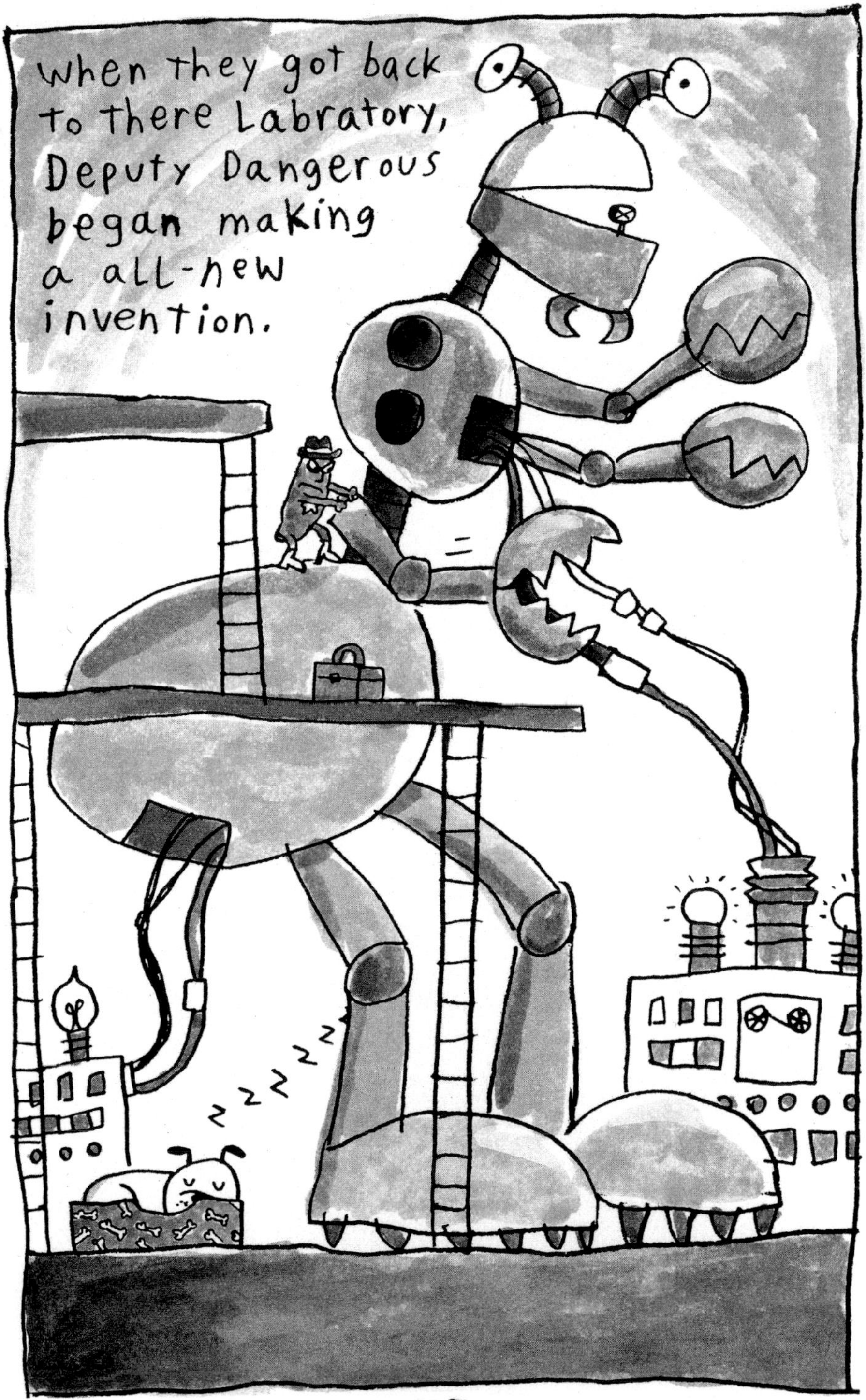
When they got back to there Labratory, Deputy Dangerous began making a all-new invention.
z z z z z z z z

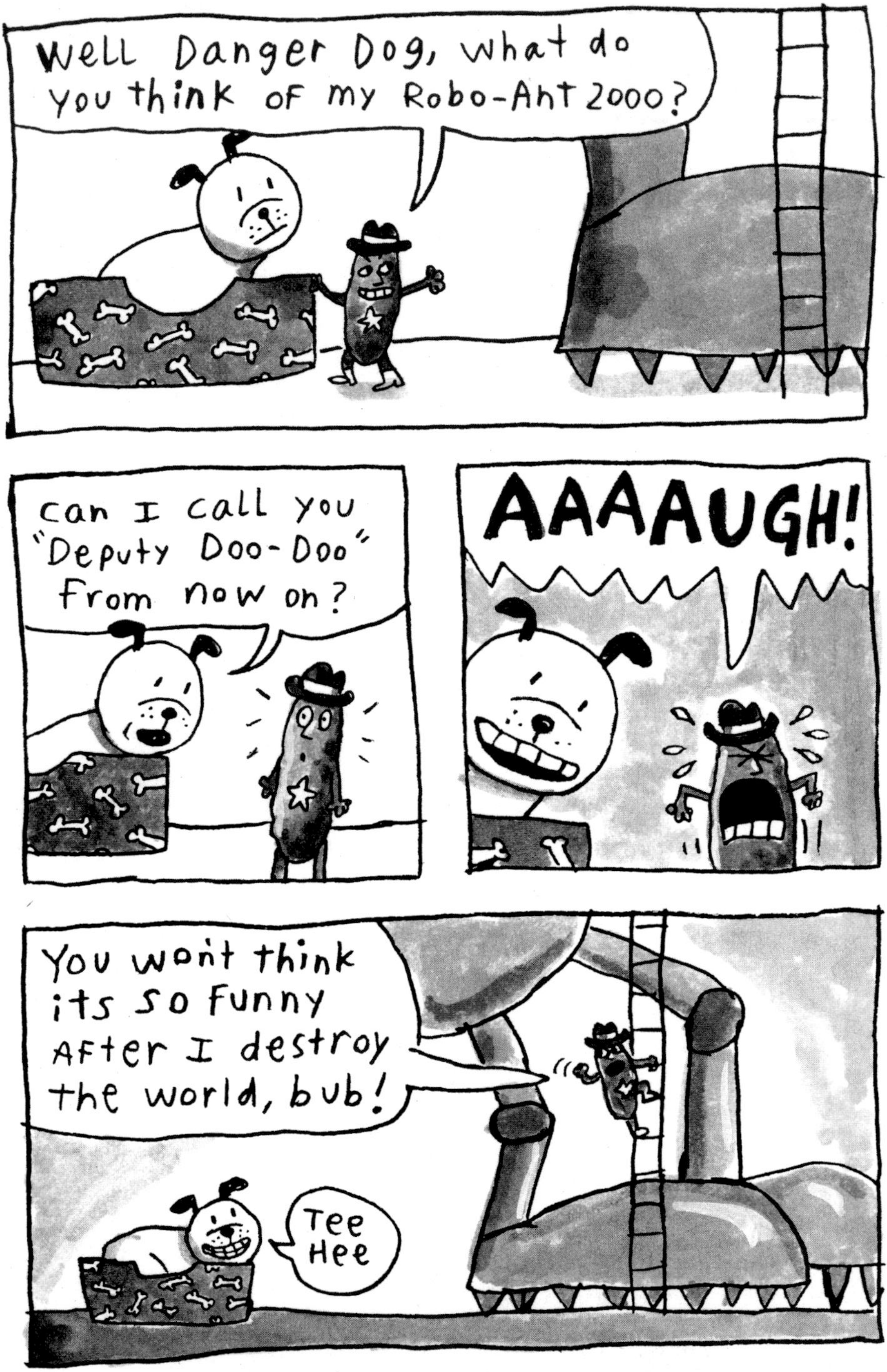
Well Danger Dog, what do you think of my Robo-Ant 2000?
Can I call you "Deputy Doo-Doo" from now on?
AAAAUGH!
You won't think its so funny after I destroy the world, bub!
Tee Hee

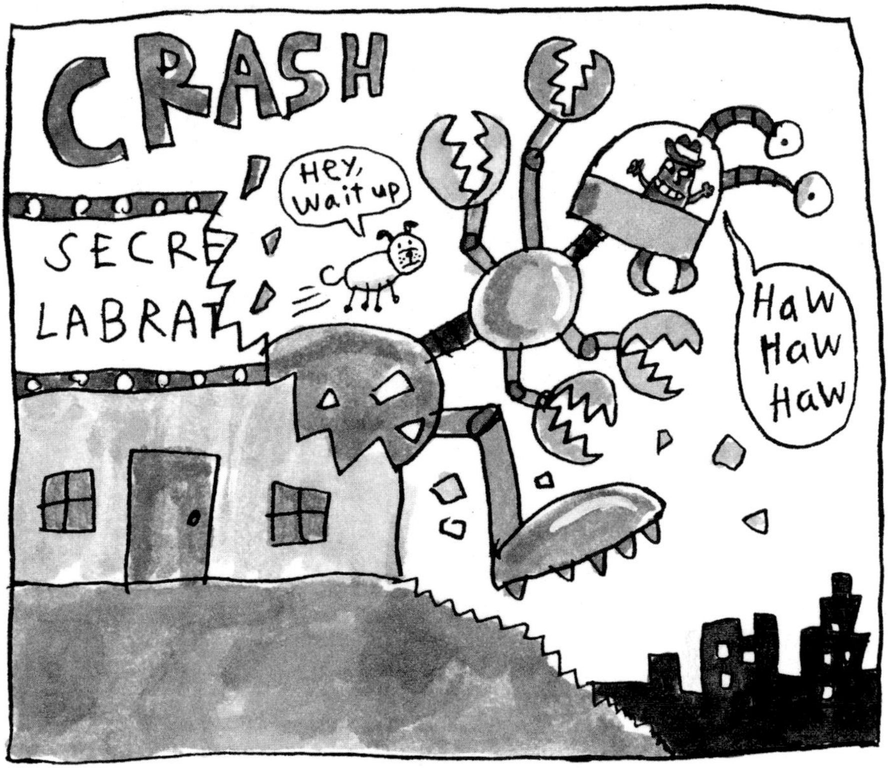
CRASH
SECRE
LABRAT
Hey, wait up
Haw Haw Haw

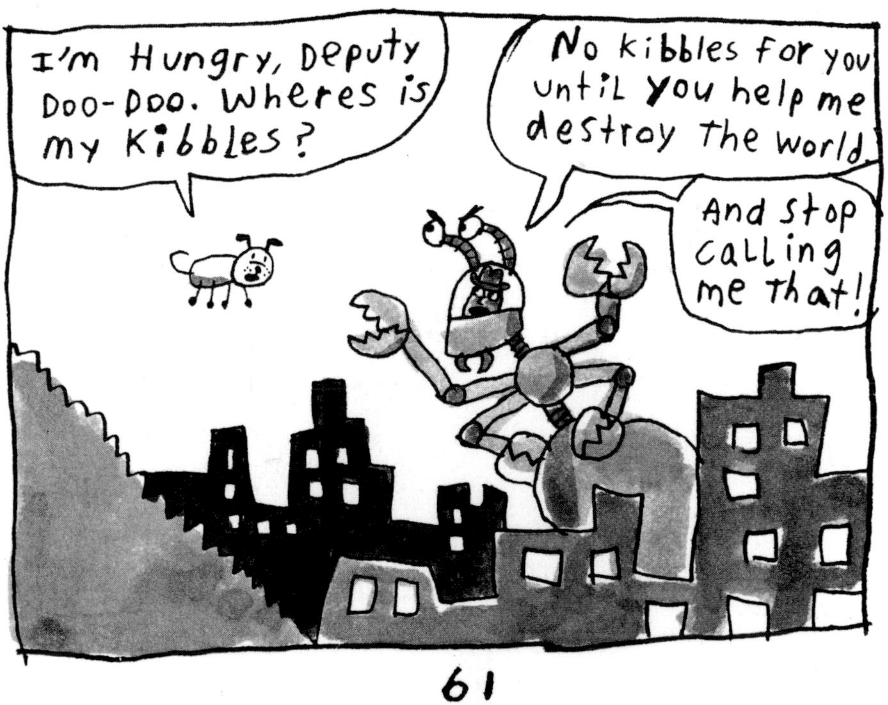
I'm Hungry, Deputy Doo-Doo. Wheres is my Kibbles?
No kibbles for you until you help me destroy the world.
And stop calling me that!

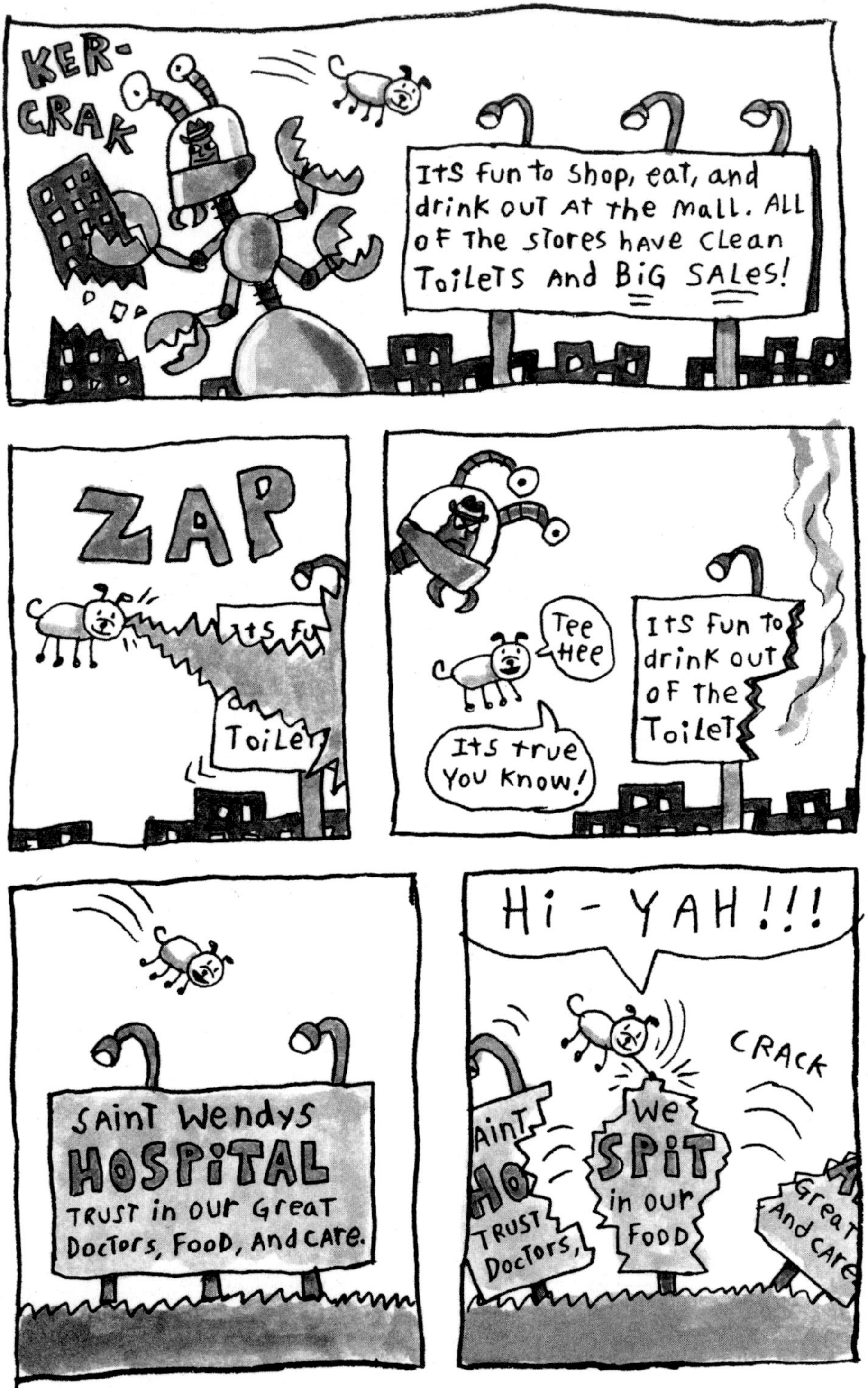
KER-CRAK
Its fun to shop, eat, and drink out at the mall. All of the stores have clean Toilets and BiG SALes!
ZAP
Its fu
Toilet
Tee Hee
Its true You Know!
Its fun to drink out of the Toilet
Saint Wendys HOSPiTAL TRUST in our Great Doctors, Food, And care.
Hi - YAH!!!
CRACK
Aint
TRUST Doctors,
We SPiT in our FOOD
Great And care

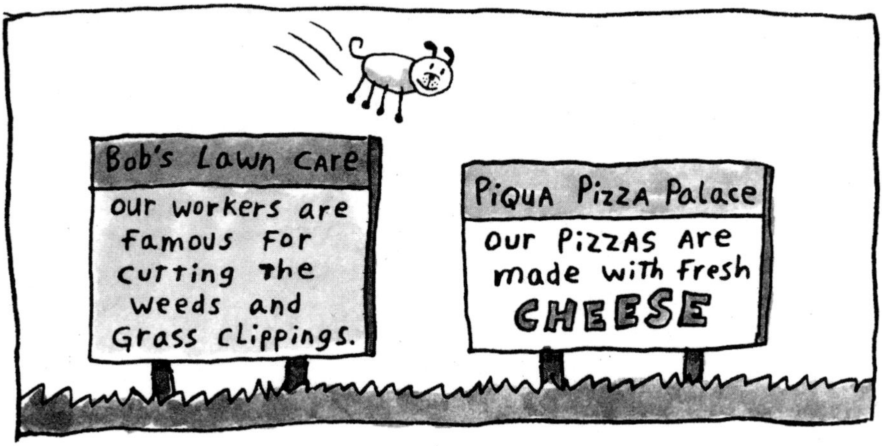
Bob's Lawn Care
our workers are famous for cutting the weeds and Grass clippings.
Piqua Pizza Palace
Our pizzas are made with fresh CHEESE

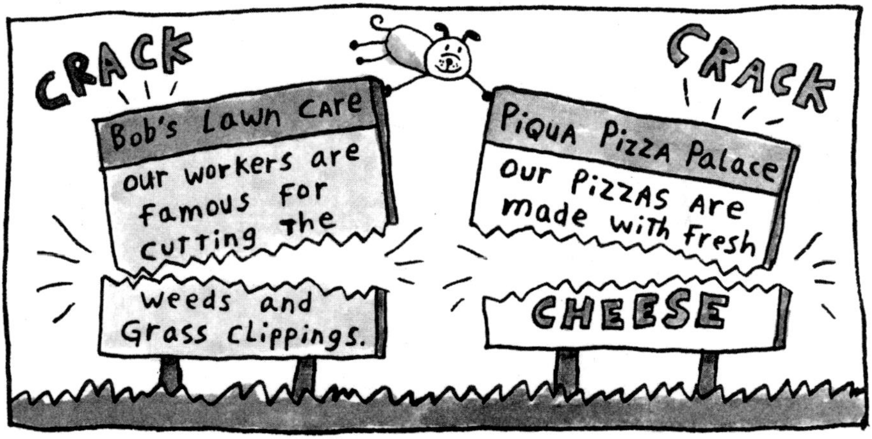
CRACK
CRACK
Bob's Lawn Care
our workers are famous for cutting the
weeds and Grass clippings.
Piqua Pizza Palace
Our pizzas are made with fresh
CHEESE

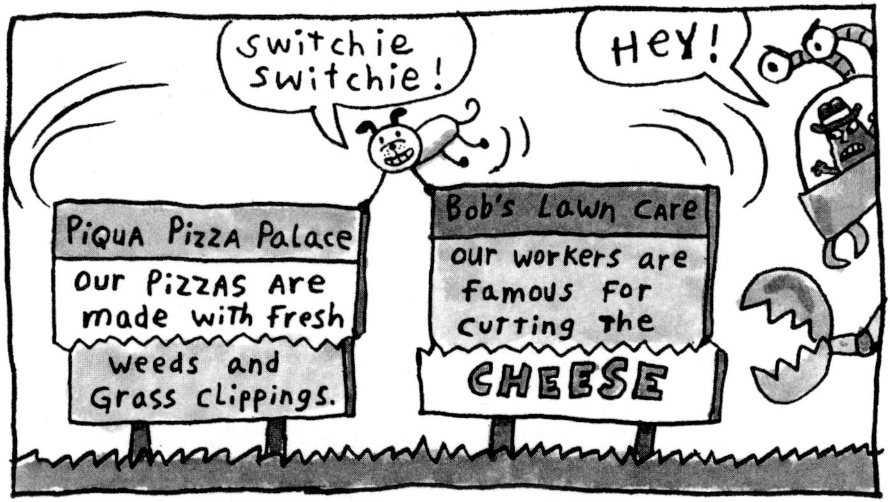
switchie switchie!
Hey!
Piqua Pizza Palace
Our pizzas are made with fresh
weeds and Grass clippings.
Bob's Lawn Care
our workers are famous for cutting the
CHEESE

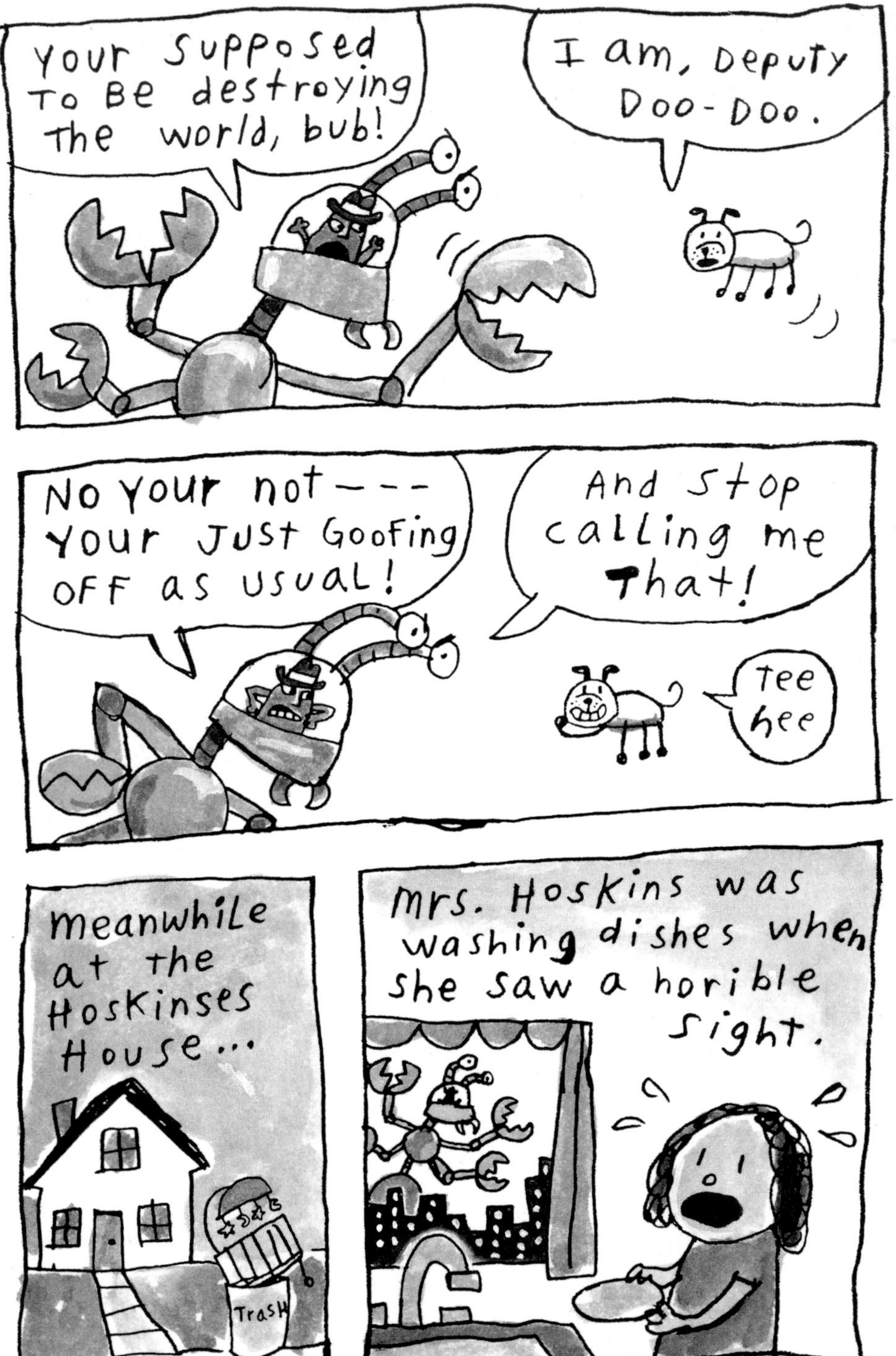

Your supposed To Be destroying the world, bub!
I am, Deputy Doo-Doo.
No your not--- your just Goofing off as usual!
And stop calling me That!
Tee hee
meanwhile at the Hoskinses House...
Trash
Mrs. Hoskins was washing dishes when she saw a horible sight.

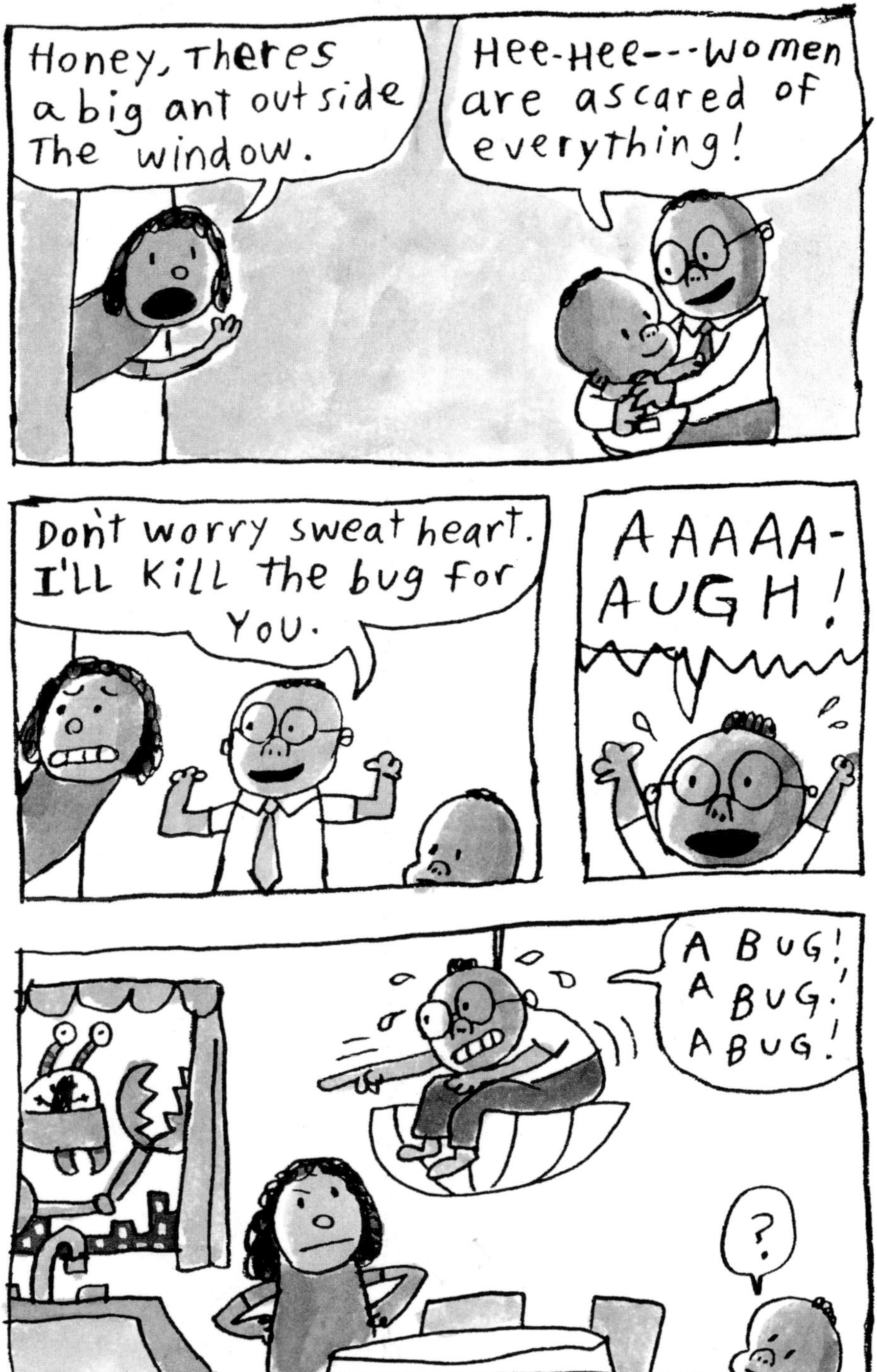
Honey, Theres a big ant outside The window.
Hee-Hee---women are ascared of everything!
Don't worry sweat heart. I'LL Kill the bug for You.
AAAAA-AUGH!
A BUG! A BUG! A BUG!
?

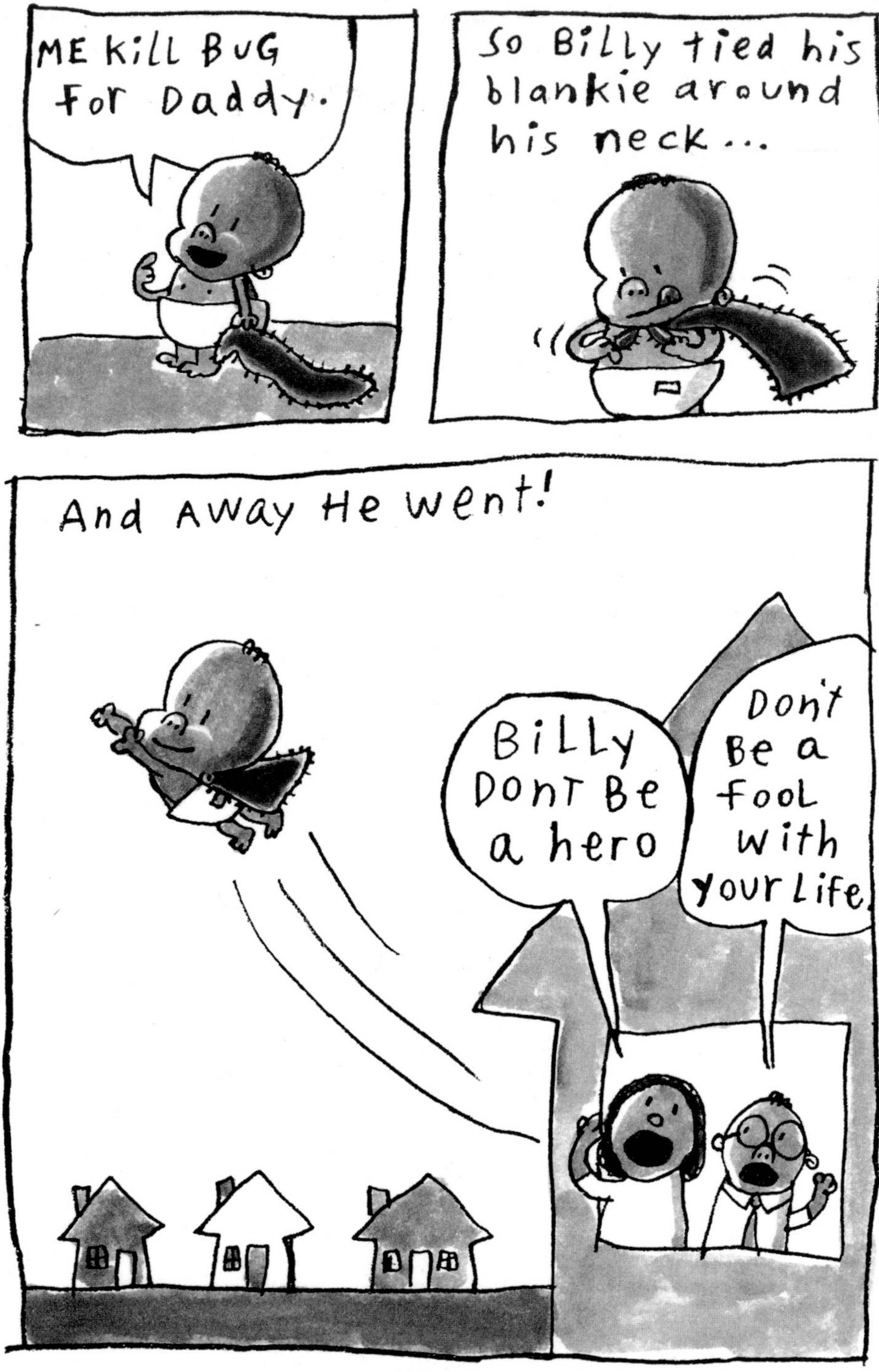
ME KiLL BuG For Daddy.
So Billy tied his blankie around his neck...
And Away He went!
BiLLy DONT Be a hero
Don't Be a FooL with your Life.

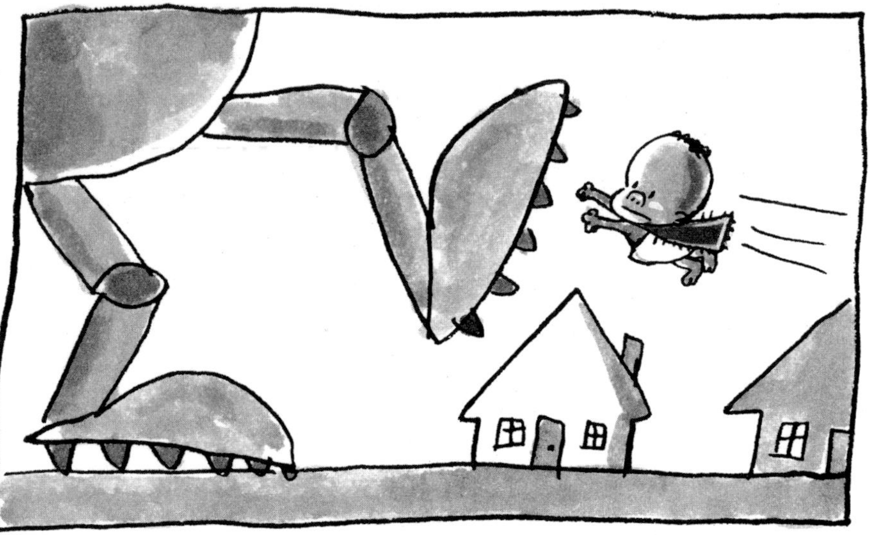

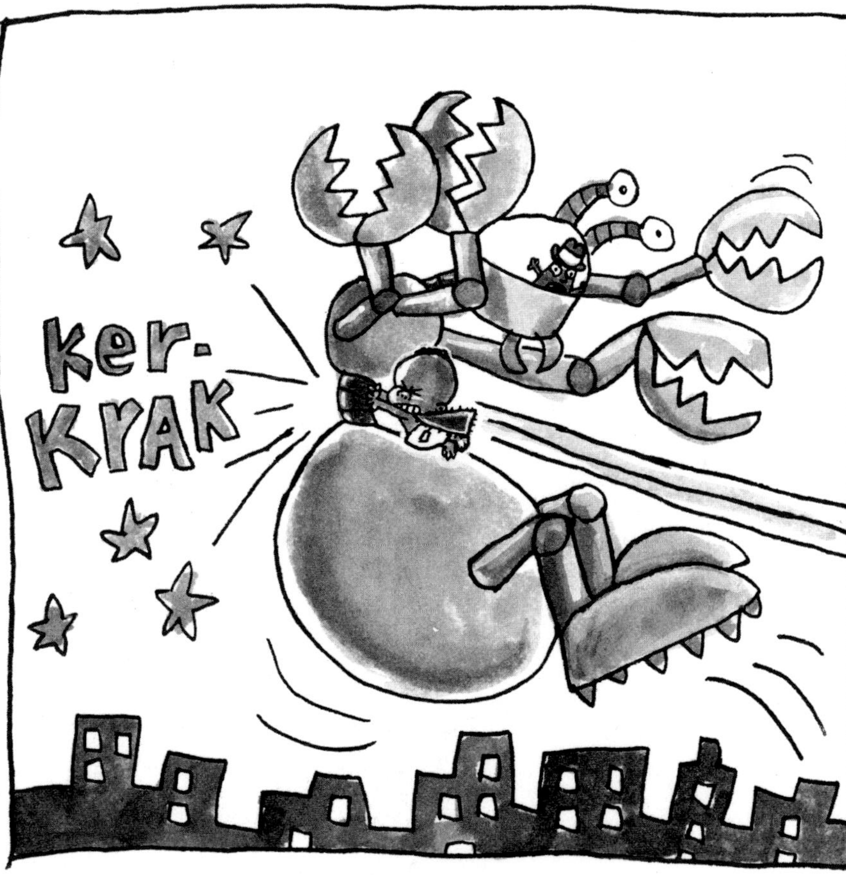

ker-
KRAK

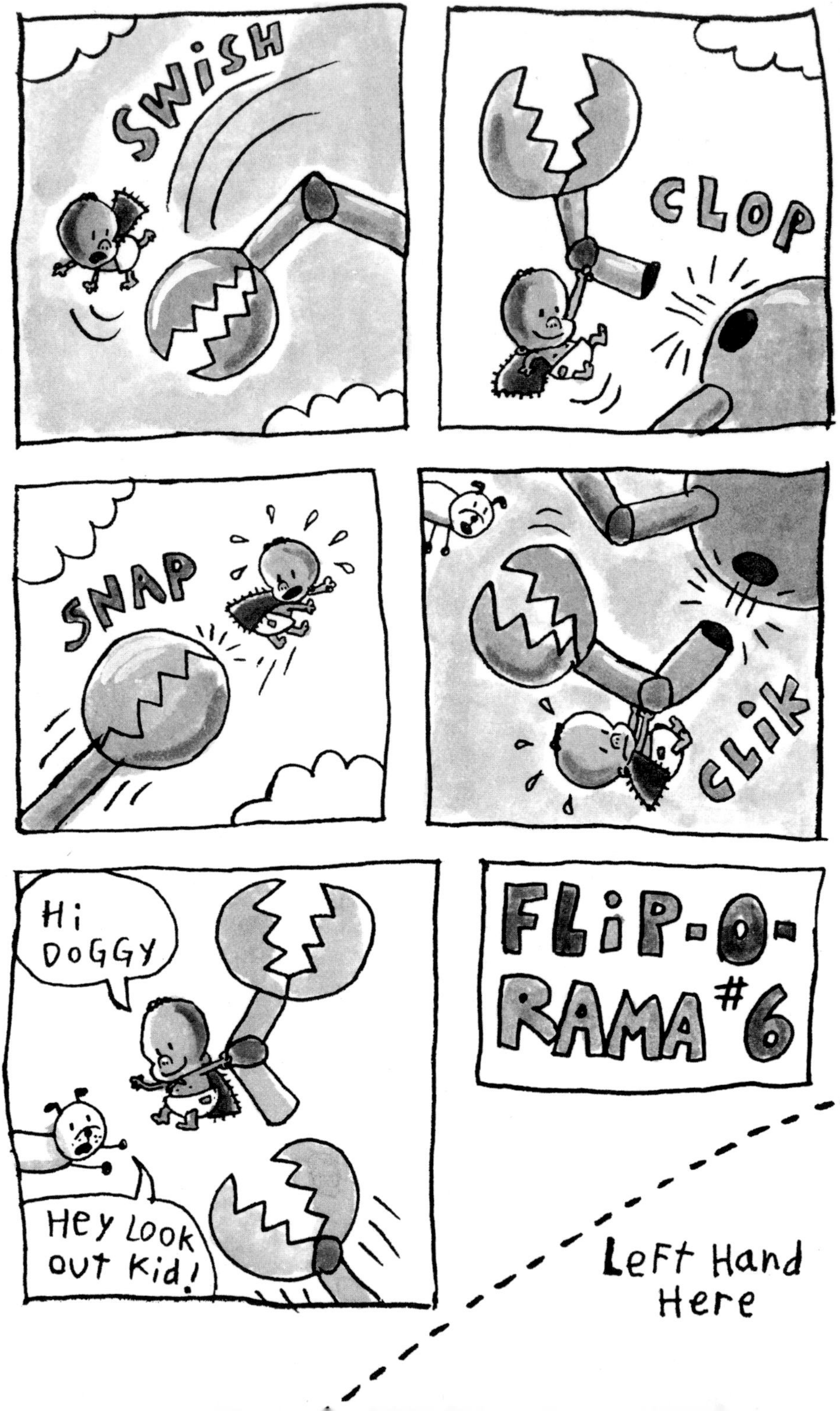
SWISH
CLOP
SNAP
CLIK
Hi DOGGY
Hey LOOK out Kid!
FLIP-O-RAMA #6
Left Hand Here

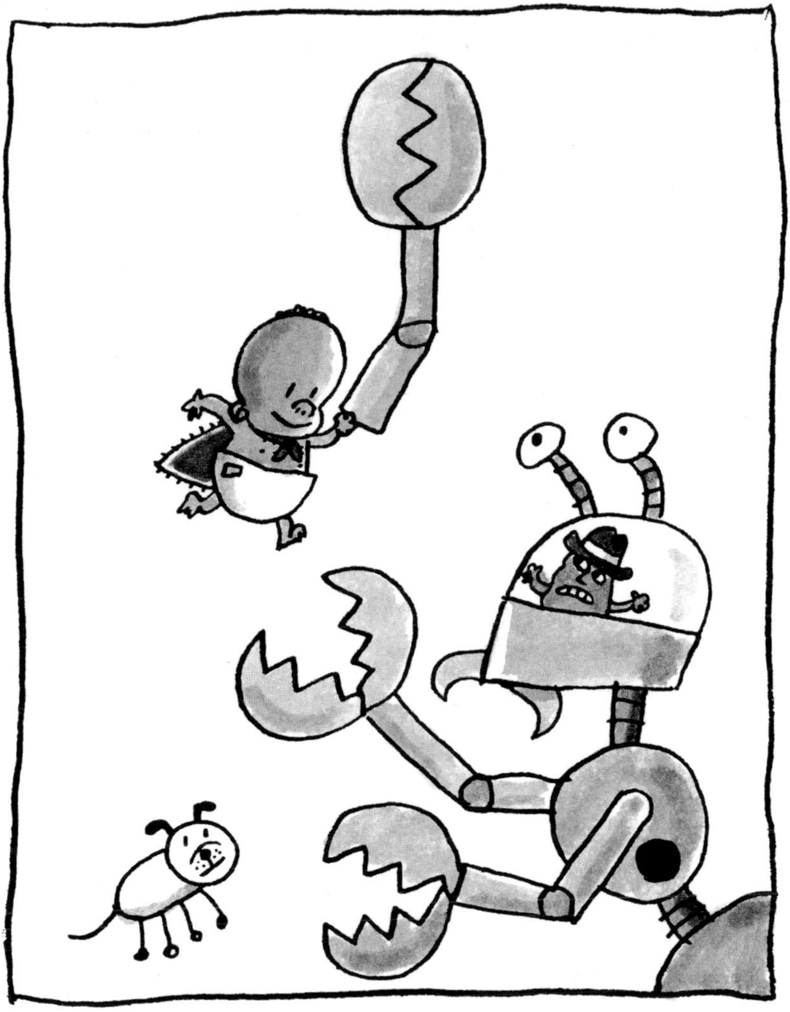

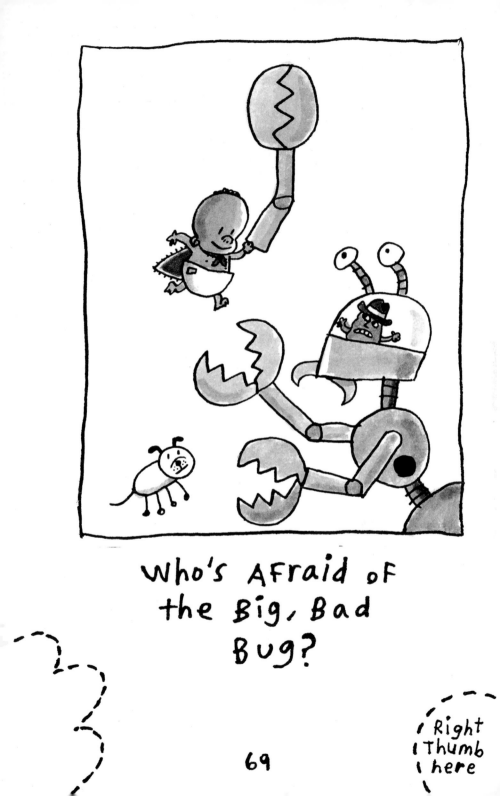

Who's AFraid of the Big, Bad Bug?

Right Thumb here

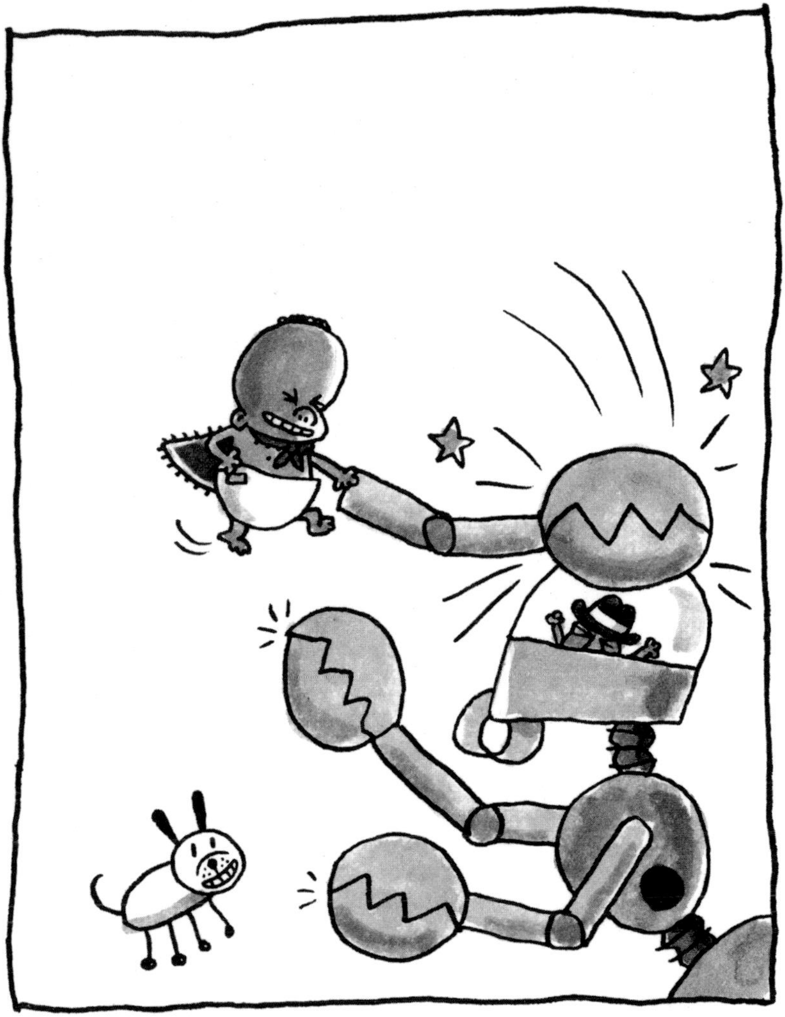

Who's Afraid of the Big, Bad Bug?

FLIP-O-RAMA #7

(pages 73 and 75.)

Remember, flip only page 73. while you are fliping, be shure to blah, blah, blah. You're not really reading this page, are you?

Well, since your here anyway, how about a gross joke? Q: What's the difference between boogers and broccoli?

A: Kids wont eat broccoli.

LeFt Hand Here

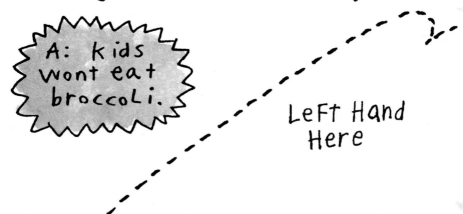

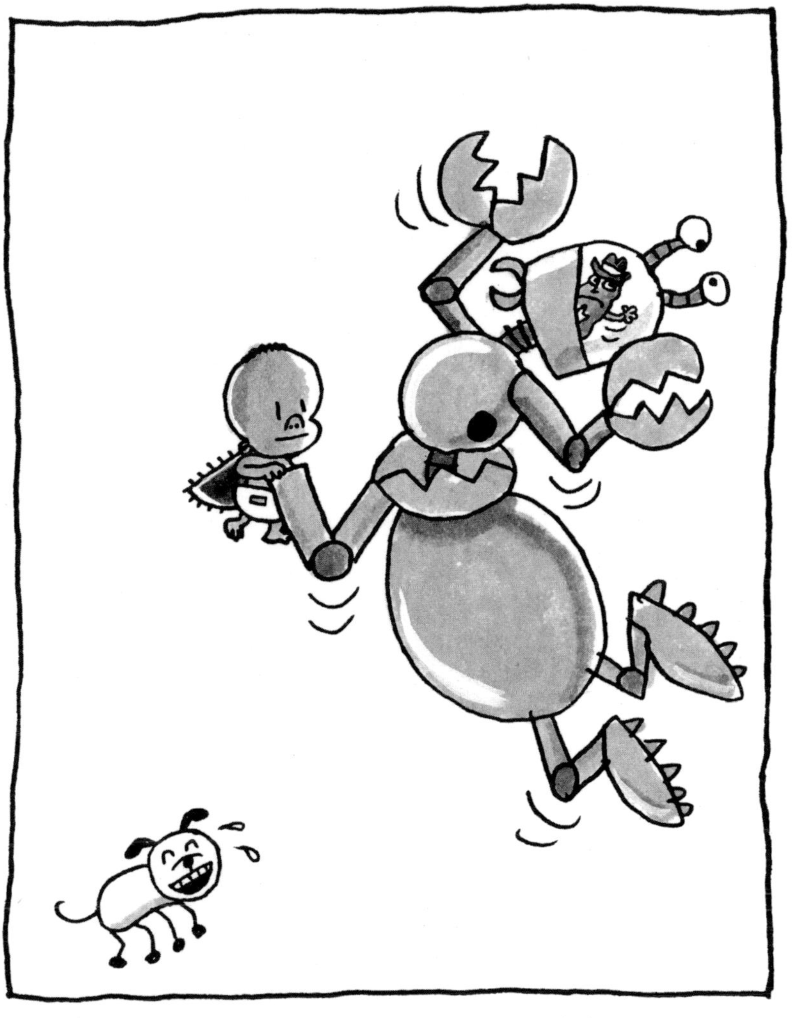

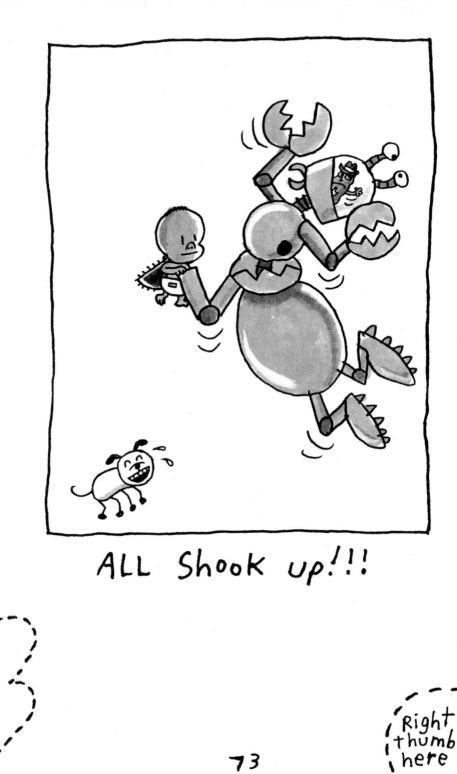

ALL Shook up!!!

Right thumb here

ALL Shook up!!!

FLIP-O-RAMA #8

(Pages **77** and **79**.)

Remember, FLip only page 77. You know, since nobody reads these pages, we figured they'd be a good place to insert subliminimal messages:

Think for yourself. Question Authority. Read banned books! Kids have the same constitutional rights as grown-ups!!!

Don't forget to boycott standardized testing!!!

LeFt Hand Here

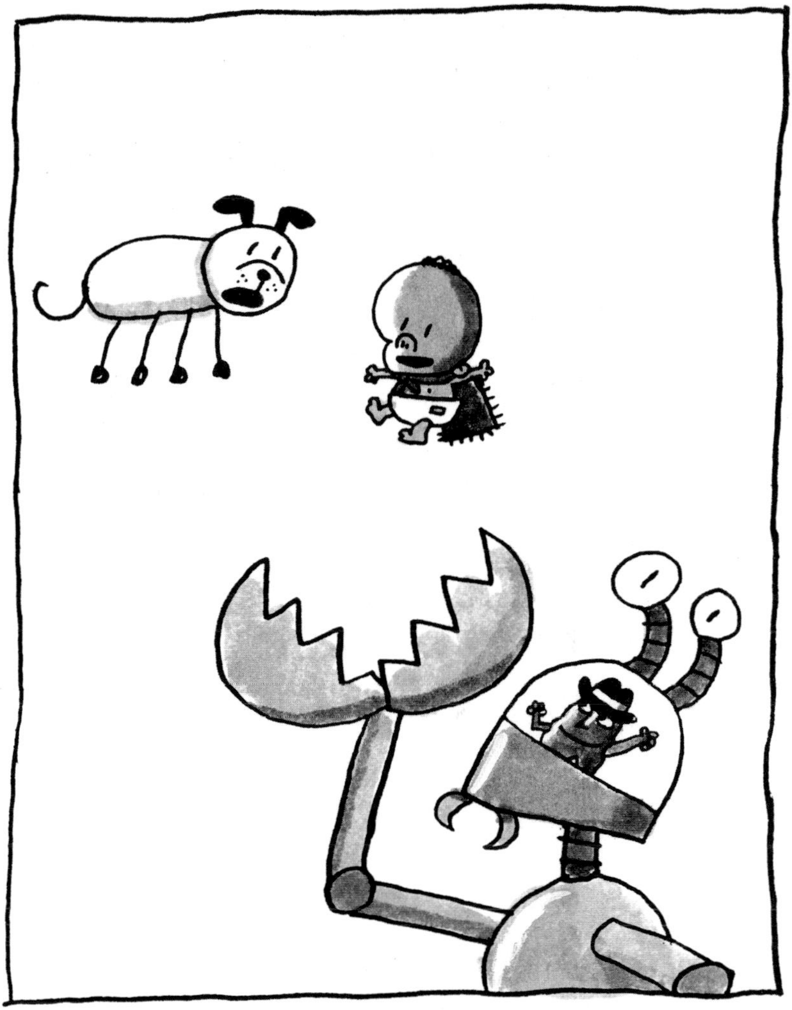

Watch out, BiLLy!!!

Right Thumb Here

Watch out, Billy!!!

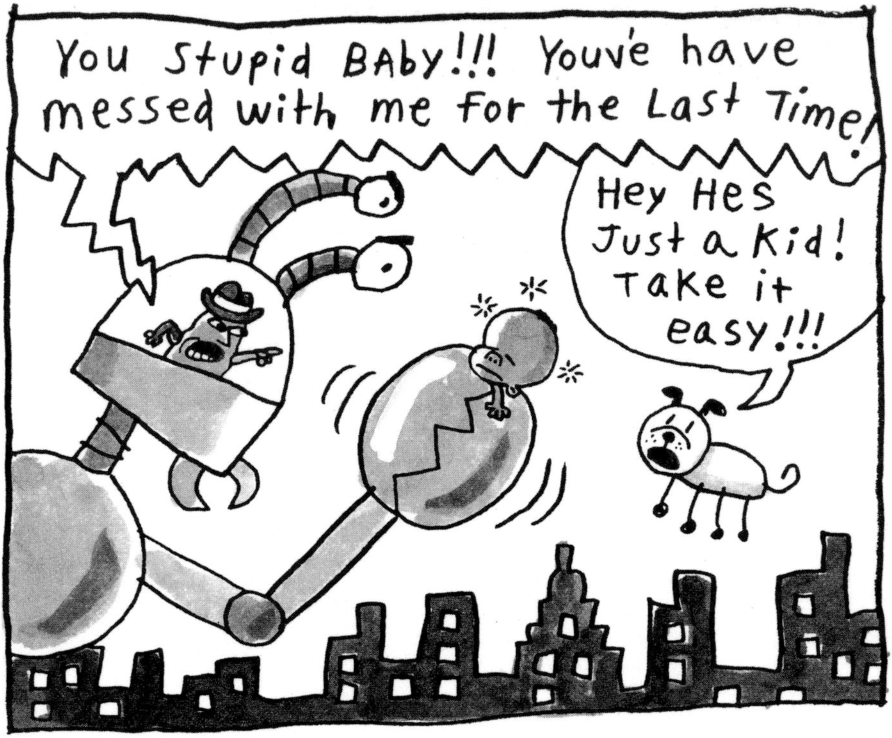
You Stupid BAby!!! Youve have messed with me For the Last Time!
Hey Hes Just a Kid! Take it easy!!!

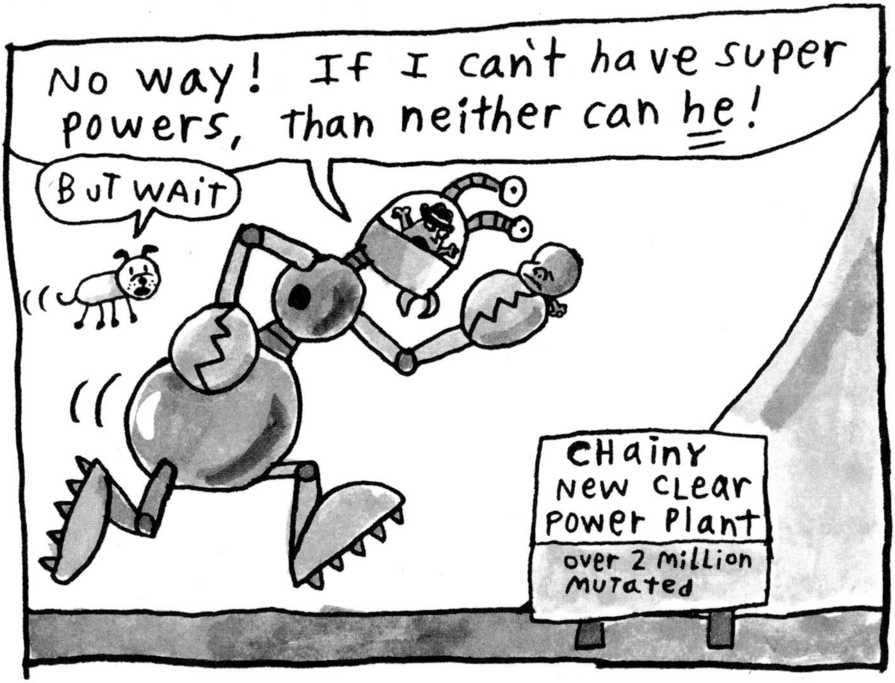
No way! If I can't have super powers, than neither can he!
BuT WAIT
CHainy New CLear Power Plant
over 2 MilLion Mutated

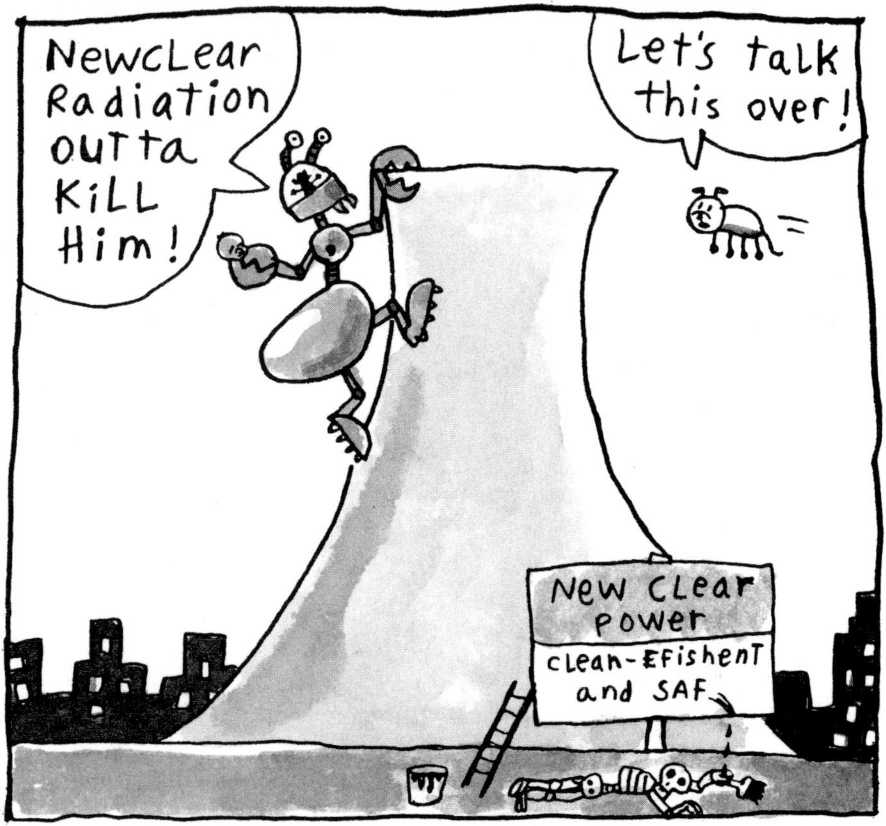
NewcLear Radiation outta KiLL Him!
Let's talk this over!
New CLear power
cLean-Efishent and SAF

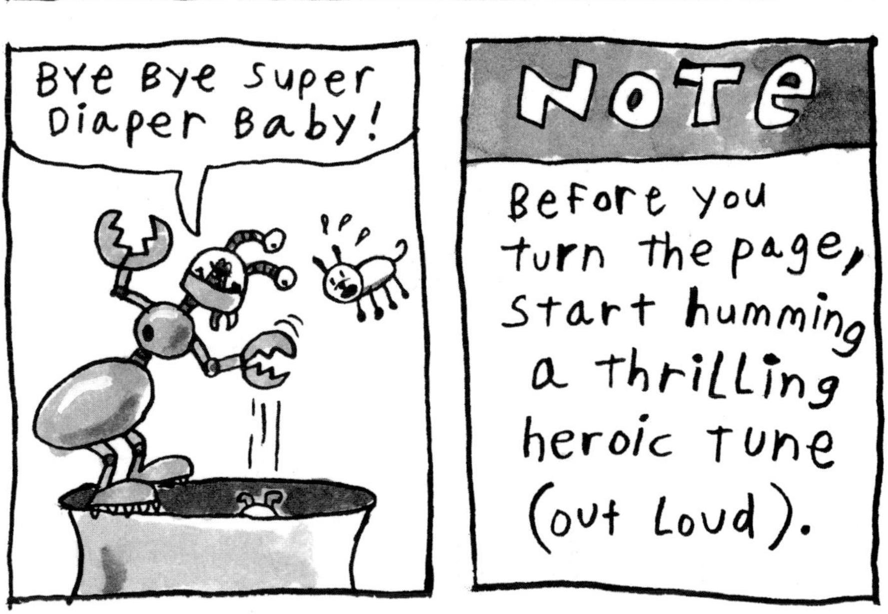
BYE Bye Super Diaper Baby!

NOTE

Before you turn the page, start humming a thrilling heroic tune (out loud).

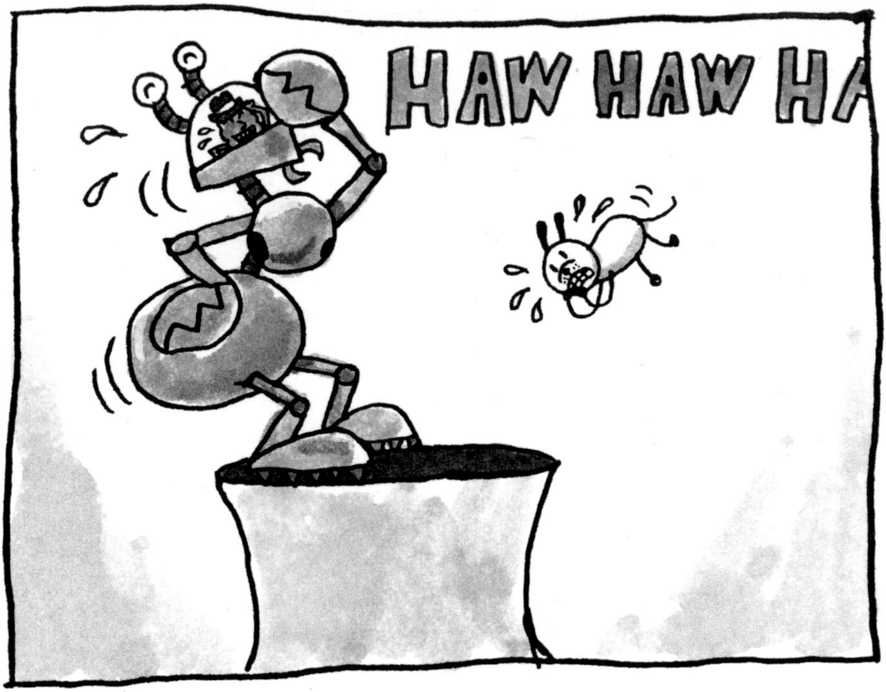
HAW HAW HA

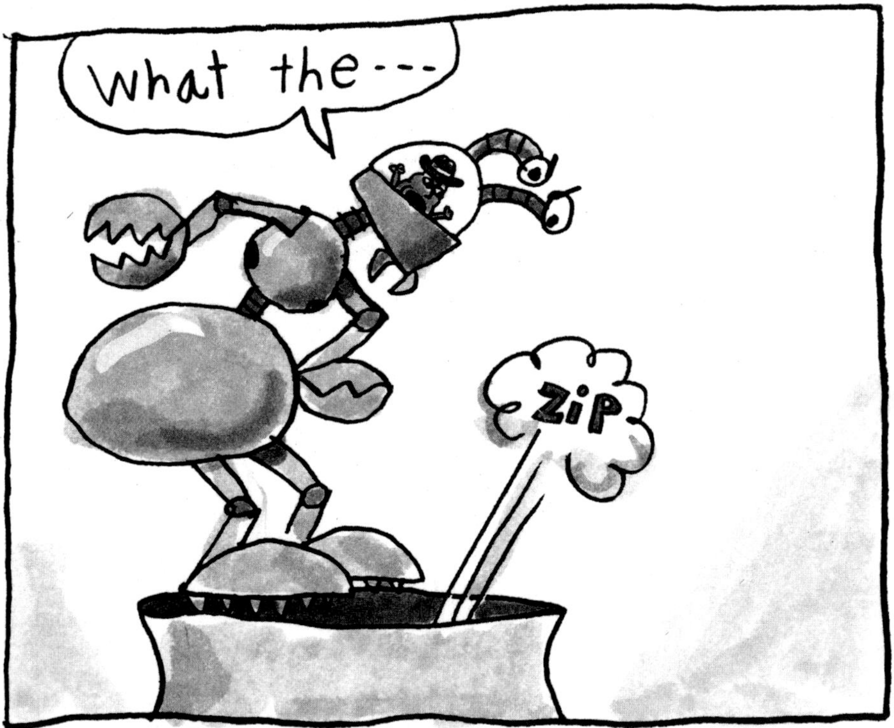
what the---
ZiP

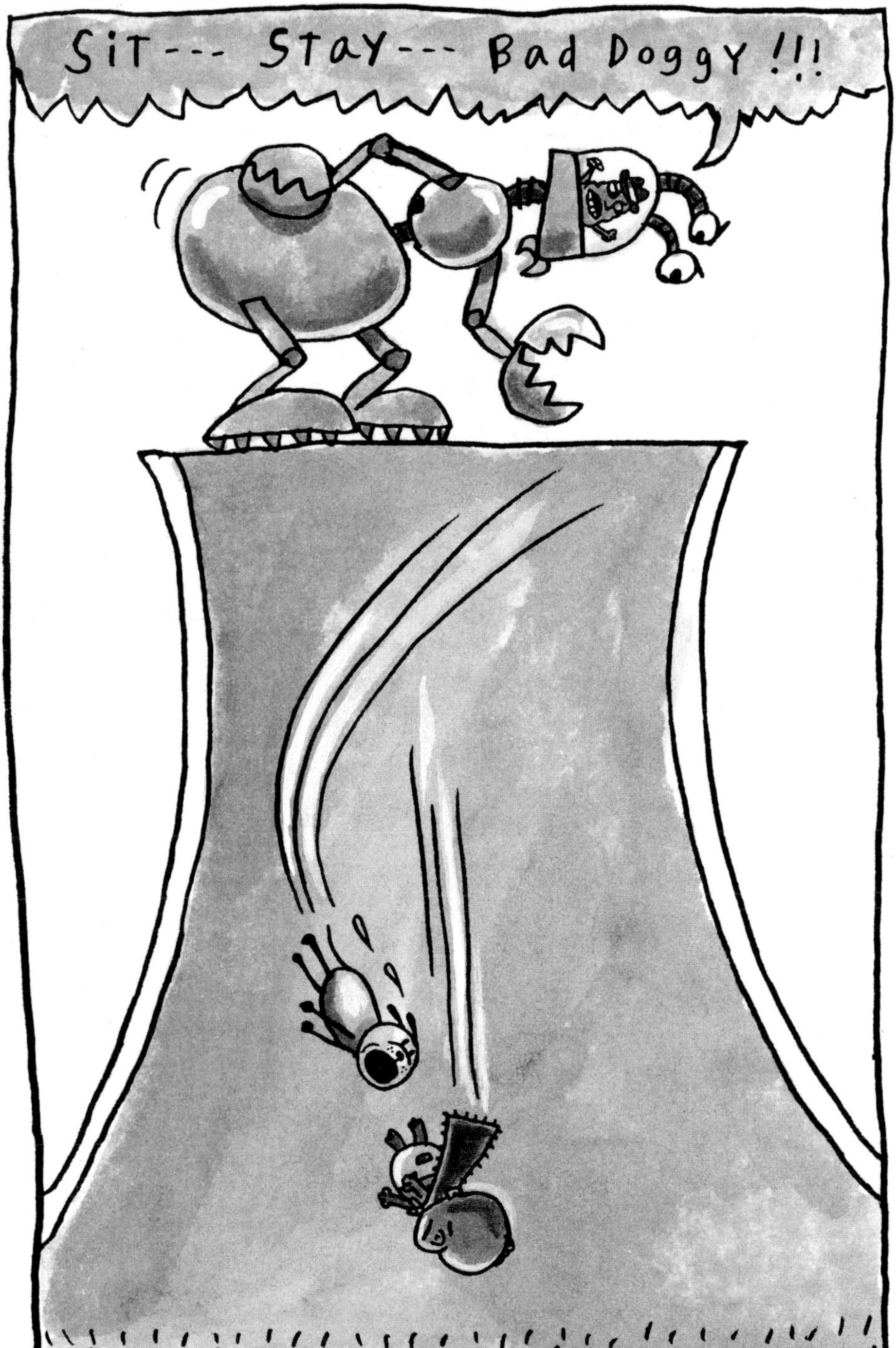
SIT--- STAY--- Bad Doggy!!!

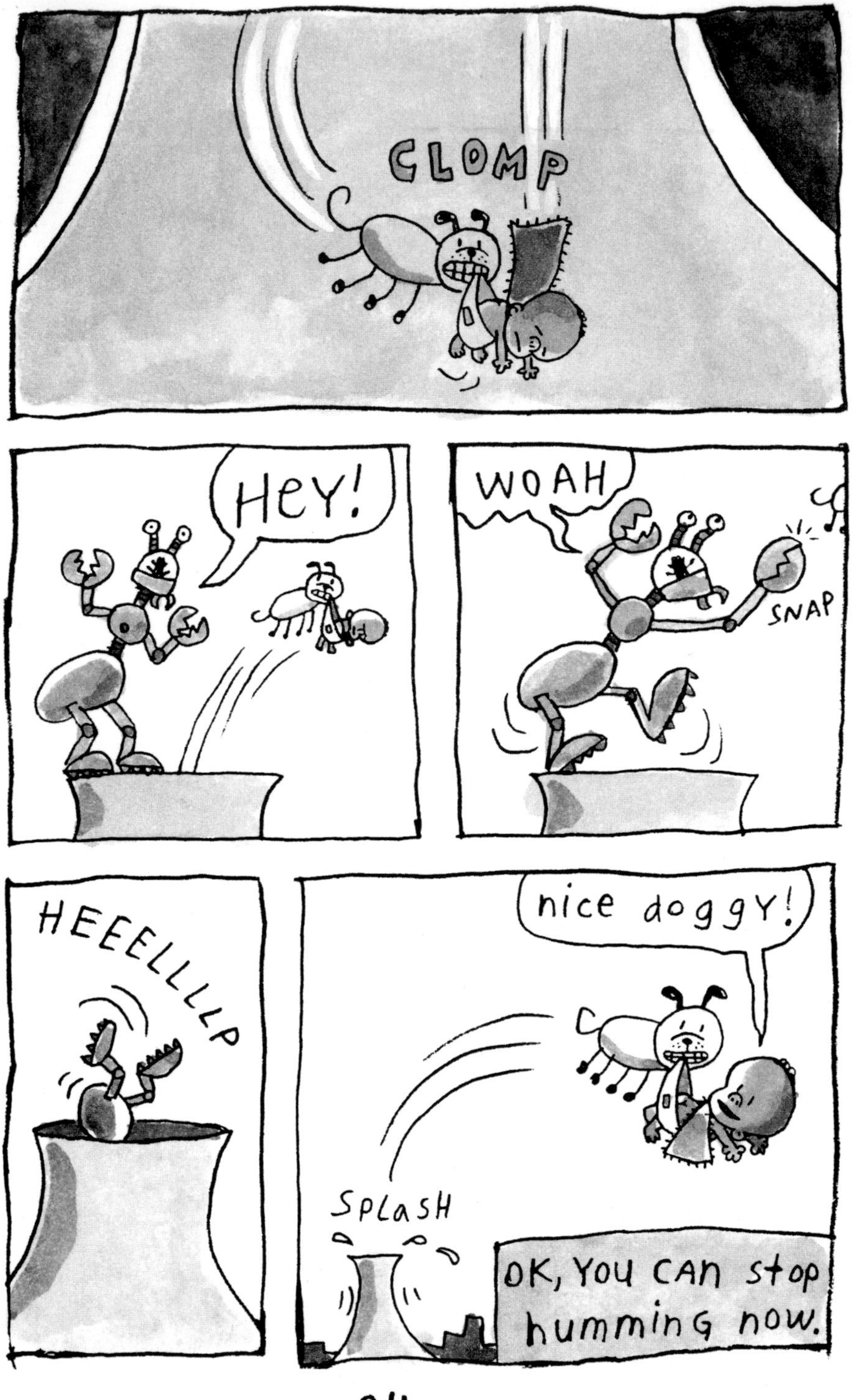
CLOMP
Hey!
WOAH
SNAP
HEEELLLLLP
nice doggy!
SPLASH
OK, YOU CAN stop humming now.

SUPER DiAPER BABY

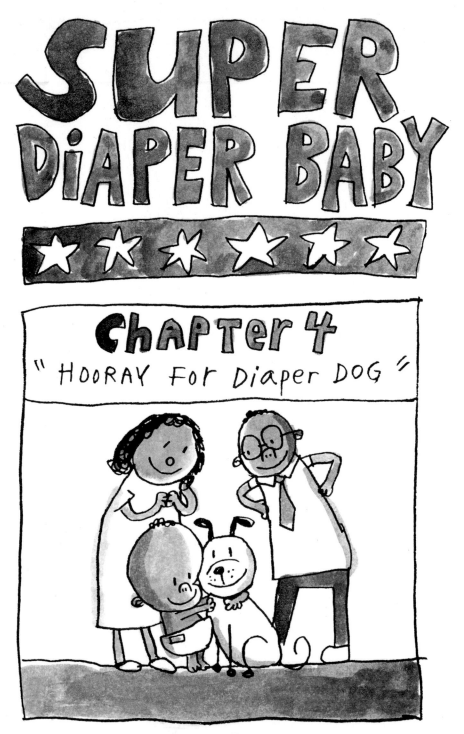

CHAPTER 4
"HOORAY FOR Diaper DOG"

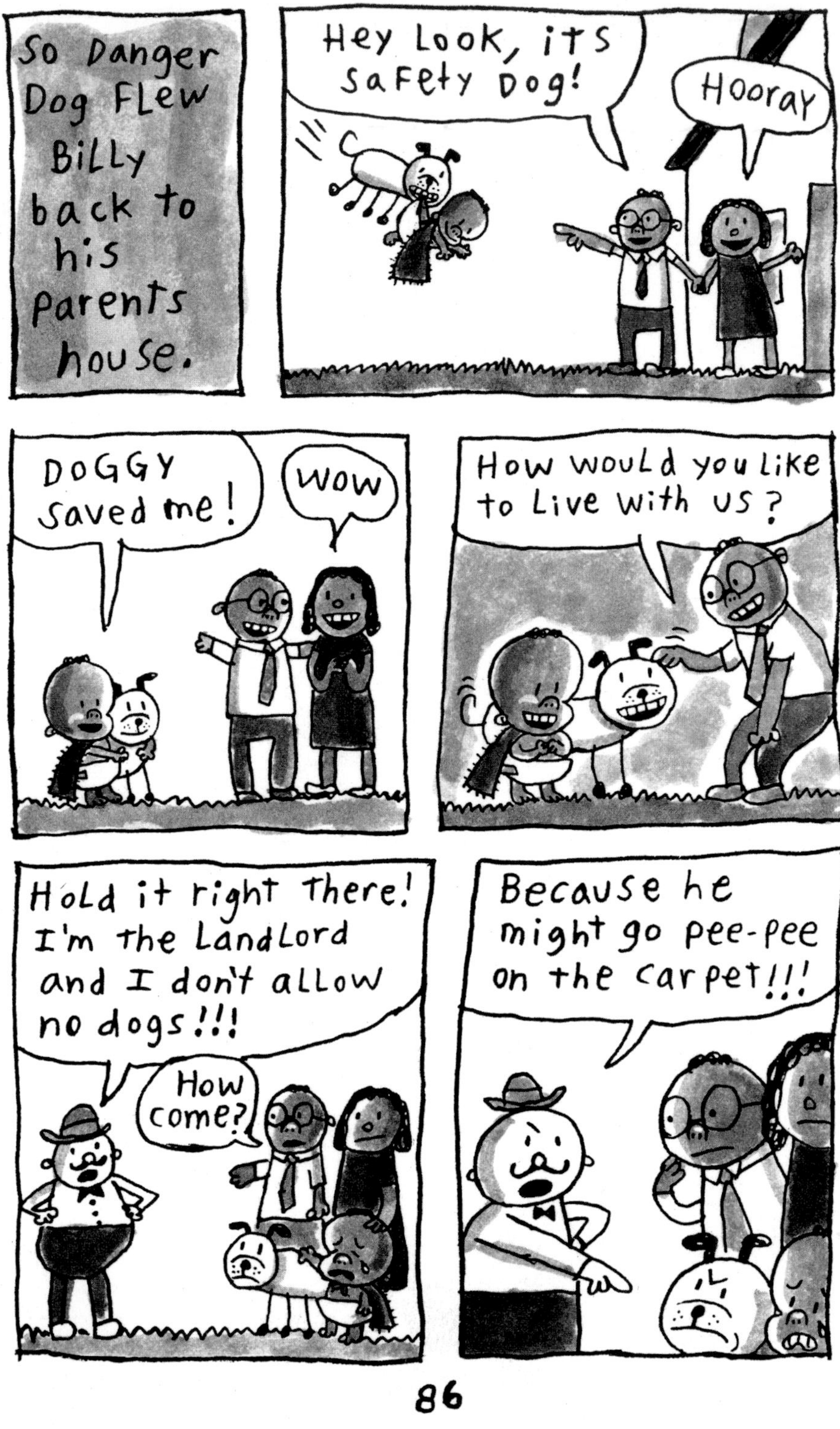
So Danger Dog Flew Billy back to his parents house.
Hey Look, its Safety Dog!
Hooray
DOGGY saved me!
WOW
How would you like to Live with us?
Hold it right there! I'm the LandLord and I don't allow no dogs!!!
How come?
Because he might go pee-pee on the carpet!!!

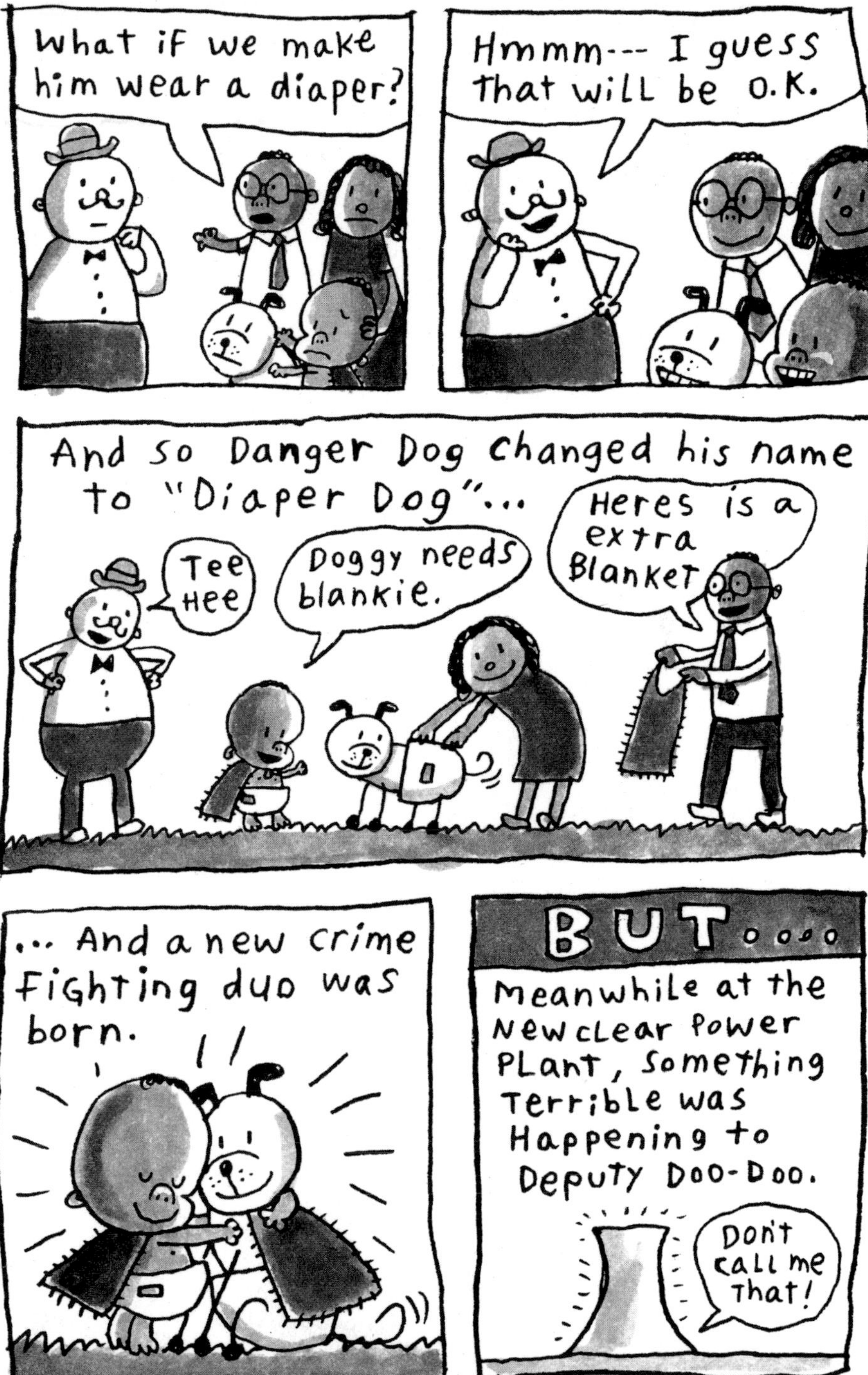
What if we make him wear a diaper?
Hmmm--- I guess That will be O.K.
And so Danger Dog changed his name to "Diaper Dog"...
Tee Hee
Doggy needs blankie.
Heres is a extra Blanket
... And a new crime Fighting duo was born.
BUT....
Meanwhile at the NewcLear Power PLant, Something Terrible was Happening to Deputy Doo-Doo.
Don't call me That!

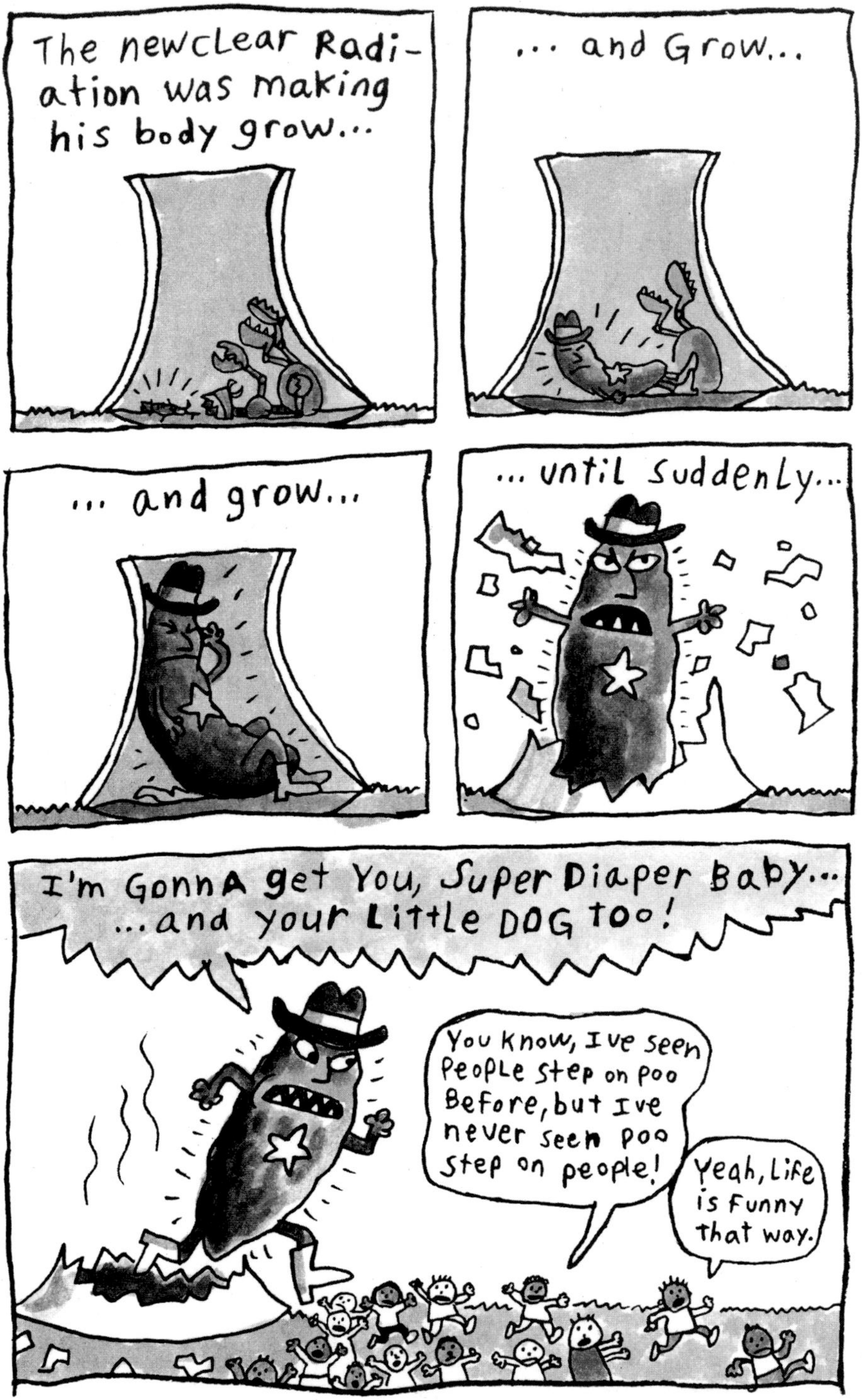
The newclear Radiation was making his body grow...
... and Grow...
... and grow...
... until suddenly...
I'm GonnA get You, Super Diaper Baby... ...and your Little DOG too!
You know, Ive seen people step on poo Before, but Ive never seen poo step on people!
Yeah, Life is Funny that way.

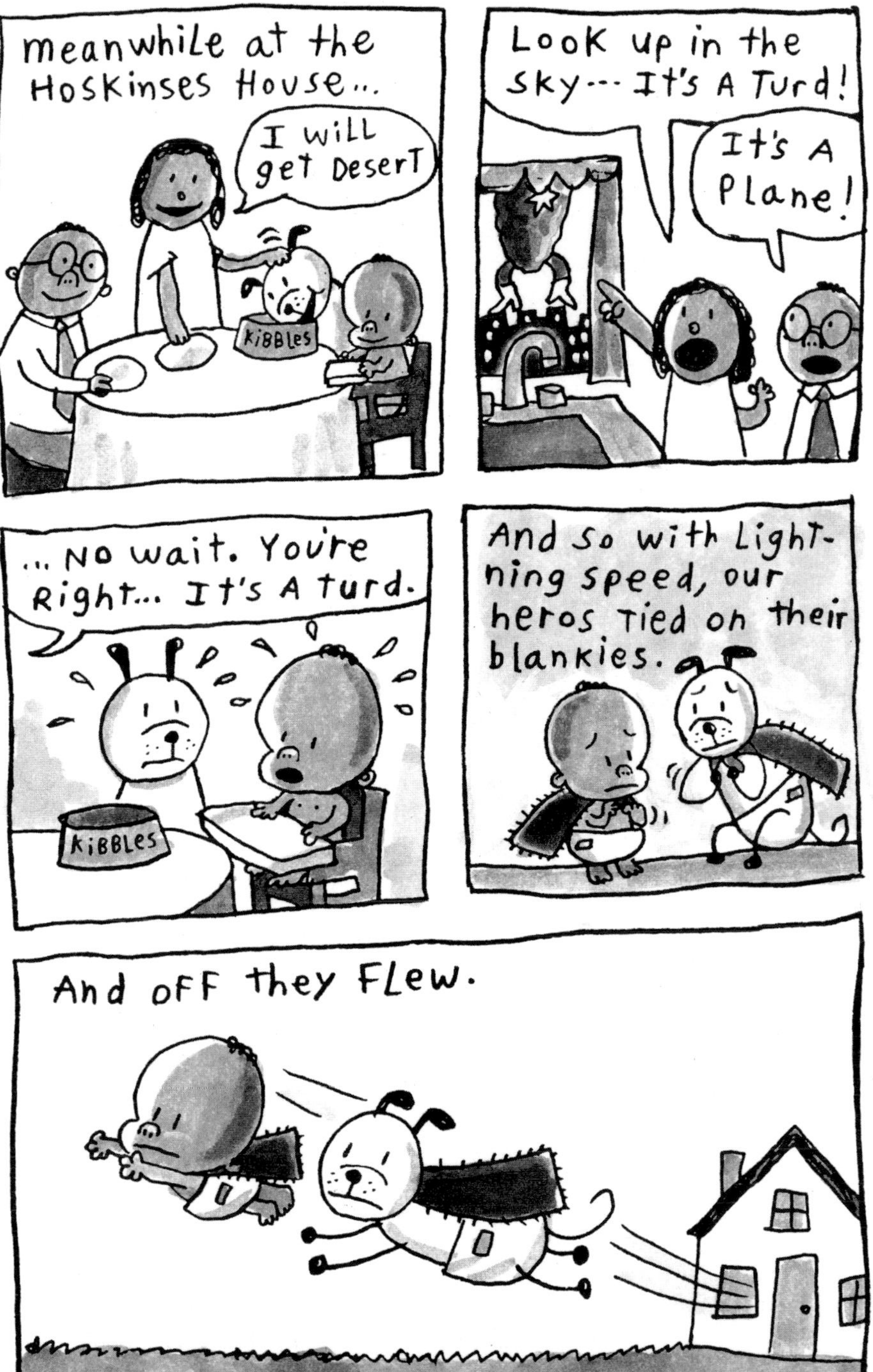
meanwhile at the Hoskinses House...
I will get DeserT
KiBBLES
Look up in the sky--- It's A Turd!
It's A Plane!
... No wait. You're Right... It's A turd.
KiBBLES
And so with Lightning speed, our heros Tied on their blankies.
And off they Flew.

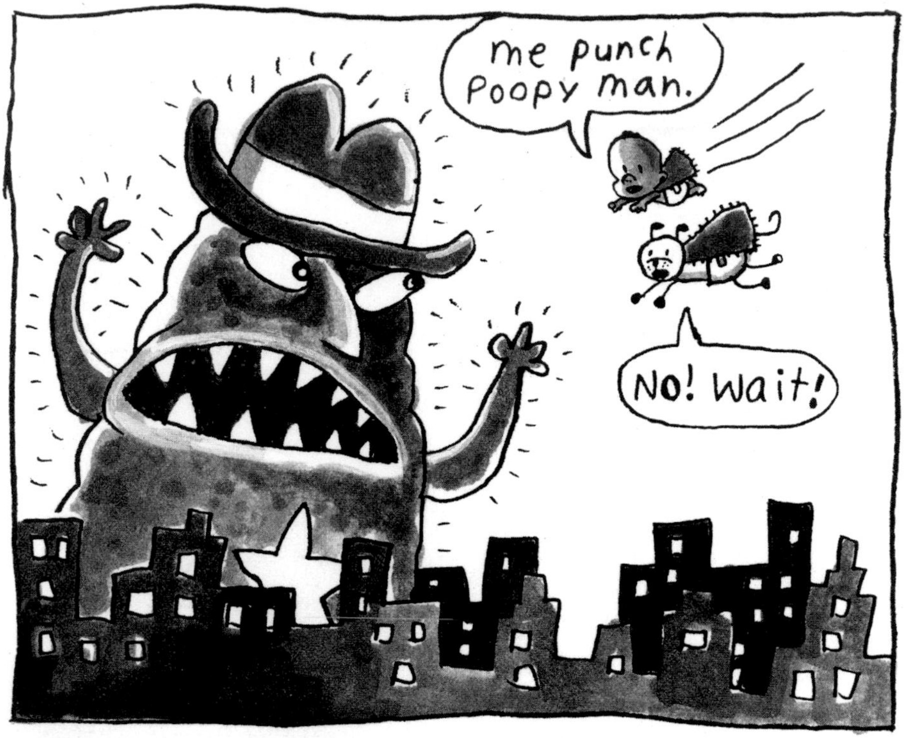
me punch Poopy man.
No! Wait!

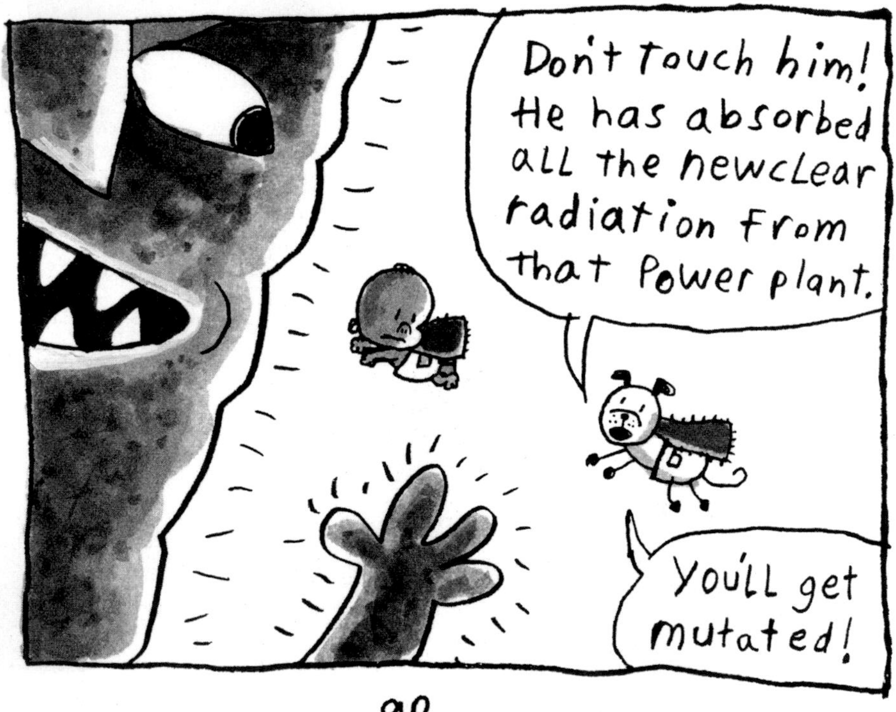
Don't touch him! He has absorbed all the newclear radiation from that Power plant.
You'll get mutated!

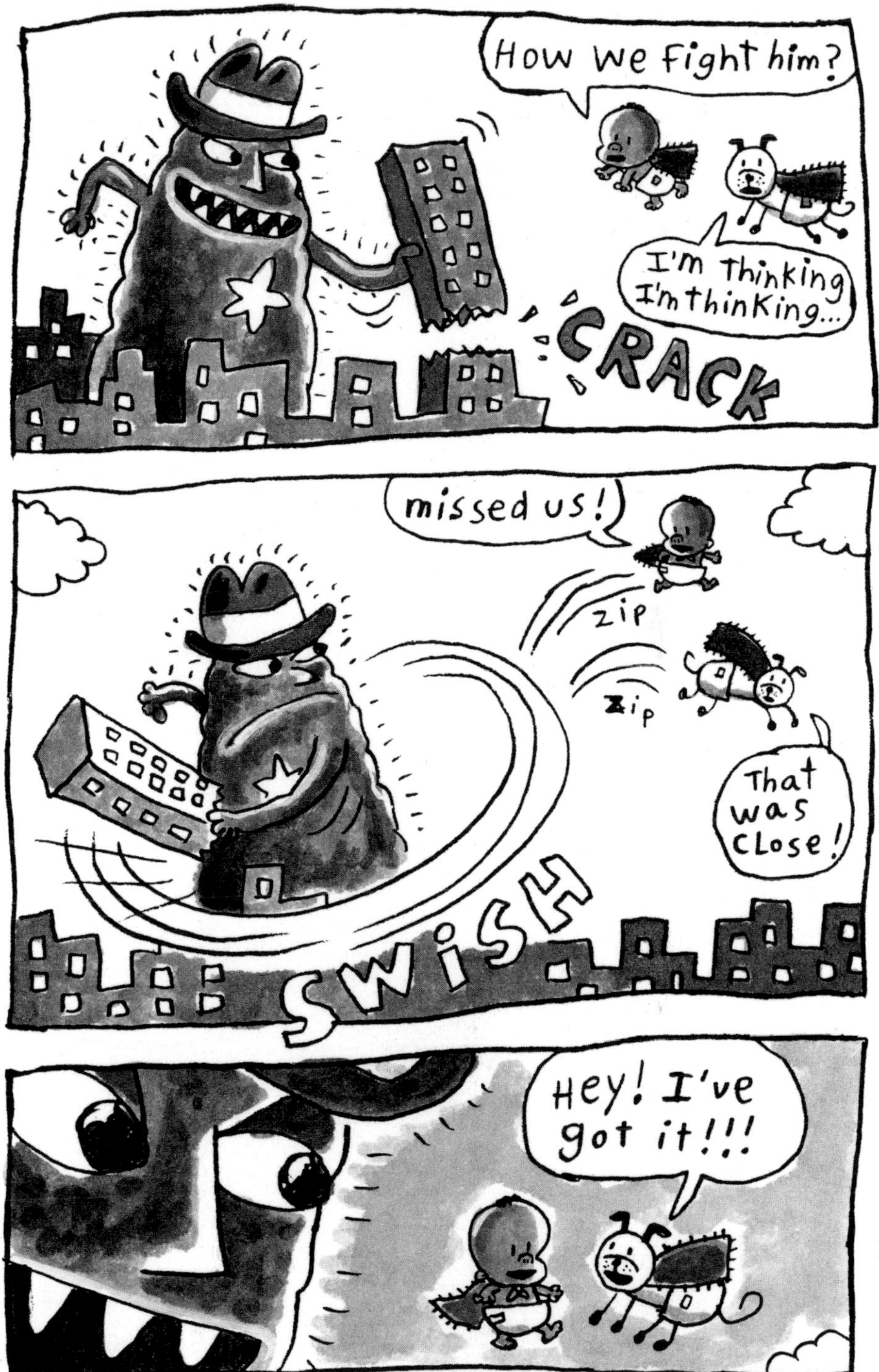
How we fight him?
I'm thinking
I'm thinking...
CRACK
missed us!
zip
zip
That was close!
SWISH
Hey! I've got it!!!

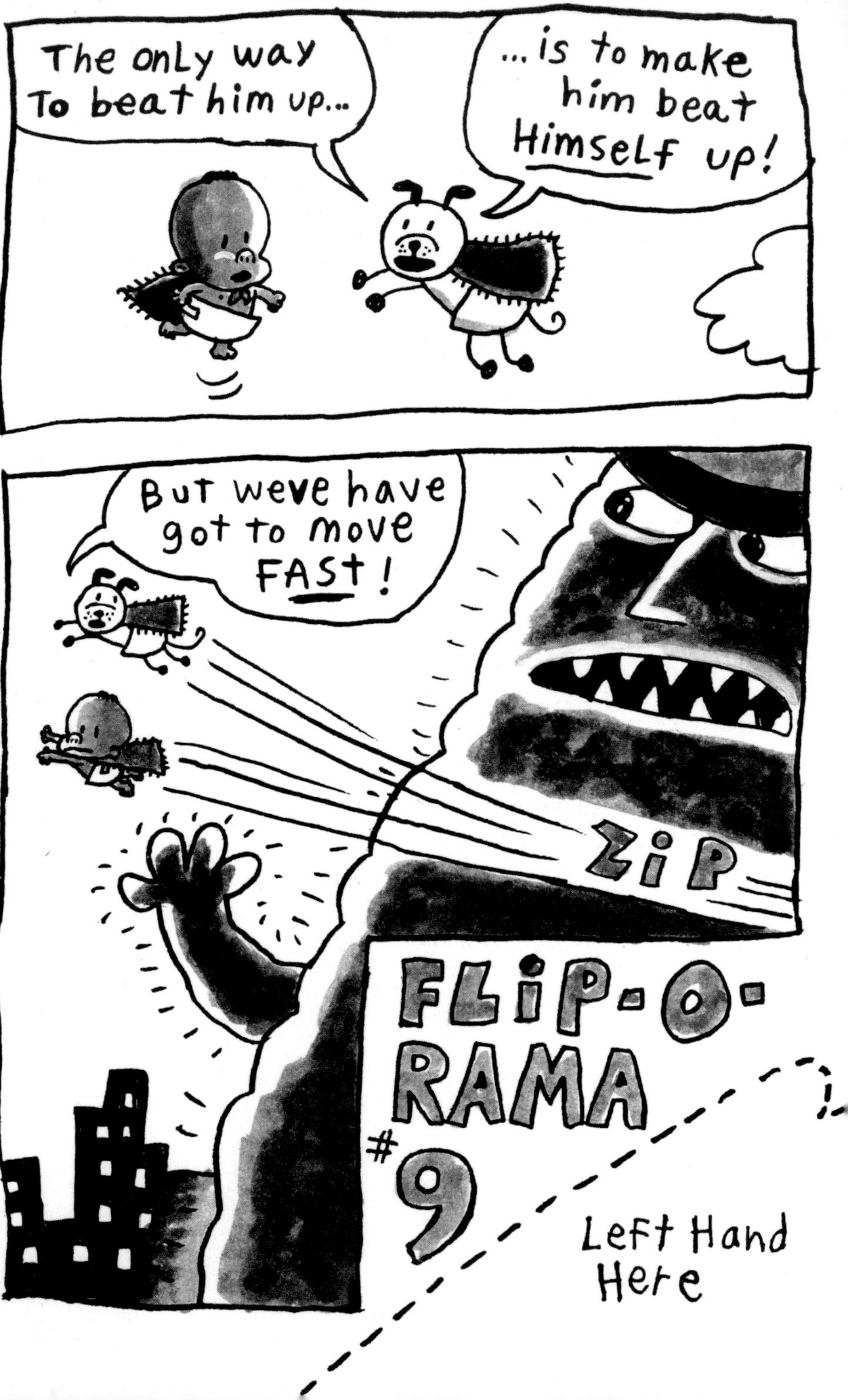
The only way To beat him up...
...is to make him beat Himself up!
But weve have got to move FAST!
ZIP
FLIP-O-RAMA
#9
Left Hand Here

"Poopy-Puncher"

Right
Thumb
here

"Poopy-Puncher"

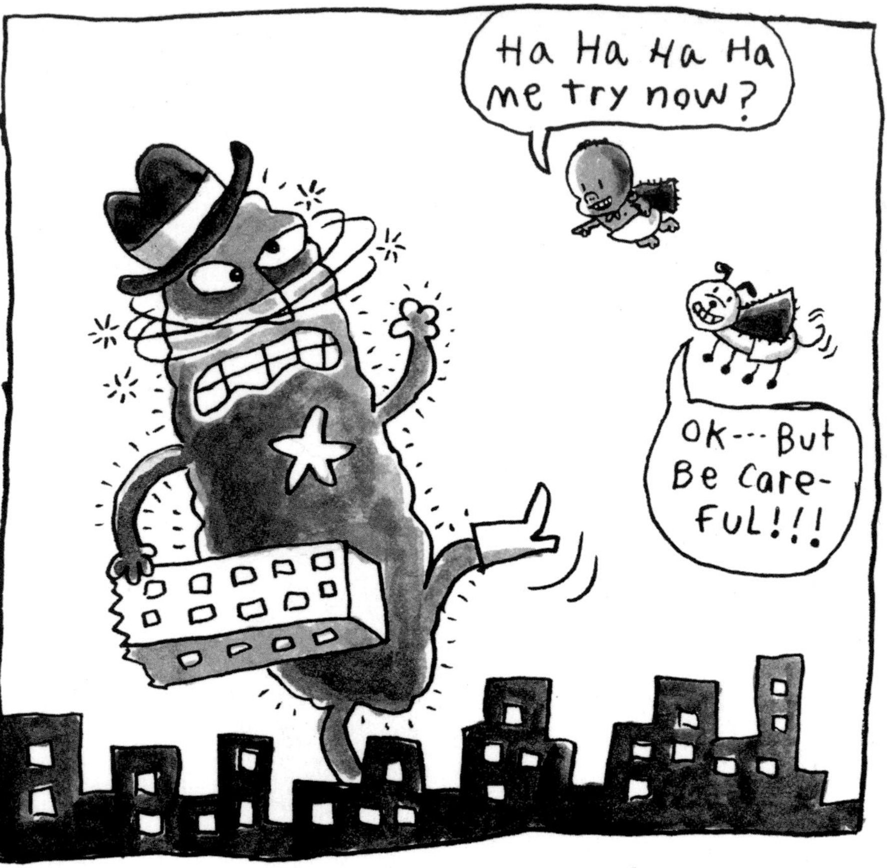
Ha Ha Ha Ha
me try now?
Ok---But
Be care-
FuL!!!

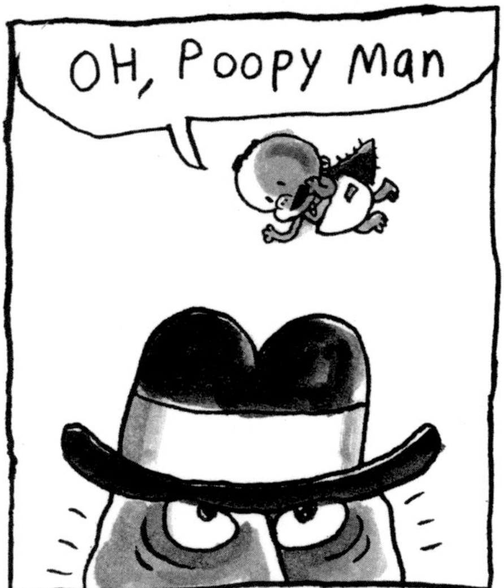
OH, Poopy Man

FLIP-O-RAMA #10

Left Hand
Here

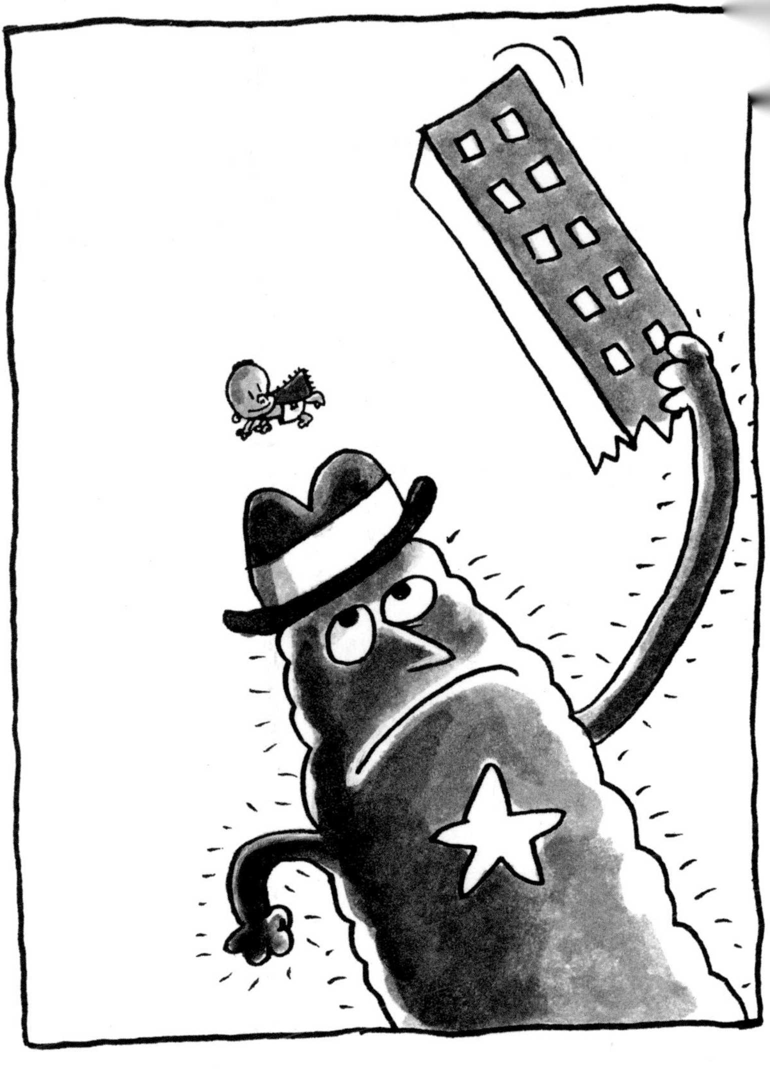

Head Banger Blues

Head Banger
Blues

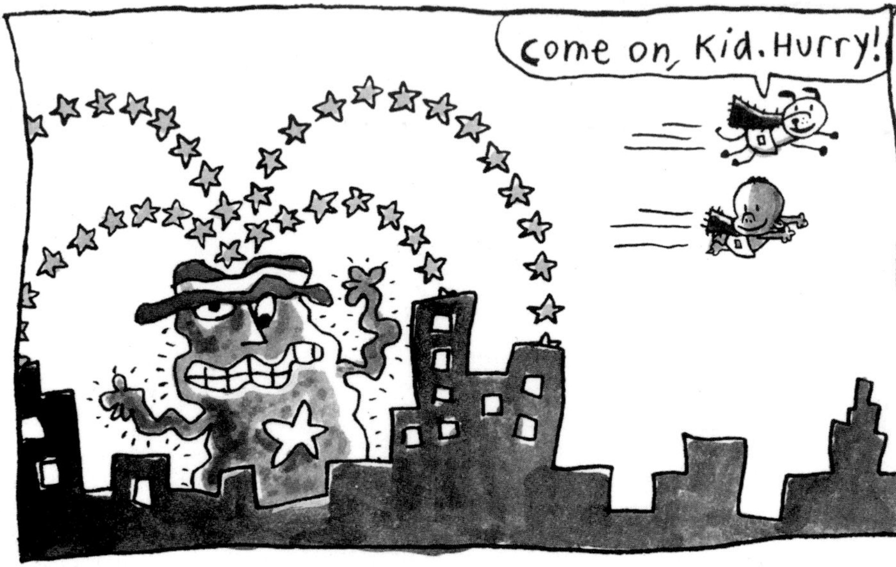
Come on, Kid. Hurry!

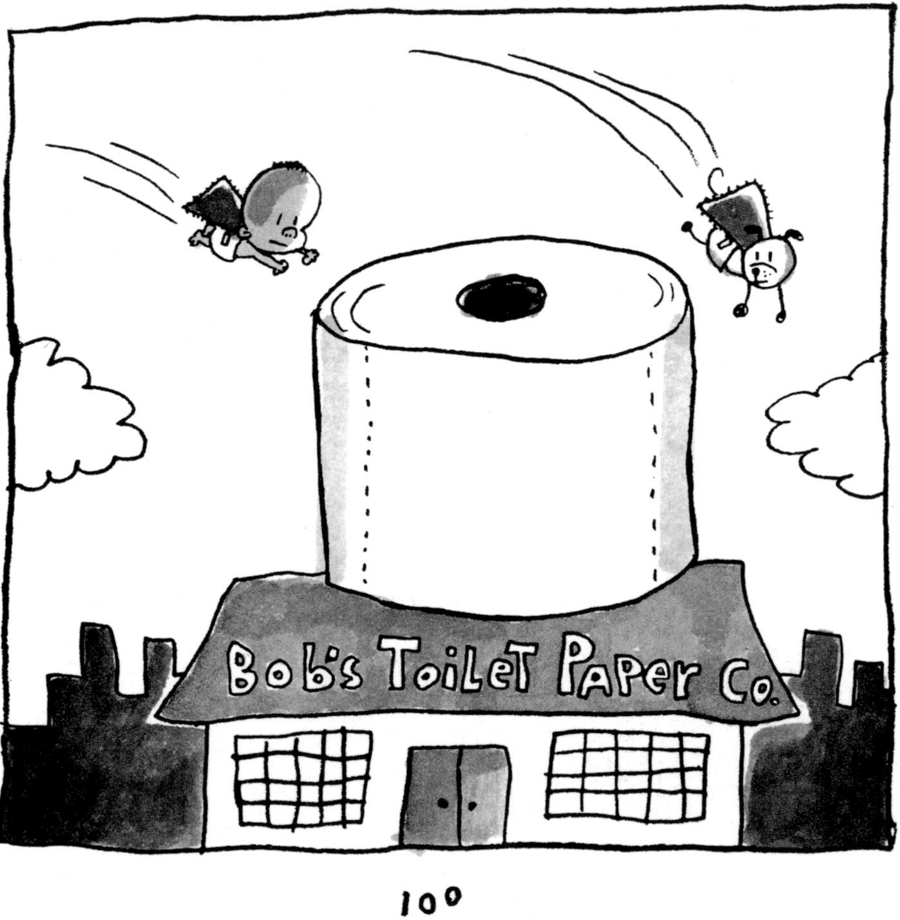
Bob's Toilet Paper Co.

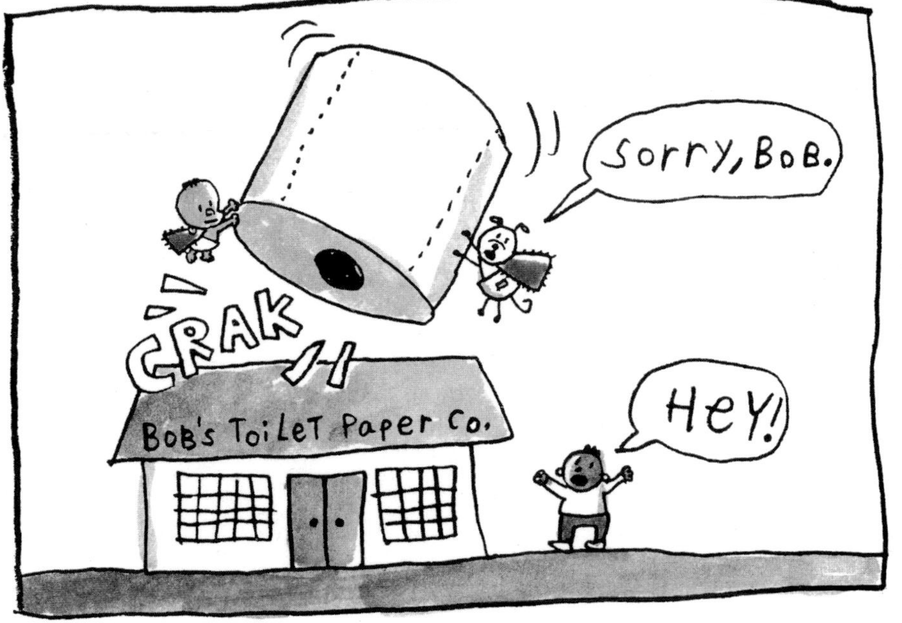
Sorry, BoB.
CRAK
BoB's ToiLeT Paper Co.
HeY!

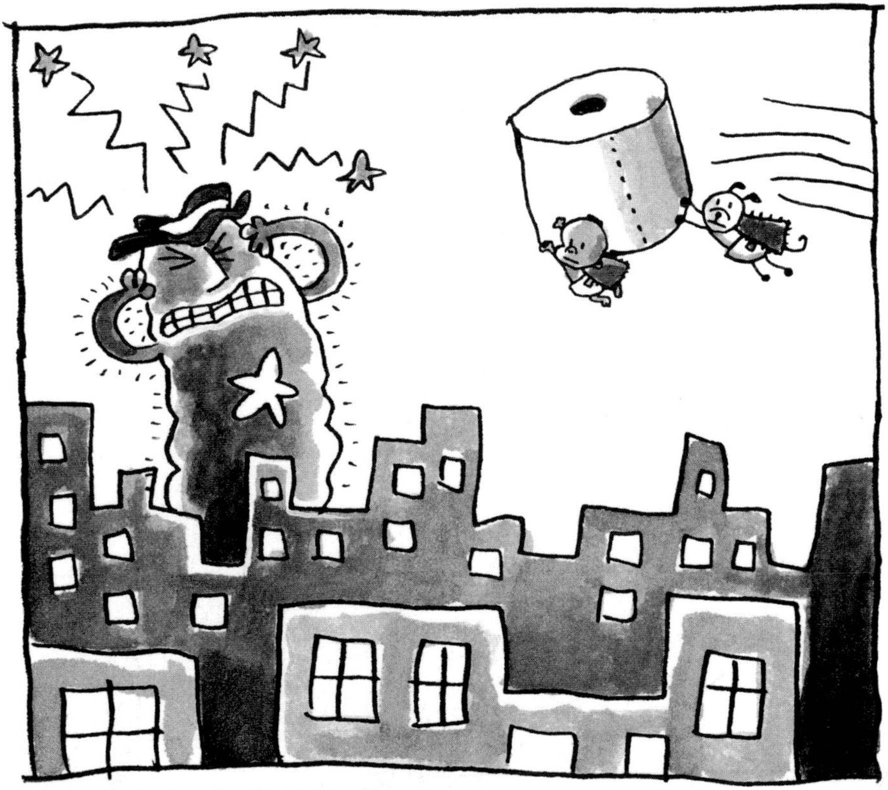

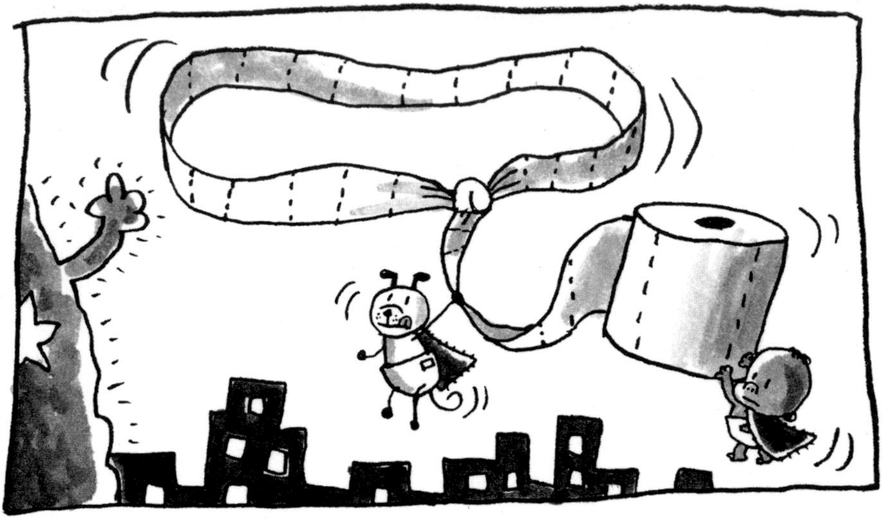

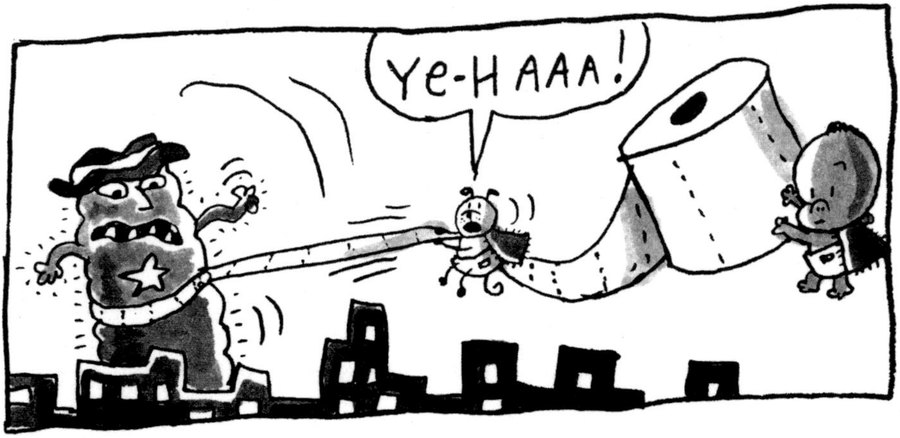
YE-HAAA!

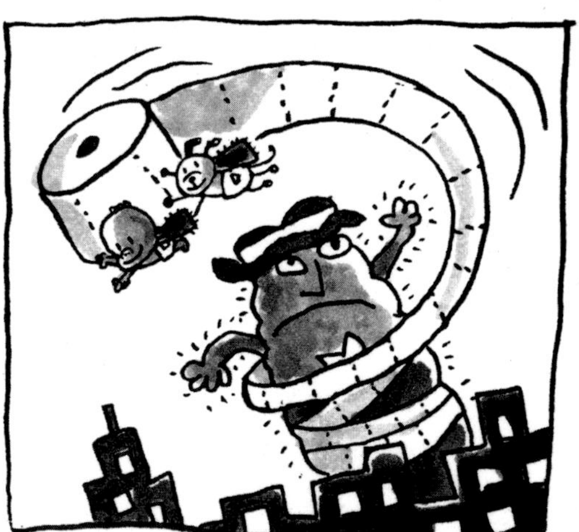

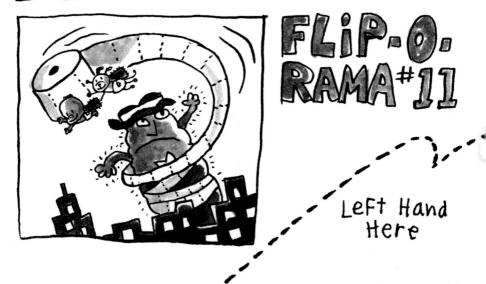

FLIP-O-RAMA #11

Left Hand Here

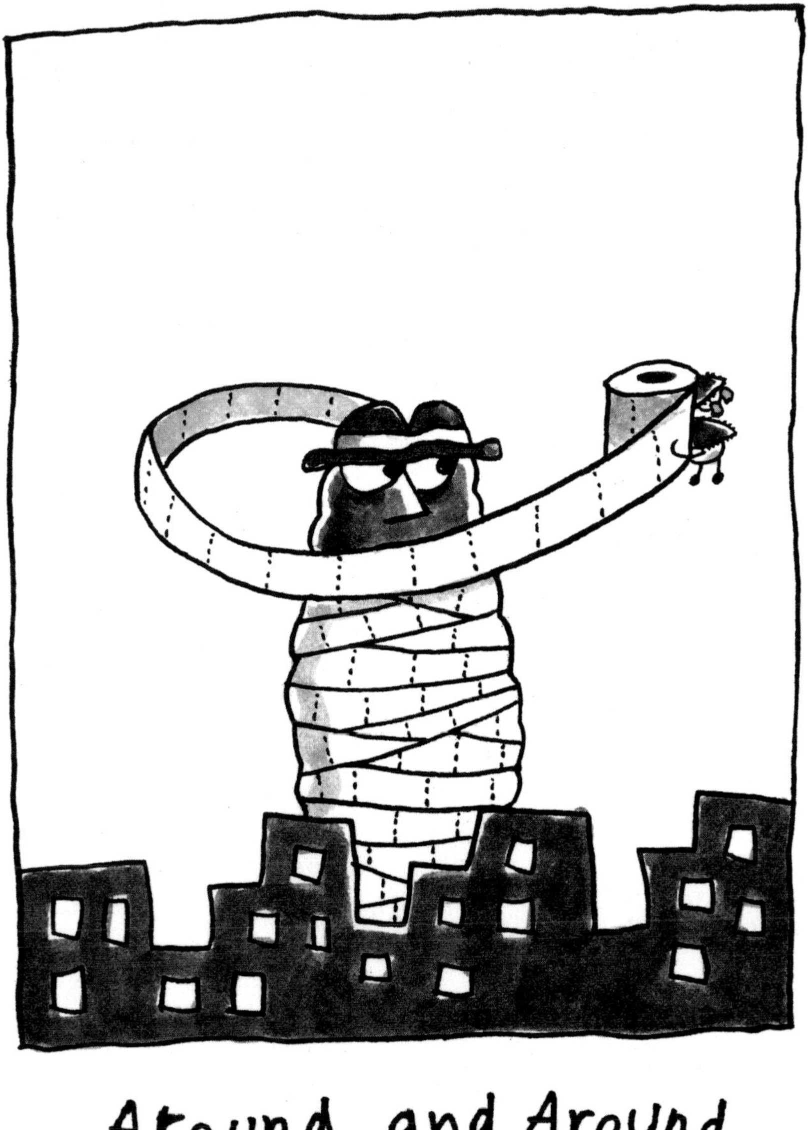

Around and Around
they went

Right
thumB
Here

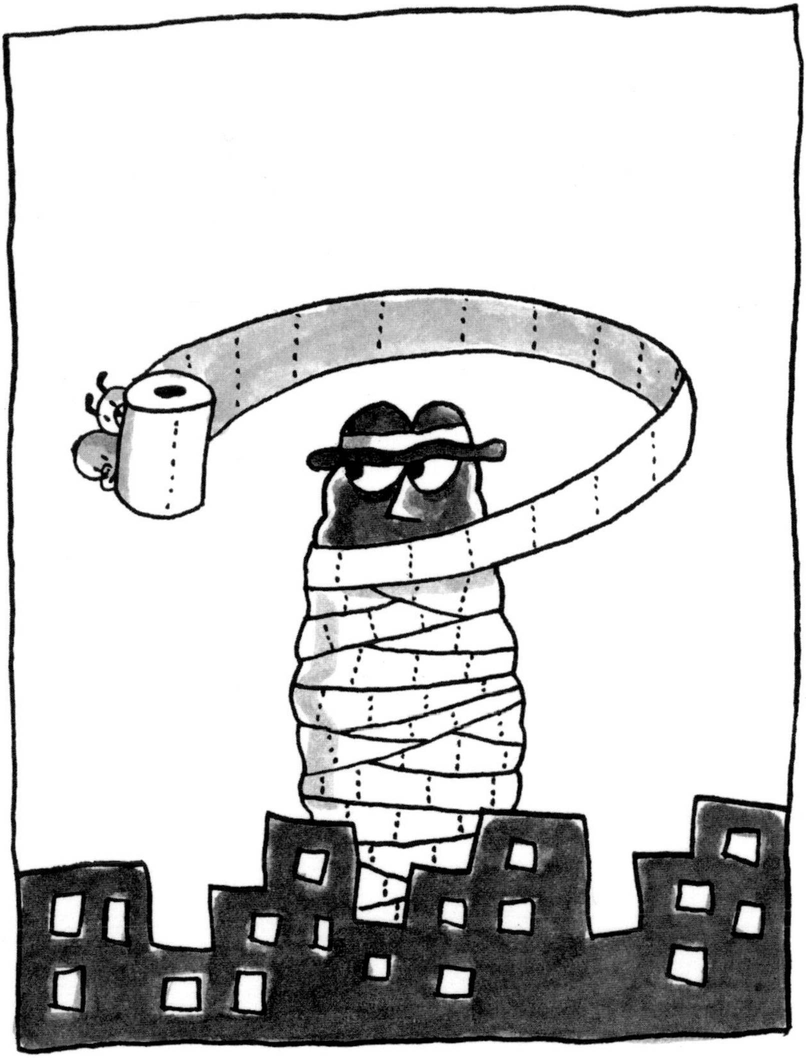

Around and Around
they went

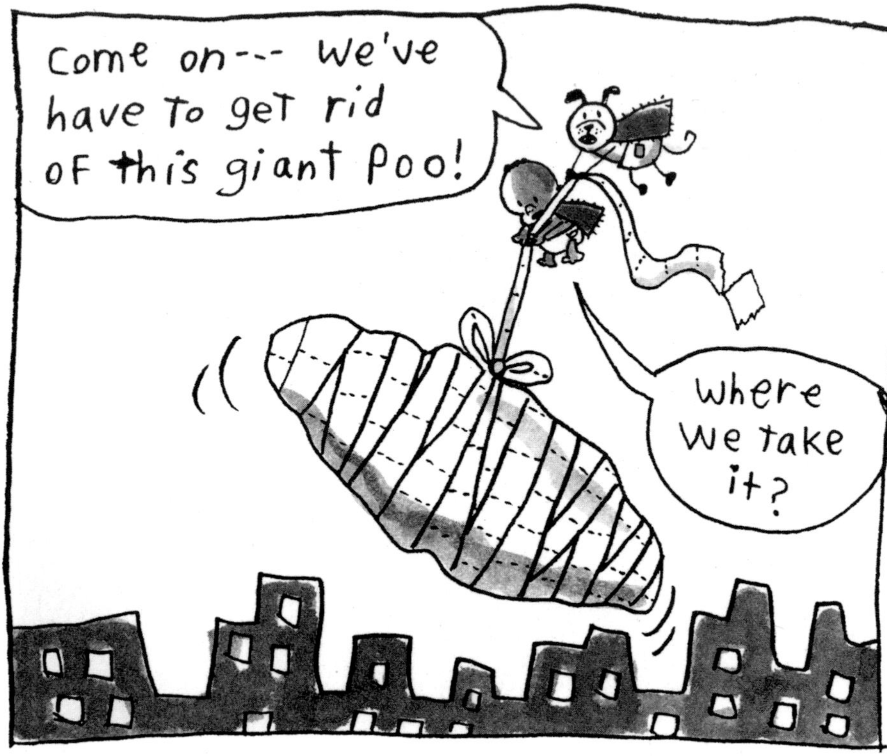
Come on--- we've have to get rid of this giant poo!
Where we take it?

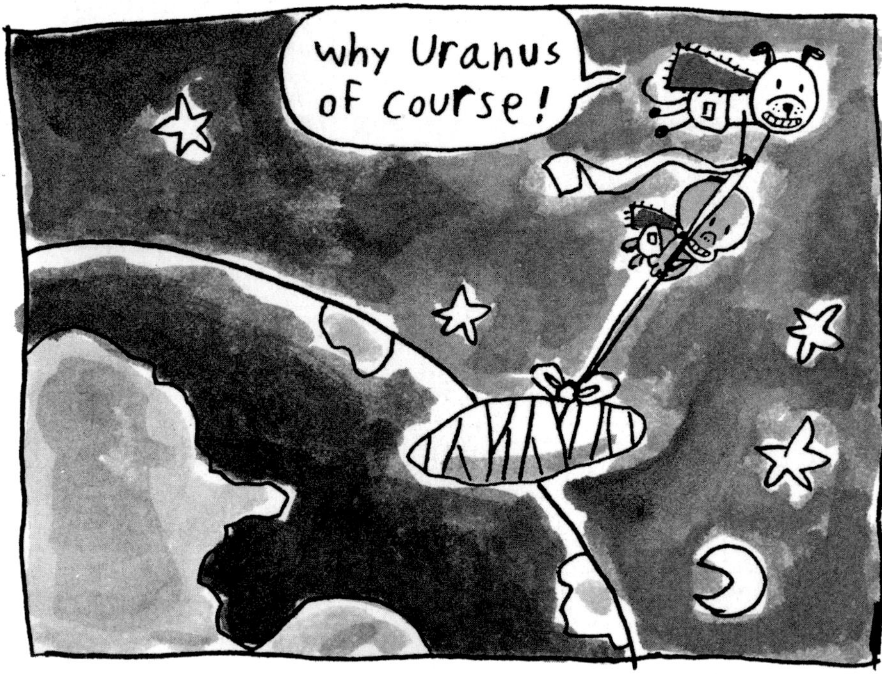
Why Uranus of course!

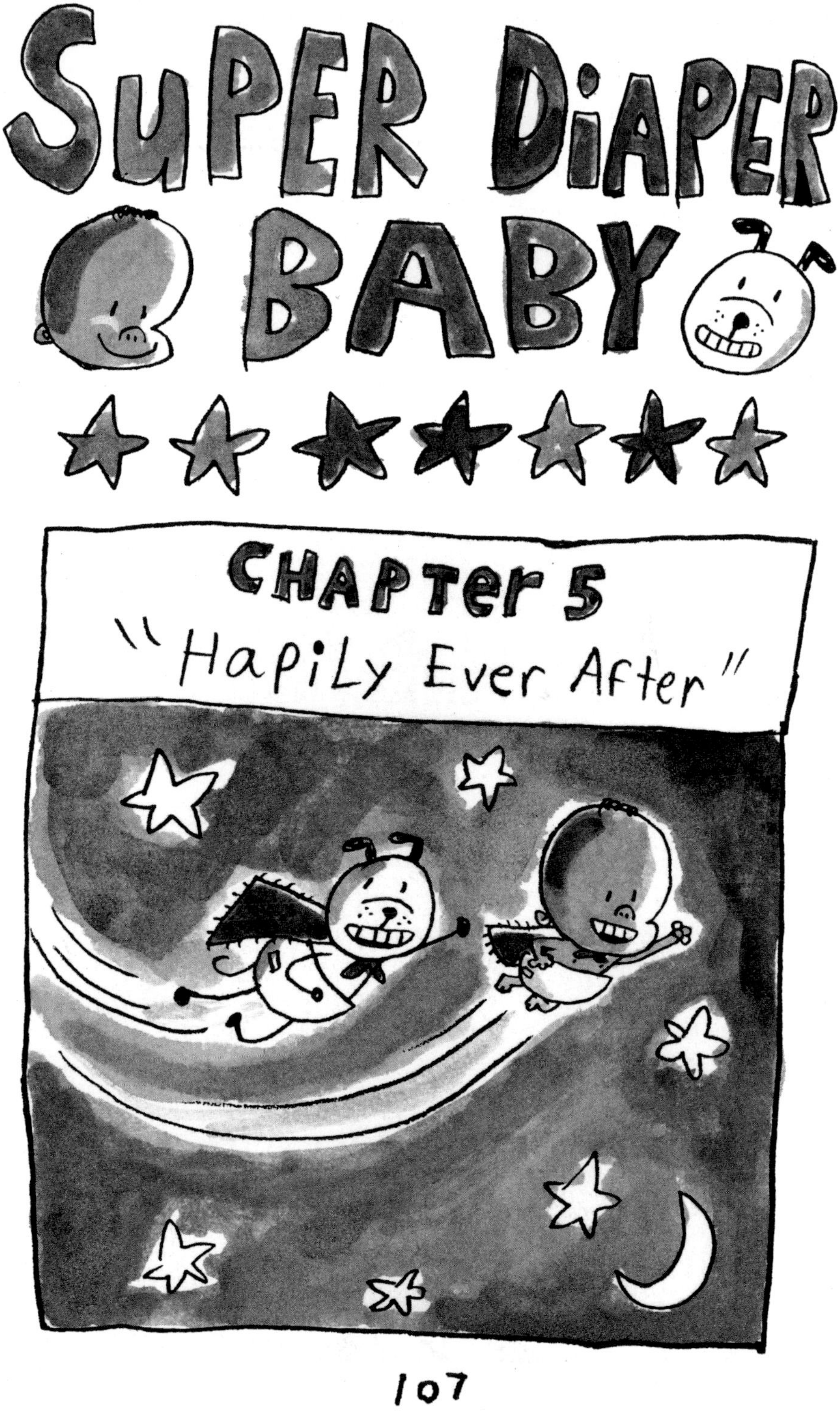
SUPER DIAPER BABY
CHAPTER 5
"HapiLy Ever After"

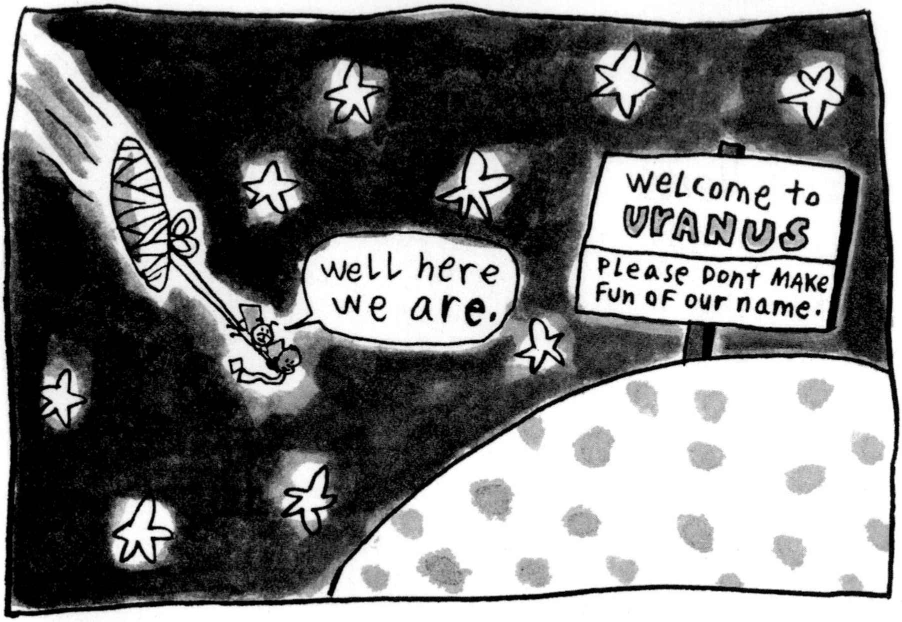
Welcome to
URANUS
Please Dont MAKE Fun of our name.
Well here we are.

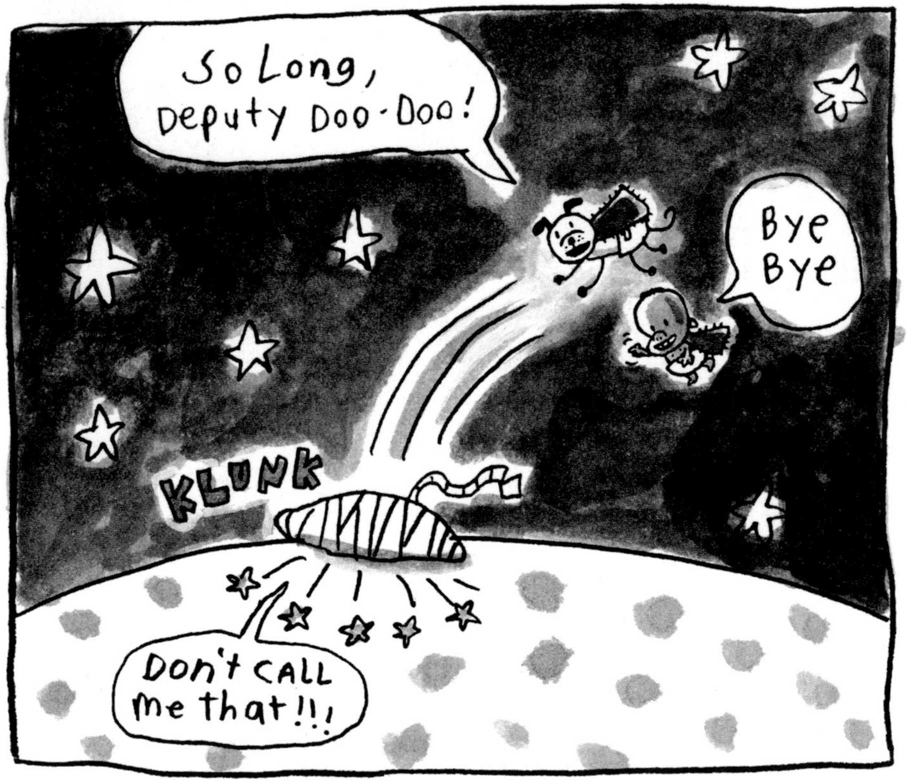
So Long, Deputy Doo-Doo!
Bye Bye
KLUNK
Don't CALL me that!!!

on there way back our Heros STopped at Mars for some refreshments.
STARB
Man, these Places are everywhere!
Can I help you?
Yeah, ILL take a Large water... and a Juice box for the Kid.
Me Like Juice box.
New Alien Super-Power Juice
Super Power Juice
Gives You super powers!
will There be anything else, Sir?
Hmmm

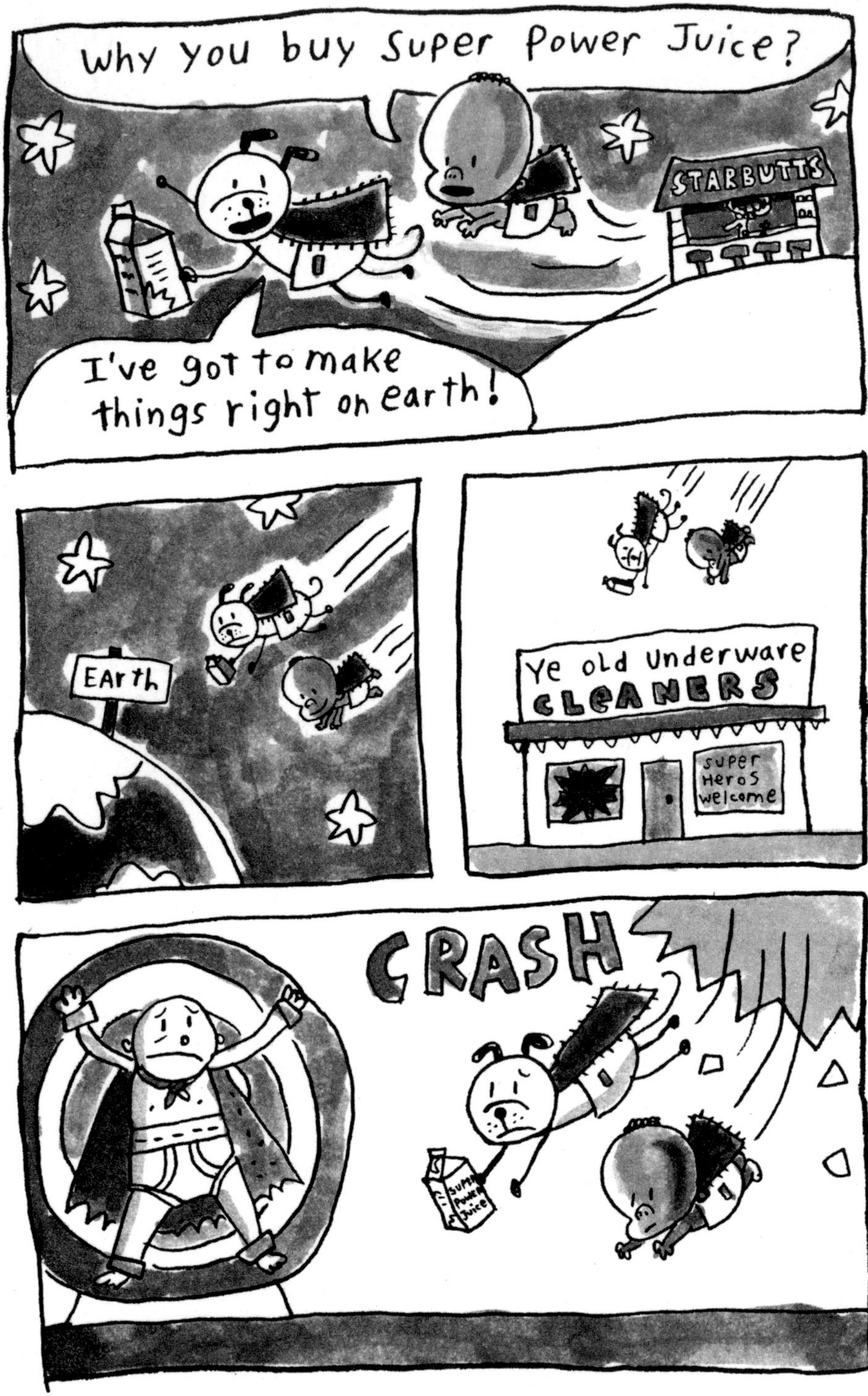

Why you buy Super Power Juice?
I've got to make things right on earth!
STARBUTTS
EArth
Ye old Underware CLEANERS
Super Heros welcome
CRASH
Super Power Juice

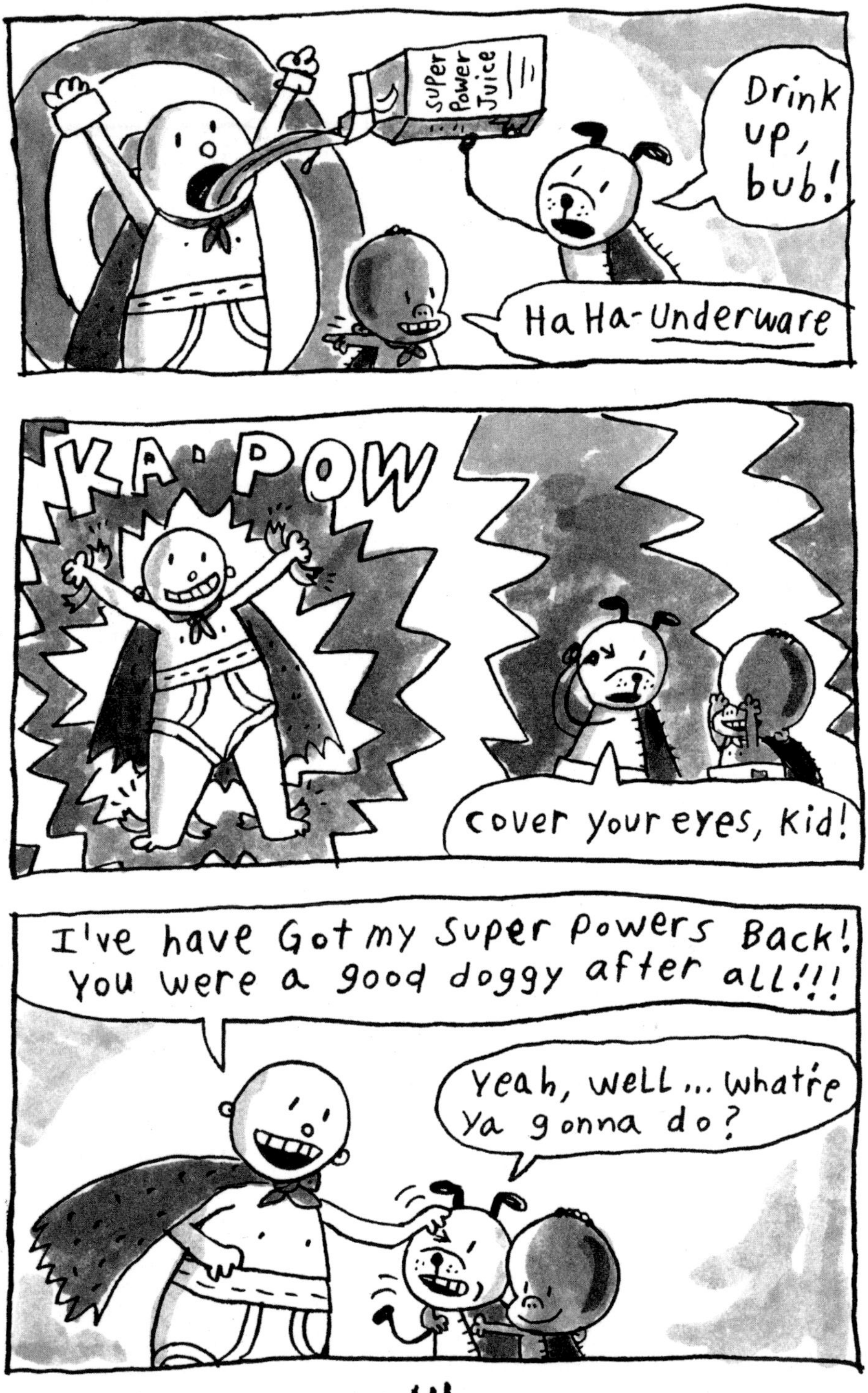
Super Power Juice
Drink up, bub!
Ha Ha-Underware
KA-POW
cover your eyes, Kid!
I've have Got my Super Powers Back! You were a good doggy after all!!!
Yeah, well... whatre ya gonna do?

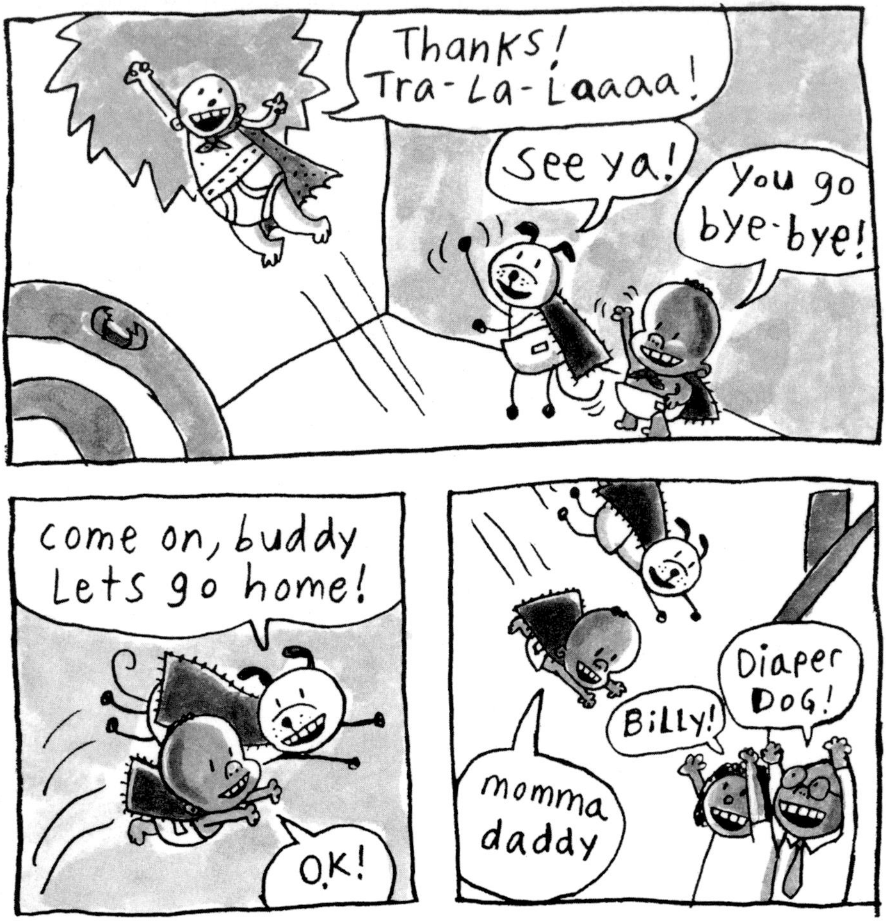
Thanks! Tra-La-Laaaa!
See ya!
You go bye-bye!
come on, buddy Lets go home!
O.K!
momma daddy
Billy!
Diaper Dog!

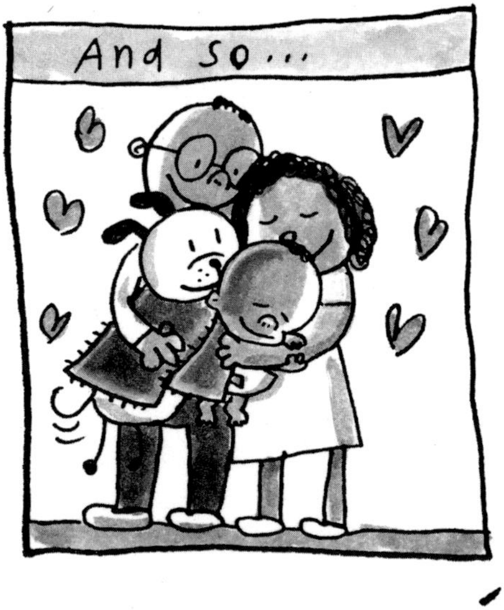
And so...

The LAST FLIP-O-RAMA

Left Hand Here

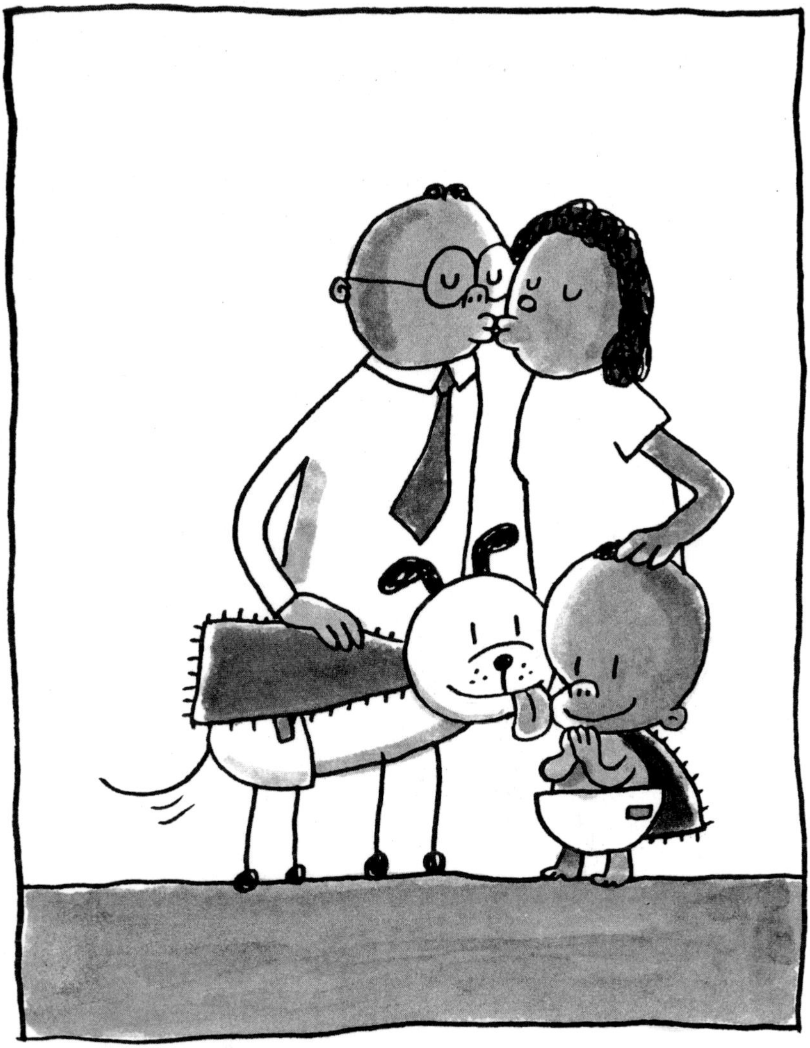

And they all lived
Hapily ever After

Right
thumb
Here

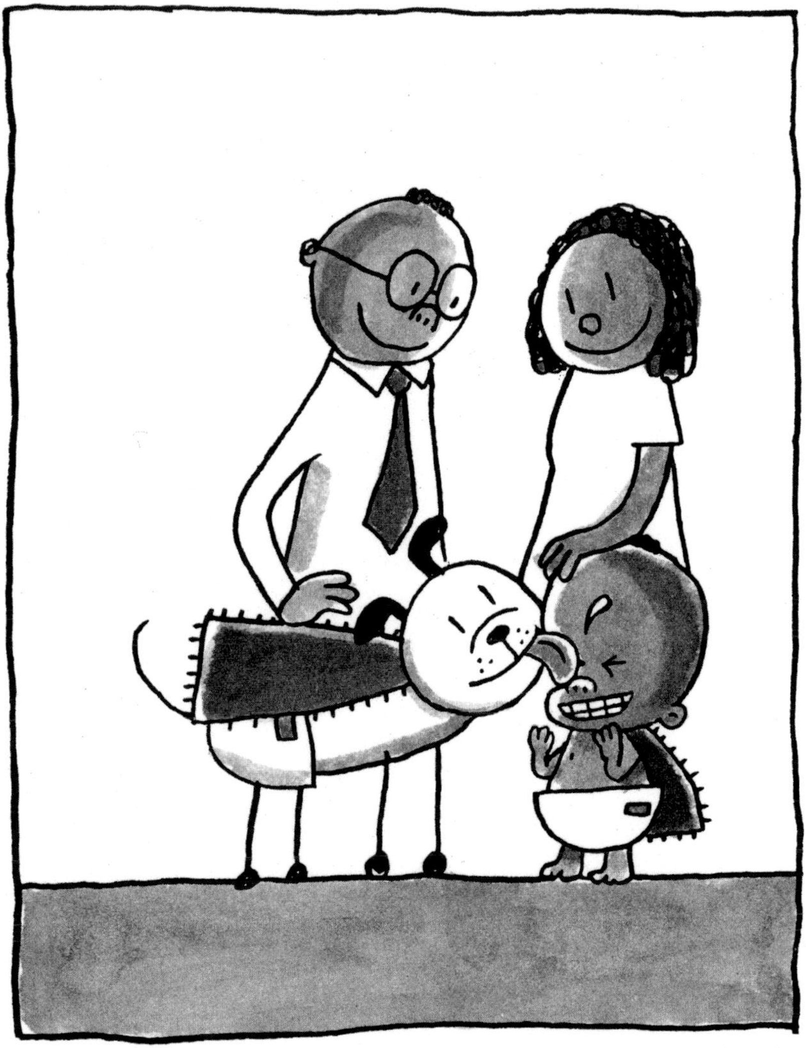

And they all Lived
HapiLy ever After

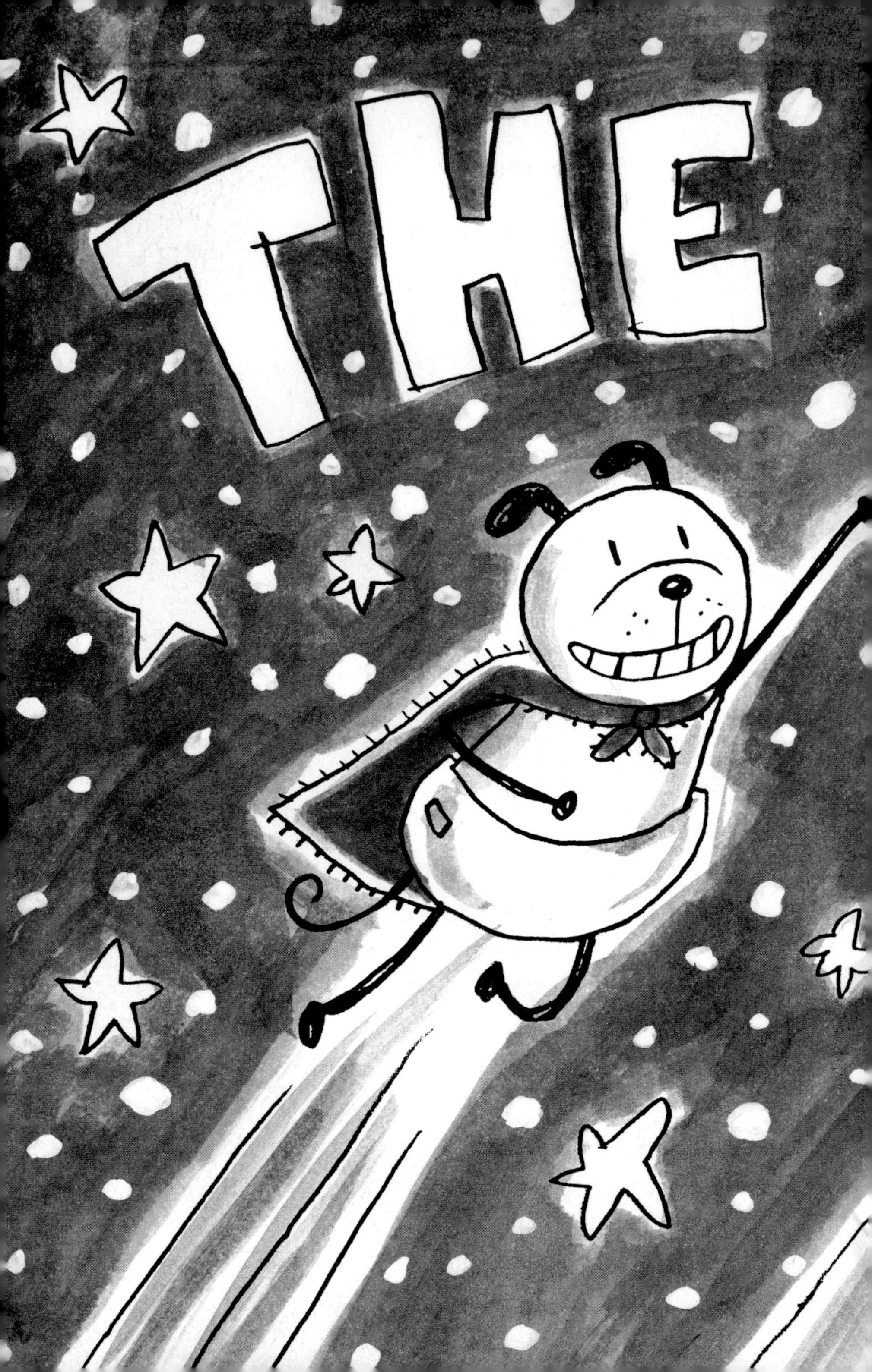
THE

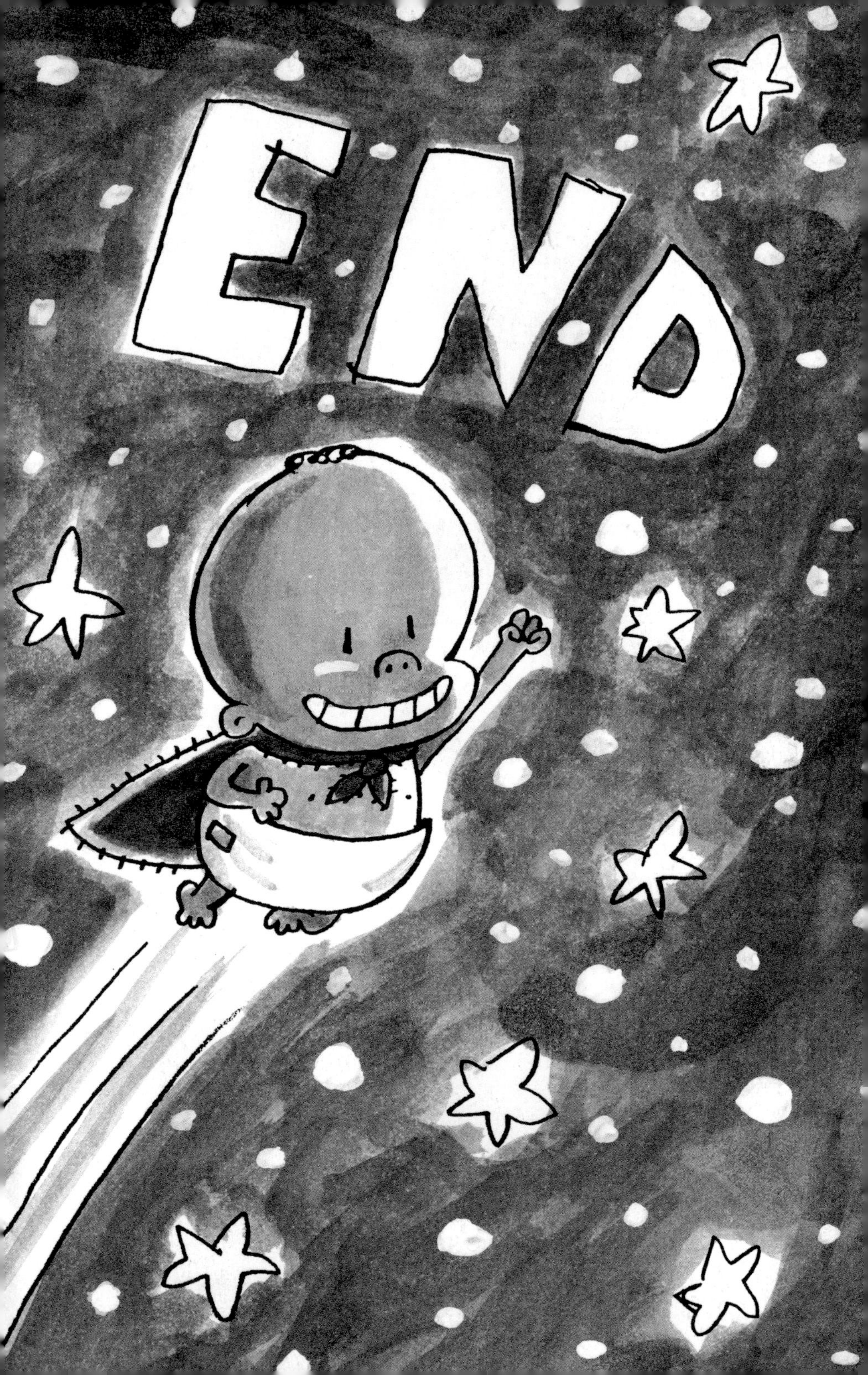
END

HOW 2 DRAW
Super Diaper Baby

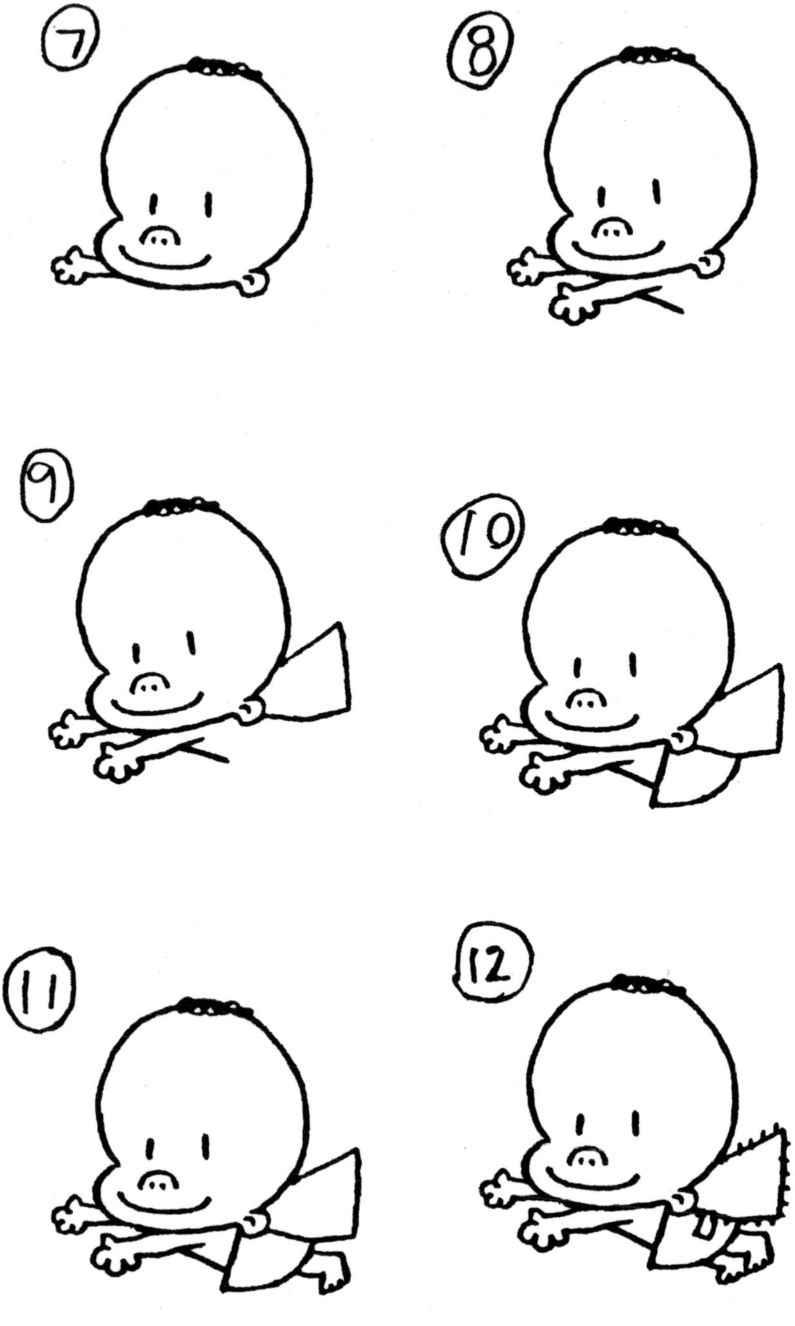
7
8
9
10
11
12

How 2 Draw Diaper Dog

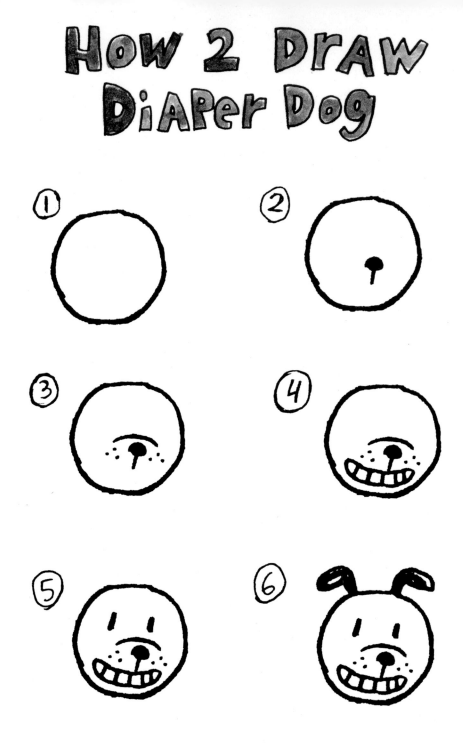

How 2 Draw Deputy Doo-Doo

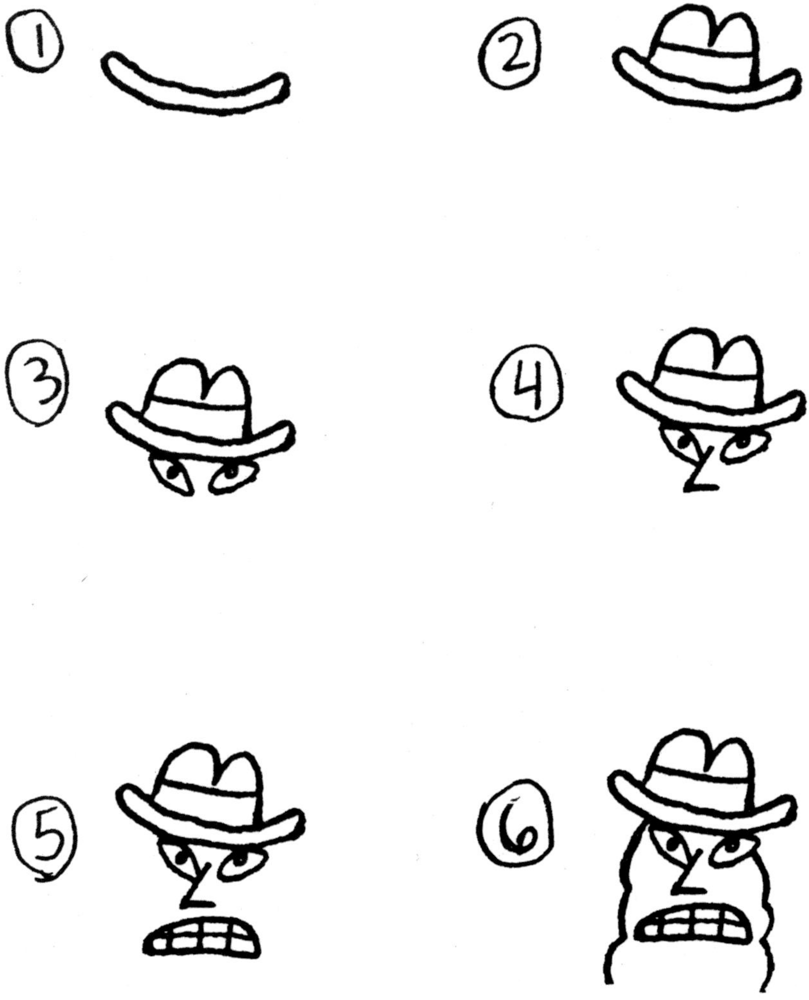

1
2
3
4
5
6

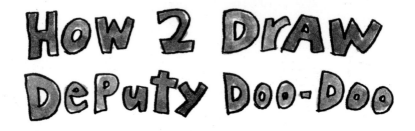

123

How 2 Draw The Robo-Ant 2000

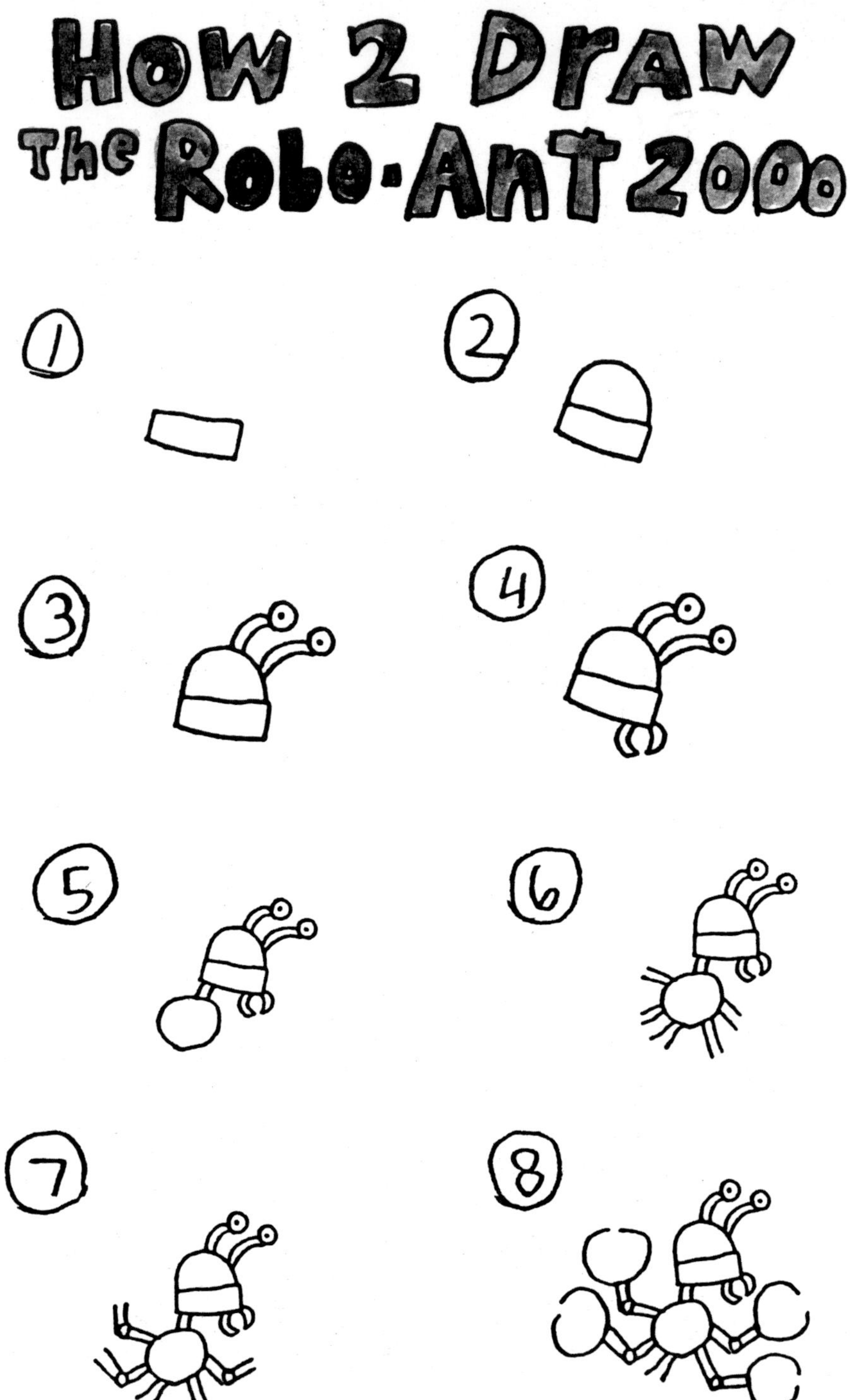
1
2
3
4
5
6
7
8

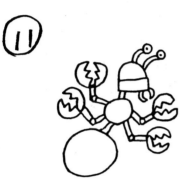

About the Author and Illustrator

GEORGE BEARD (age 9 ¾) is the co-creator of such wonderful comic book characters as Captain Underpants, Timmy the Talking Toilet, and The Amazing Cow Lady.

Besides making comics, George enjoys skateboarding, watching TV, playing video games, pulling pranks, and saving the world. His favorite food is chocolate chip cookies.

George lives with his mom and dad, and his two cats, Porky and Buckwheat. He is currently a fourth grader at Jerome Horwitz Elementary School in Piqua, Ohio.

HAROLD HUTCHINS (age 10) has co-written and illustrated more than 30 comic books with his best pal (and next-door neighbor), George Beard.

When he is not making comics, Harold can usually be found drawing or reading comics. He also enjoys skateboarding, playing video games, and watching Japanese monster movies. His favorite food is gum.

Harold lives with his mom and his little sister, Heidi. He has five goldfish named Moe, Larry, Curly, Dr. Howard, and "Superfang."

We're Sorry!!!

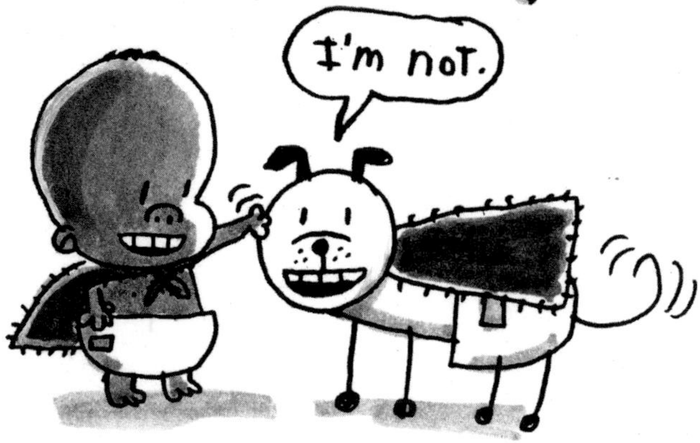
I'm not.

If you were offended by this book, please visit

www.scholastic.com/captainunderpants/funstuff

to download more offensive stuff!

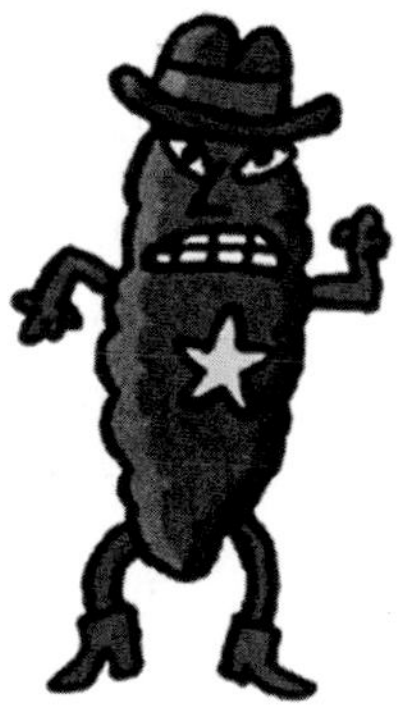

MORE EPIC NOVELS BY GEORGE AND HAROLD

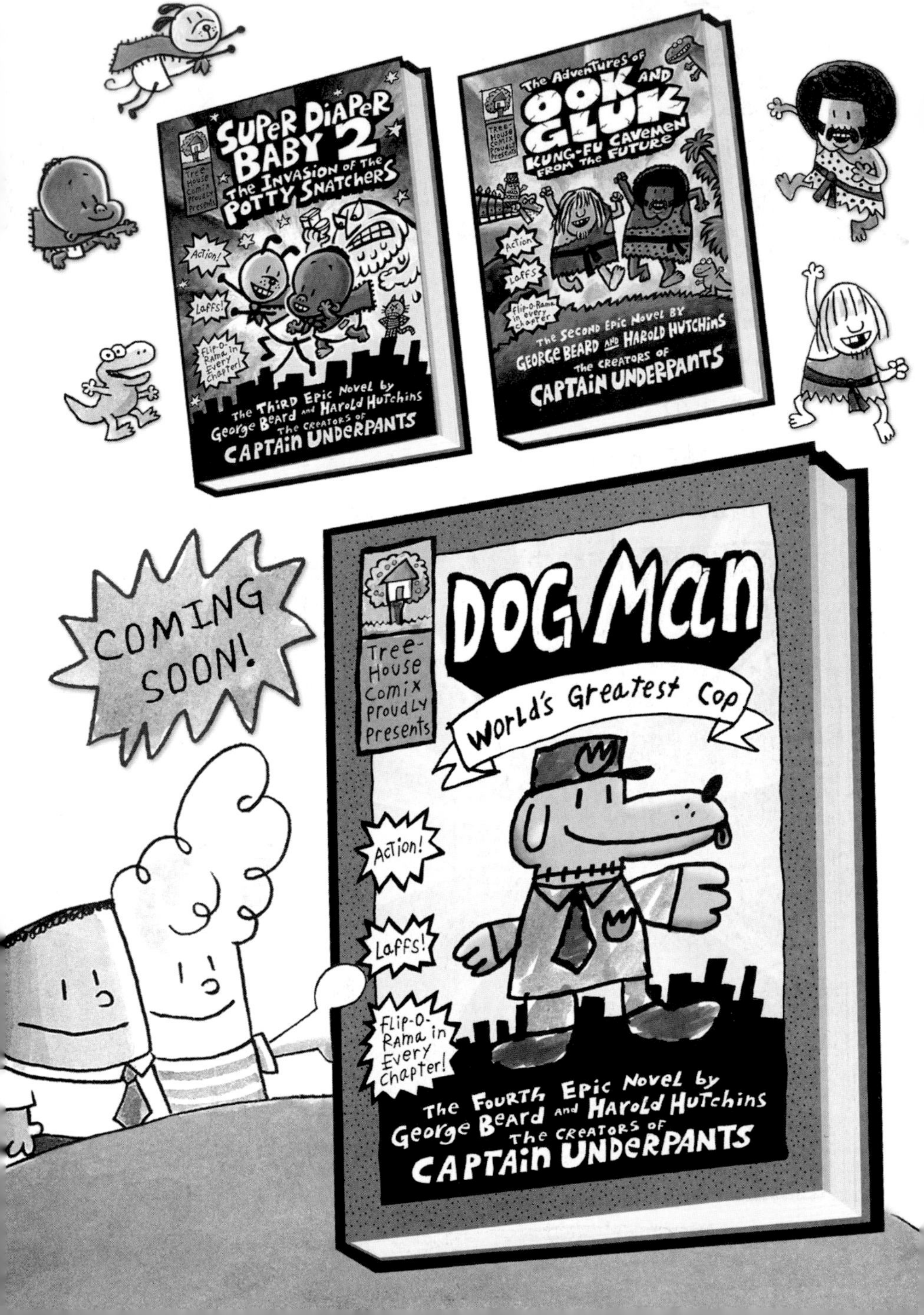

Super Diaper Baby 2
The Invasion of the Potty Snatchers
Tree House Comix Proudly Presents
Action!
Laffs!
Flip-O-Rama in Every Chapter!
The Third Epic Novel by George Beard and Harold Hutchins
The Creators of Captain Underpants
The Adventures of Ook and Gluk
Kung-Fu Cavemen from the Future
Action
Laffs
Flip-O-Rama in every chapter
The Second Epic Novel by George Beard and Harold Hutchins
The Creators of Captain Underpants
COMING SOON!
Tree-House Comix Proudly Presents
DOG MAN
World's Greatest Cop
Action!
Laffs!
Flip-O-Rama in Every Chapter!
The Fourth Epic Novel by George Beard and Harold Hutchins
The Creators of CAPTAIN UNDERPANTS

The Adventures of SUPER DiAPER BABY
Behind the Baby

Read on for the behind-the-scenes story about the making of this book, pages from Dav Pilkey's sketchbook, and more!

THE STORY BEHIND THE STORY

In case you didn't know, this book was really written by George and Harold's alter ego—me! My name is Dav Pilkey. That's me on the right.

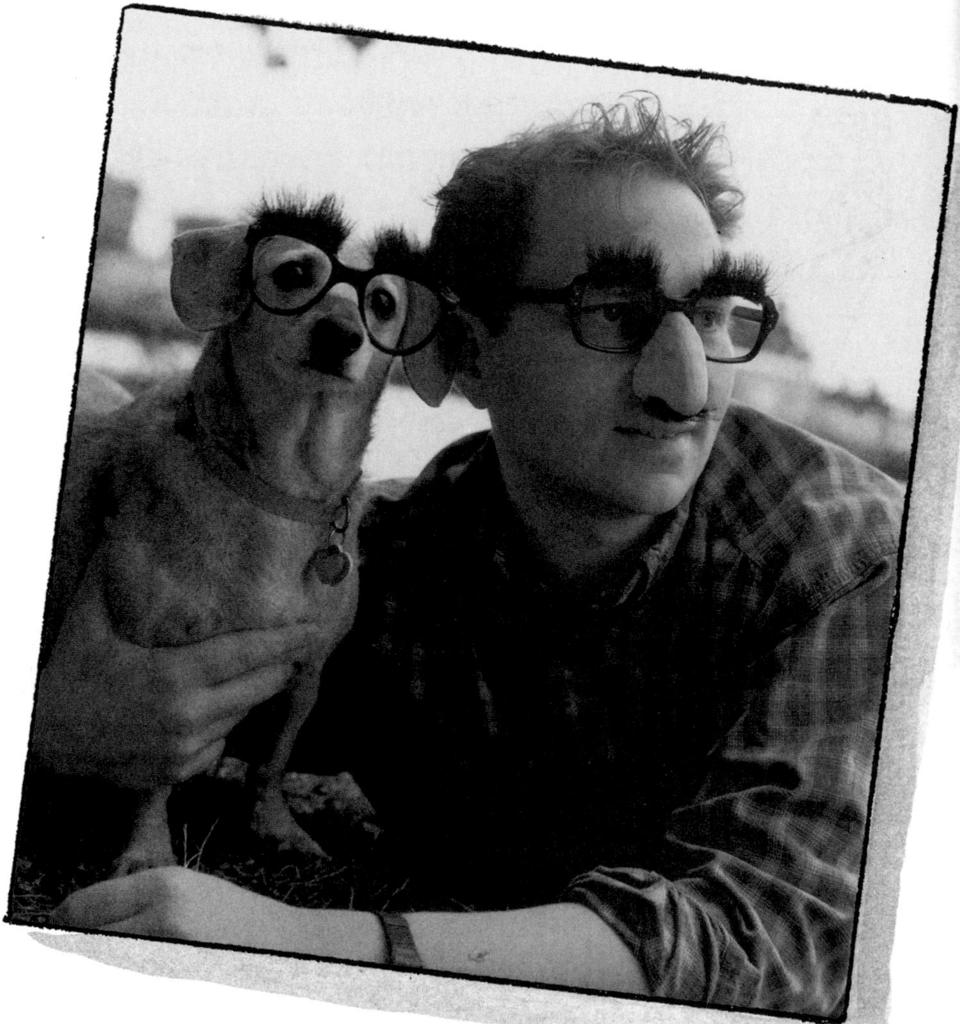

George and Harold are very real characters to me. I based both of them on myself when I was a kid. So when I started working on this book, I needed to "become" George and Harold. In my imagination, I stopped being me, and sort of let them take over. I let them create the story they wanted, without worrying about spelling, or grammar, or moralistic plots that would please adults.

I was also inspired by the homemade comic books I receive from kids every day. Their comics sometimes contain poor grammar and misspelled words, and usually have bad guys who are disgusting in one way or another.

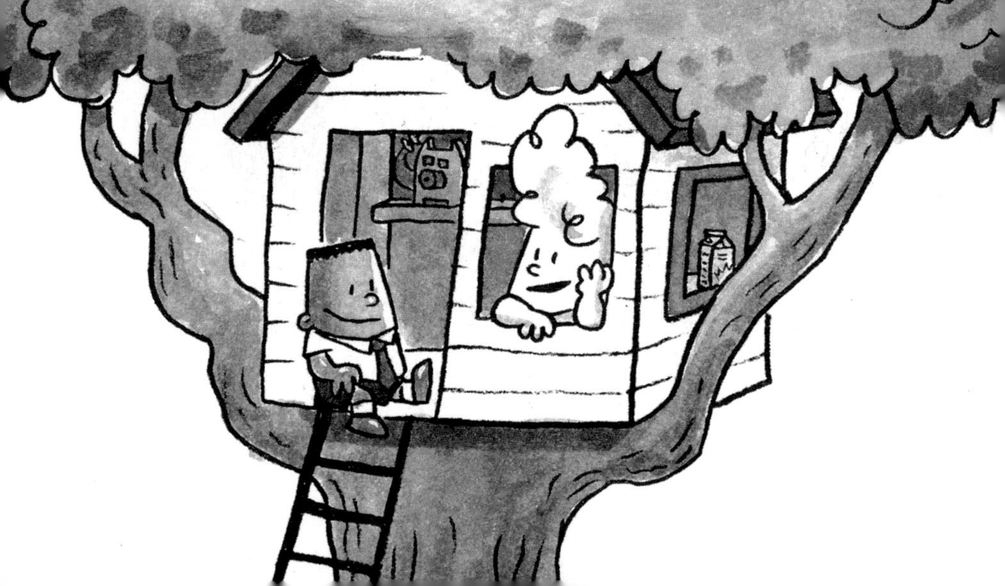

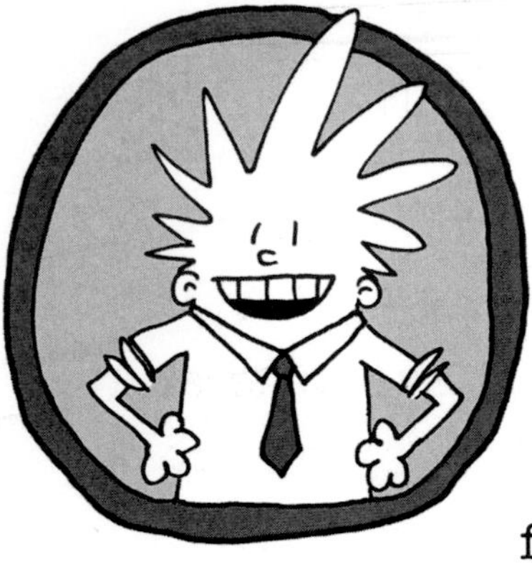

But the amazing thing is that these comics are all made voluntarily. Nobody forces those kids to make comic books. They just do it for fun. And there's always something wonderful about that kind of unprompted creativity. I really tried to capture some of that energy in this book.

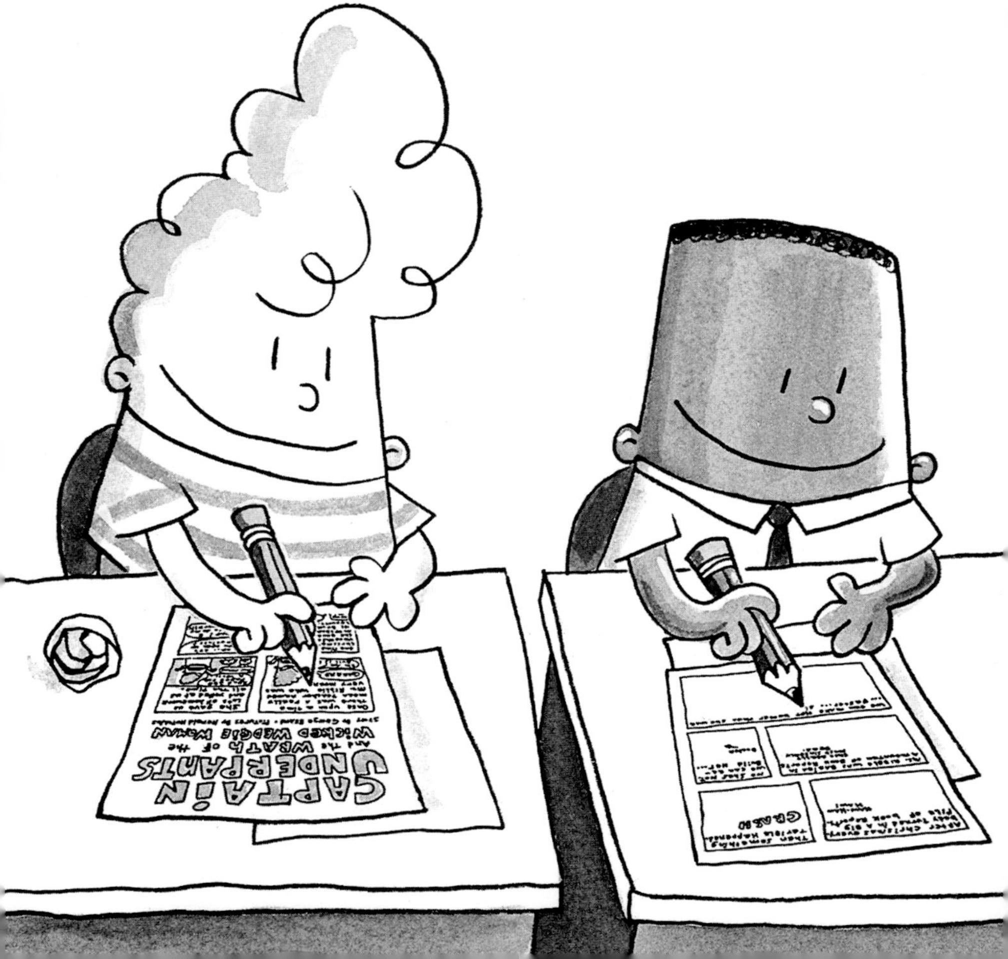
CAPTAIN UNDERPANTS

Part 1: THE INSPIRATION

When I was making *Captain Underpants and the Wrath of the Wicked Wedgie Woman* (which contains three comics by George and Harold), I began to imagine how much fun it would be to do an entire book of comics.

At first, I wanted to do a collection of short, unrelated comic stories by George and Harold. I wrote down a bunch of ideas and titles. But Super Diaper Baby didn't really appear until I began to draw sketches. This sketch was the beginning of everything. I liked the way the baby looked so much that I immediately decided to do a whole book about him.

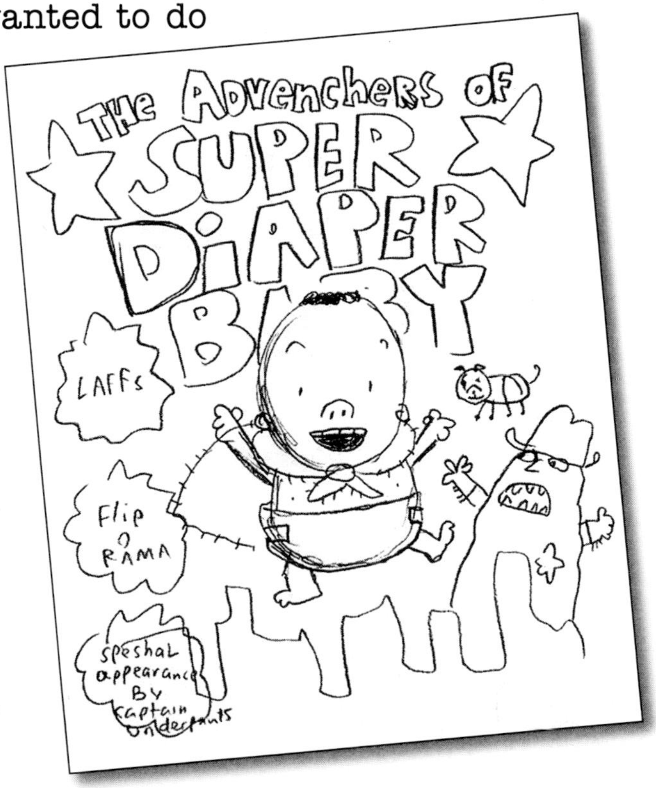
The Advenchers of
SUPER DiAPER BABY
LAFFs
Flip O RAMA
speshal appearance By Captain Underpants

Part 2: THE SKETCHES

When I first begin to work out a story (which I usually do in my head), it helps me to have visual references. So I like to draw sketches of the main characters, and write down who they are and what role they will play in the story.

Here are my first character sketch sheets:

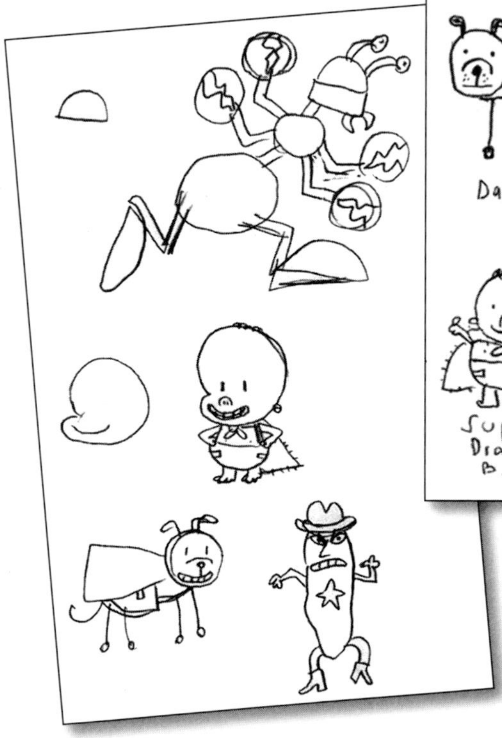

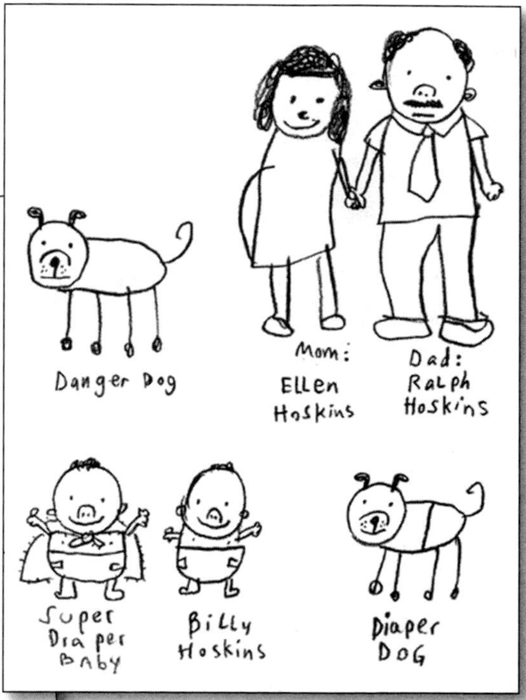
Danger Dog
Mom:
Ellen
Hoskins
Dad:
Ralph
Hoskins
Super
Draper
Baby
Billy
Hoskins
Diaper
DOG

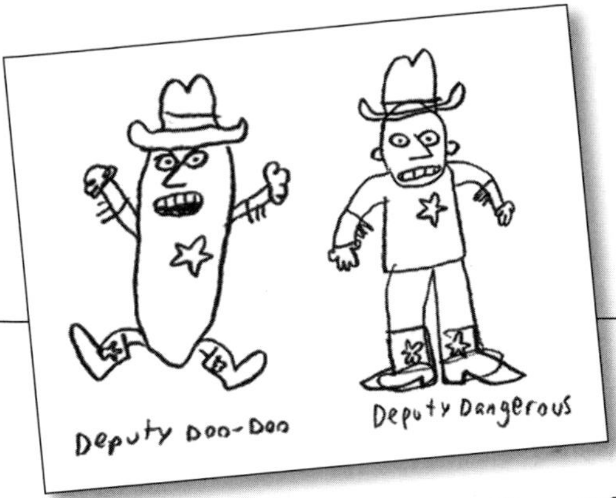
Deputy Doo-Doo
Deputy Dangerous

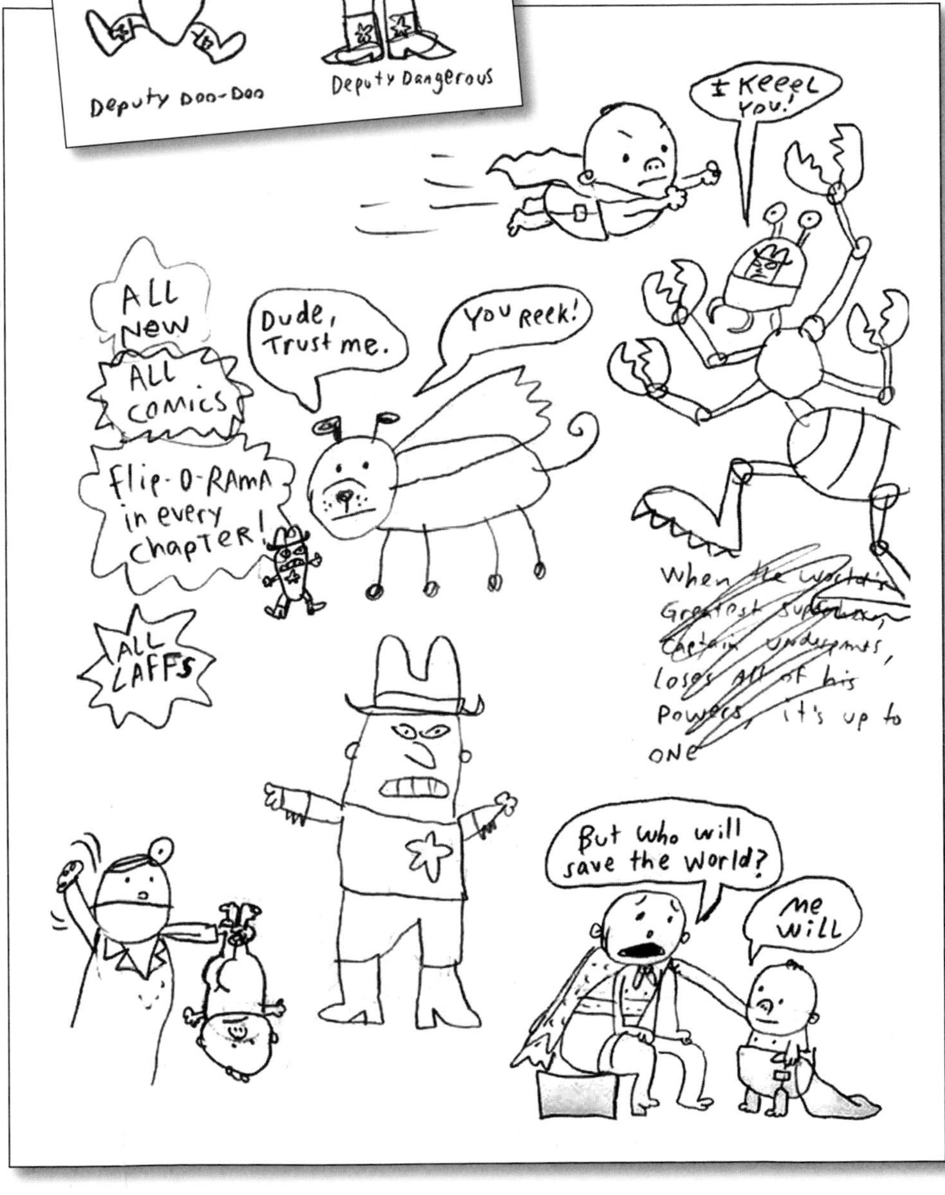
I Keeel You!
ALL New
ALL COMICS
Flip-O-RAMA in every chapter!
ALL LAFFS
Dude, Trust me.
You Reek!
When the world's Greatest Superhero, Captain Underpants, loses All of his Powers, it's up to ONE
But who will save the world?
Me will

Part 3: FIGURING OUT THE STORY

Usually, I find it helpful to make notes on a story BEFORE I write it. The next two pages are from an early draft.

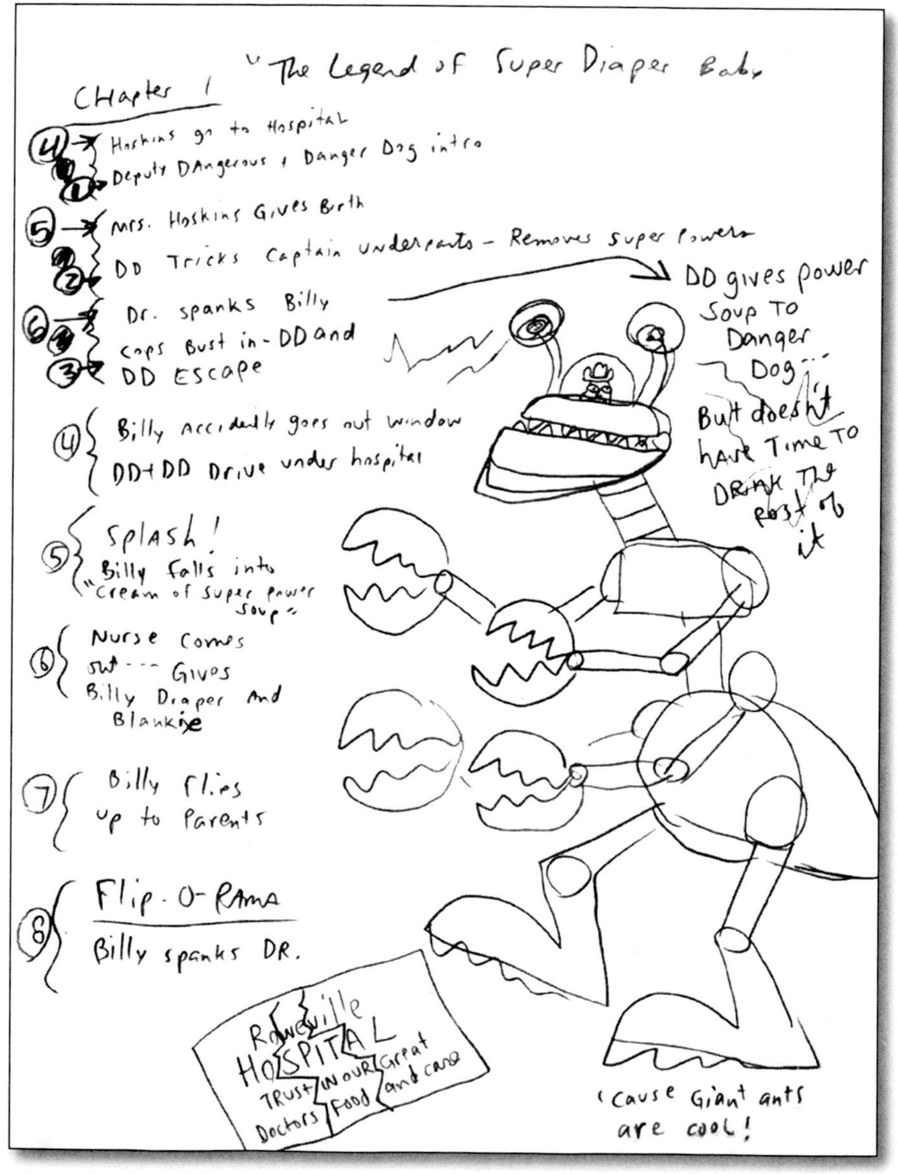
"The Legend of Super Diaper Baby
Chapter 1
4 → Hoskins go to Hospital
1 → Deputy DAngerous + Danger Dog intro
5 → Mrs. Hoskins Gives Birth
2 → DD Tricks Captain Underpants – Removes Super Powers
6 → Dr. spanks Billy
3 → cops Bust in - DD and DD Escape
DD gives power Soup to Danger Dog... But doesn't have Time to DRINK THE Rest of it
4 Billy accidently goes out window
DD+DD Drive under hospital
5 Splash!
Billy Falls into "Cream of Super Power Soup"
6 Nurse Comes out --- Gives Billy Diaper And Blankie
7 Billy Flies up to Parents
8 Flip-O-Rama
Billy spanks DR.
Rawsville HOSPITAL
TRUST Doctors
IN OUR Food
Great and care
'cause Giant ants are cool!

You'll notice that these pages have pictures in the margins.

I find that it's helpful to draw while I write, because I often get good ideas from my sketches.

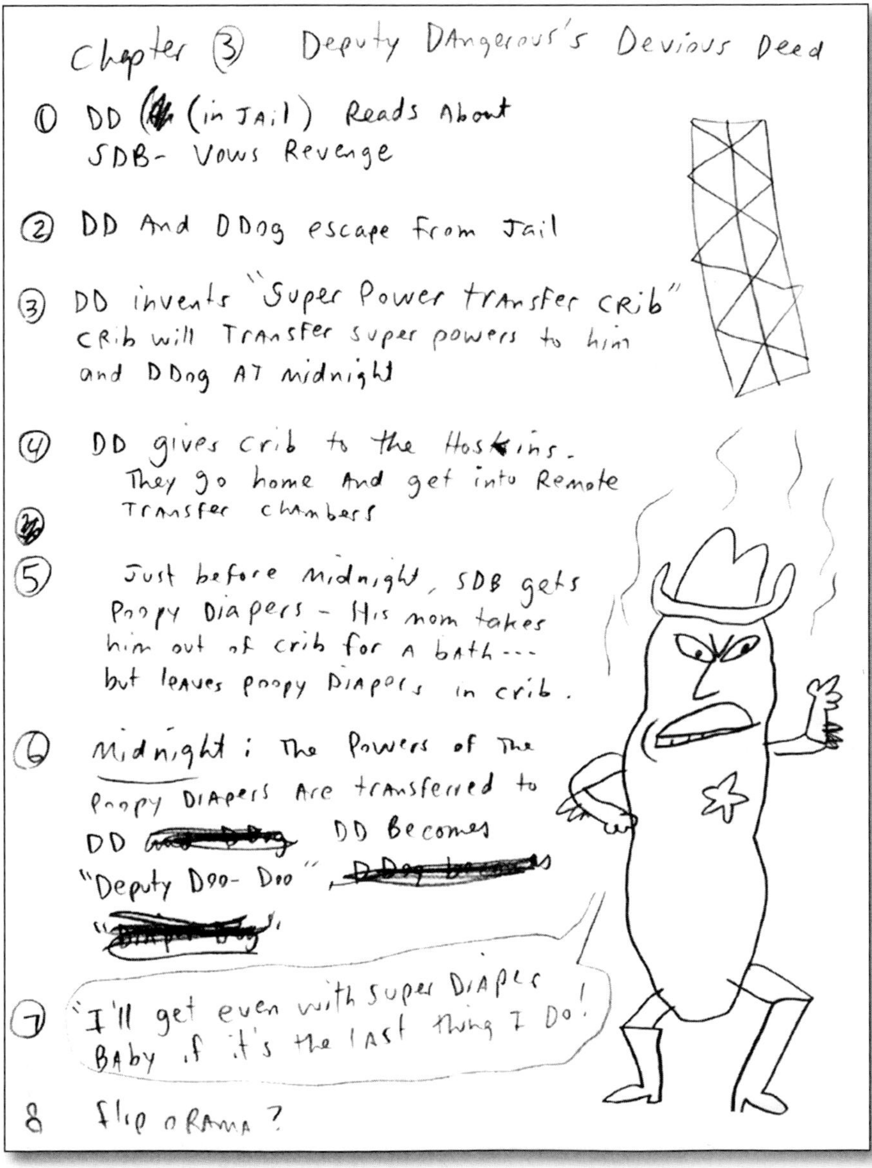
Chapter 3 Deputy DAngerous's Devious Deed
1 DD (in JAil) Reads About SDB- Vows Revenge
2 DD And DDog escape from Jail
3 DD invents "Super Power transfer cRib" cRib will TrAnsFer super powers to him and DDog AT midnight
4 DD gives crib to the Hoskins. They go home And get into Remote TrAnsfer chAmbers
5 Just before midnight, SDB gets Poopy DiApers - His mom takes him out of crib for A bath --- but leaves poopy DiApers in crib.
6 Midnight: The Powers of The Poopy DiApers Are trAnsferred to DD DD Becomes "Deputy Doo-Doo"
7 "I'll get even with Super DiAper BAby if it's the LAst thing I Do!
8 flip oRAmA?

Part 4: THE STORYBOARDS

I created this book in a different way from most of my other books because the story and art were more important than the writing. In fact, I didn't even write the text for this book until I had figured out where the drawings were going to go.

To do this, I created storyboards, which are like a map of the book. They show an illustrator all of the pages of a book at once. Each little box on the next page represents a page in the book. The sketches inside each little box helped me to decide how much room I had to put words on each page.

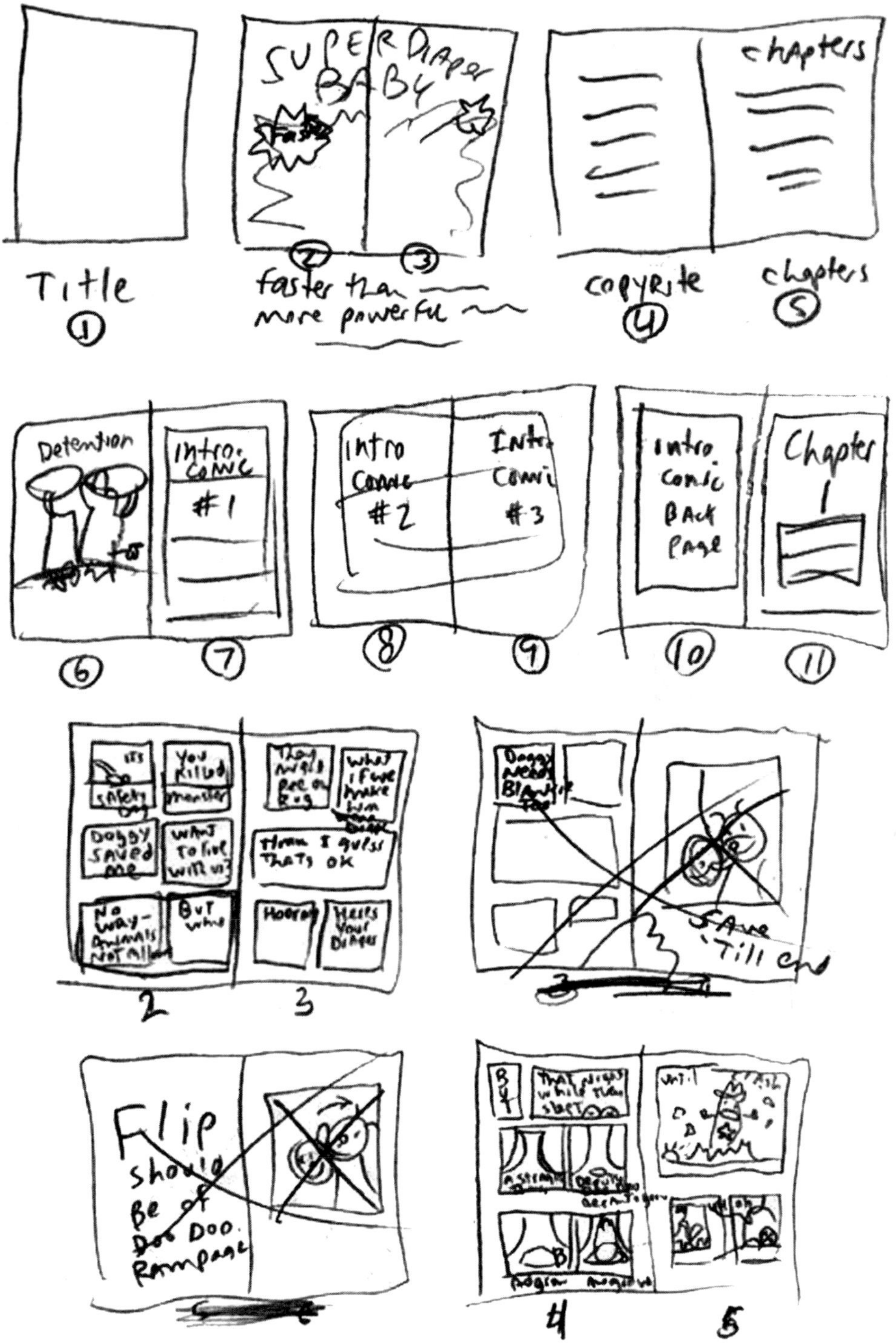

Title
1
SUPER DIAPER BABY
2
3
faster than
more powerful
copyrite
4
chapters
chapters
5
Detention
Intro comic
#1
Intro comic
#2
Intro comic
#3
Intro comic
Back page
Chapter
1
6
7
8
9
10
11
It's
safety day
You killed
monster
Doggy
saved
me
Want
to live
with us?
No
way—
Animals
not allowed
But
who
They might
pee on
rug
Hmm I guess
thats ok
Hooray
Here's
your
diaper
2
3
Doggy
needs
Blankie
too
Save
'till end
Flip
should
be of
Doo Doo
Rampage
That night
while they
slept
4
5

Part 5: THE DUMMY

After the storyboards were completed, I made a dummy, which is kind of like a rough draft. This is where I did most of the work on the book. If you look closely at the next group of pictures, you'll see that I was still trying to figure out parts of the story at this stage.

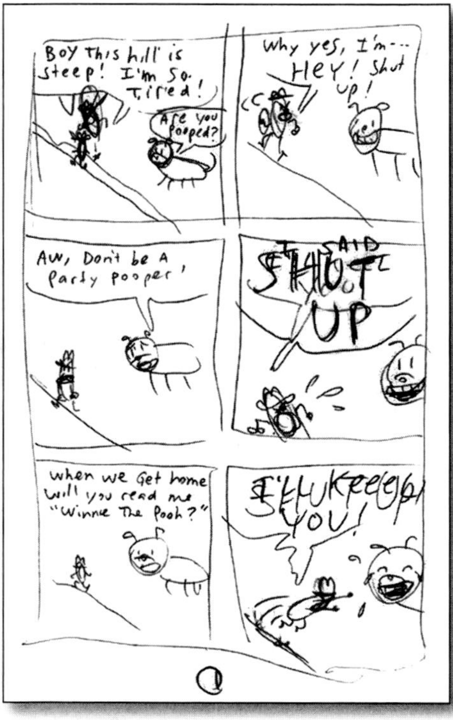
Boy This hill is steep! I'm So Tired!
Are you Pooped?
Why yes, I'm---
HEY! Shut up!
Aw, Don't be A Party pooper!
I SAID
SHUT UP
When we Get home will you read me "Winnie The Pooh?"
1

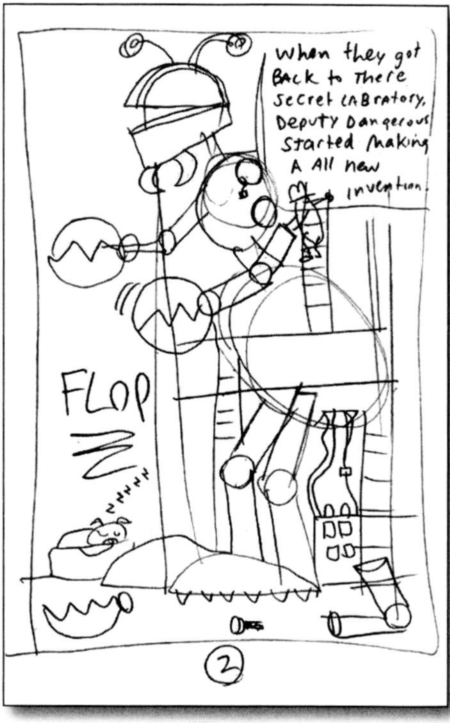
When they got Back to There secret LABratory, Deputy Dangerous Started Making A All new invention.
FLOP
2

There are many differences between what appears in the dummy and what ended up in the book.

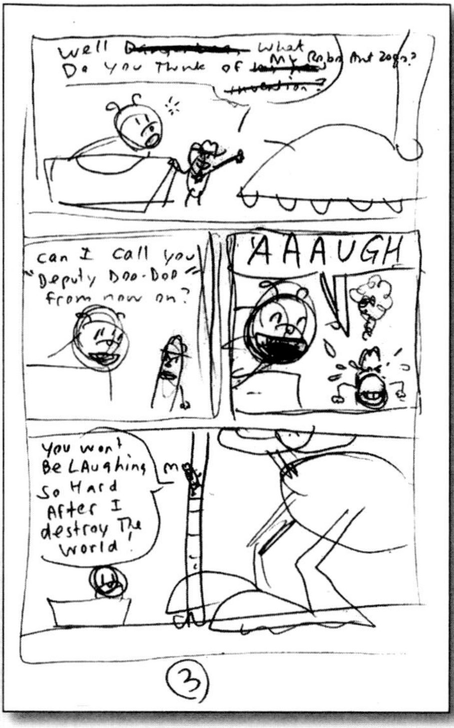
Well What Do You Think of My Robo Ant 2000?
Can I call you "Deputy Doo-Doo" from now on?
AAAUGH
You won't Be Laughing So Hard After I destroy The World!
3

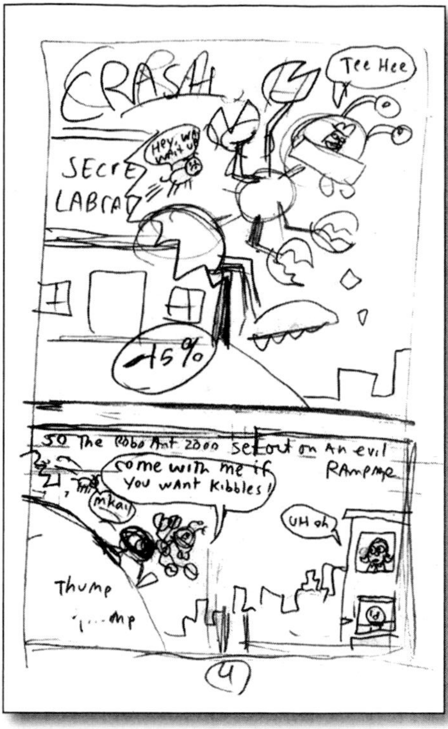
CRASH
Tee Hee
Hey, Wait up!
SECRE LABRA
15%
So The Robo Ant 2000 set out on An evil Rampage
Come with me if You want Kibbles!
mkay
Uh oh
Thump
4

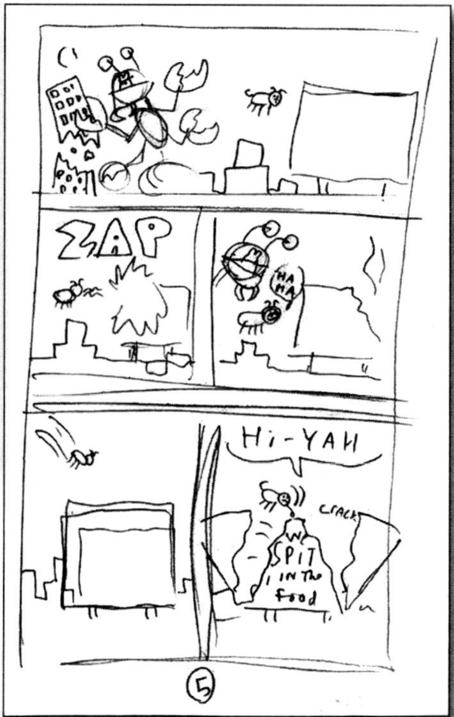
ZAP
HA HA
Hi-YAH
Crack
We SPIT IN The food
5

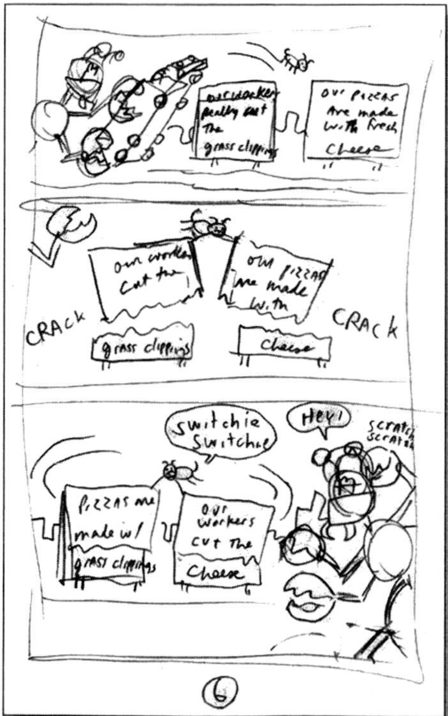
Our workers really cut the grass clippings
Our Pizzas Are made with fresh Cheese
Our workers Cut the
Our pizzas are made With
CRACK
grass clippings
Cheese
CRACK
Switchie Switchie
Hey!
Scratch Scratch
Pizzas are made w/ grass clippings
Our Workers Cut The Cheese
6

Part 6: THE EDITING

During the editing process, changes often need to be made. I decided to drop several panels from chapter 1 because I felt that they slowed down the pace of the story.

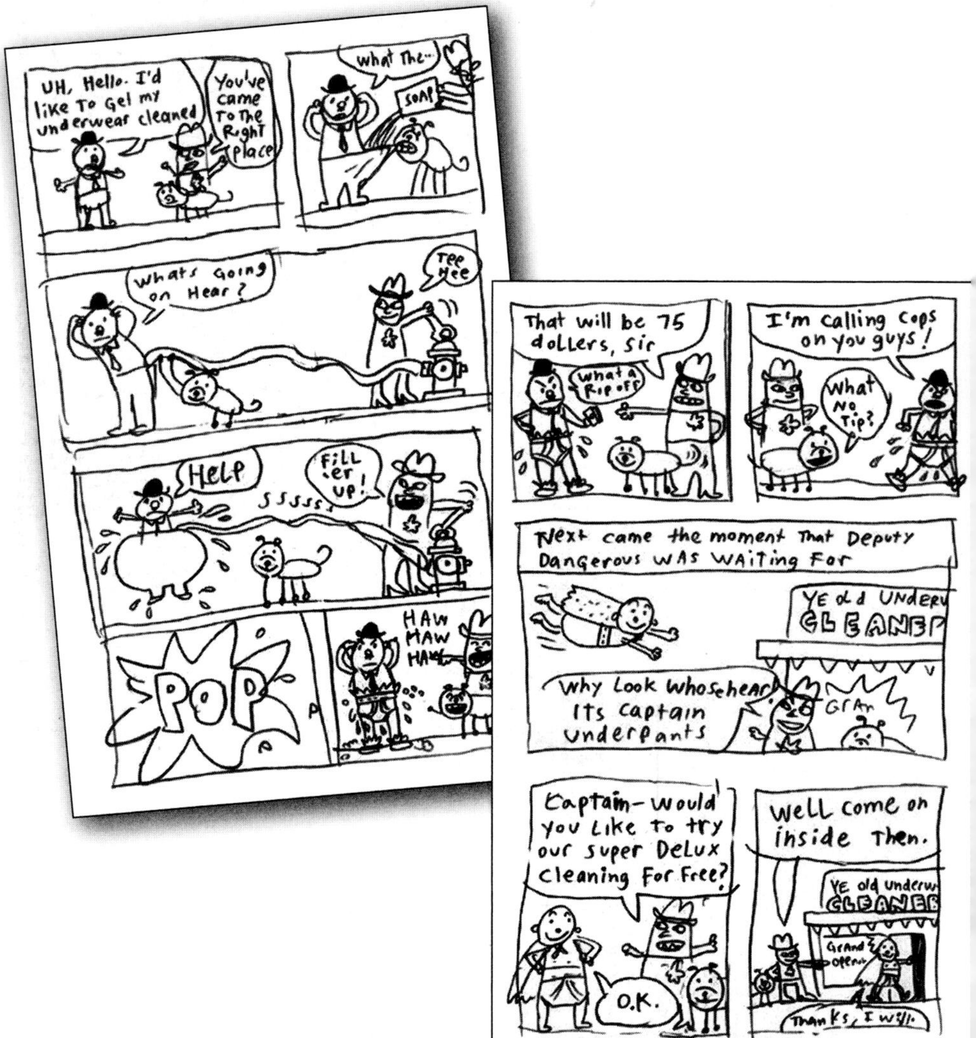

UH, Hello. I'd like To Get my underwear cleaned
You've came To The Right place
what The...
SOAP
Whats Going on Hear?
Tee Hee
HELP
SSSSS
Fill er up!
POP
HAW HAW HAW
That will be 75 dollers, sir
what a Rip off
I'm calling cops on you guys!
What No Tip?
Next came the moment That Deputy Dangerous WAS WAiting For
YE old UNDERW
CLEANER
Why Look whosehear its captain underpants
GRRR
Captain- would you Like to try our super DeLux cleaning For Free?
O.K.
Well come on inside Then.
YE old underw
CLEANER
Grand opening
Thanks, I will.

Part 7: THE COVER

Then it was time to draw the cover.

Here is a pencil sketch:

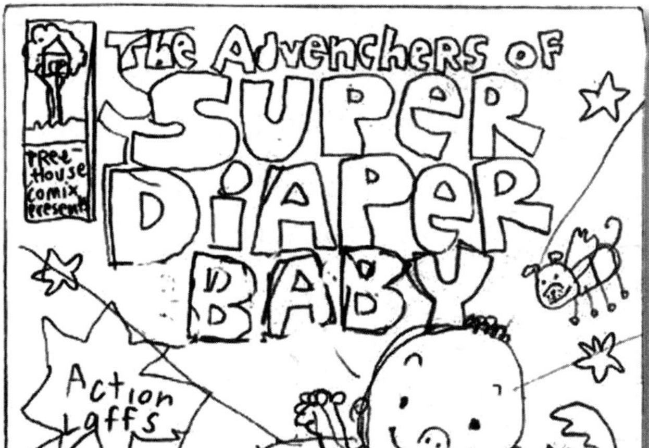
The Advenchers of
SUPER DIAPER BABY
Tree-House Comix Presents
Action Laffs
Inapropriet Laffs Humor
Speshal Guest Star Captain Underpants
THE FIRST GRAPHIC NOVEL BY
GEORGE BEARD

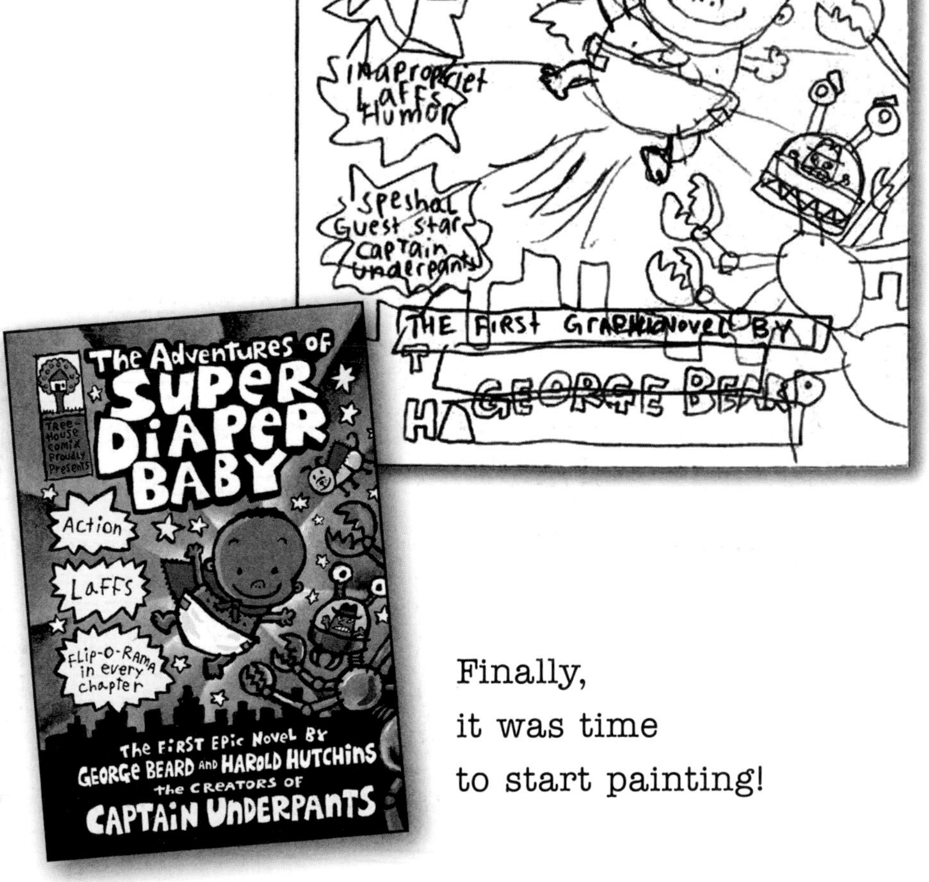
The Adventures of
SUPER DIAPER BABY
Tree-House Comix Proudly Presents
Action
Laffs
Flip-O-Rama in every chapter
The First Epic Novel By
GEORGE BEARD and HAROLD HUTCHINS
the creators of
CAPTAIN UNDERPANTS

Finally, it was time to start painting!

HAVE YOU READ YOUR UNDERPANTS TODAY?

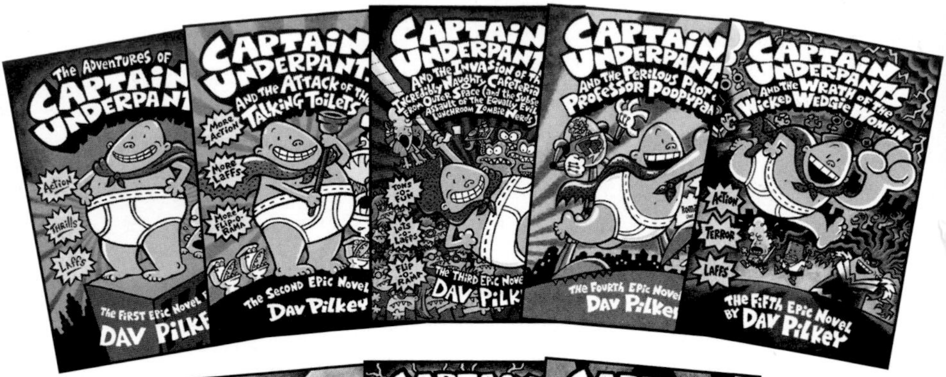
The Adventures of Captain Underpants
The First Epic Novel by Dav Pilkey
Captain Underpants and the Attack of the Talking Toilets
The Second Epic Novel by Dav Pilkey
Captain Underpants and the Invasion of the Incredibly Naughty Cafeteria Ladies from Outer Space
The Third Epic Novel by Dav Pilkey
Captain Underpants and the Perilous Plot of Professor Poopypants
The Fourth Epic Novel by Dav Pilkey
Captain Underpants and the Wrath of the Wicked Wedgie Woman
The Fifth Epic Novel by Dav Pilkey

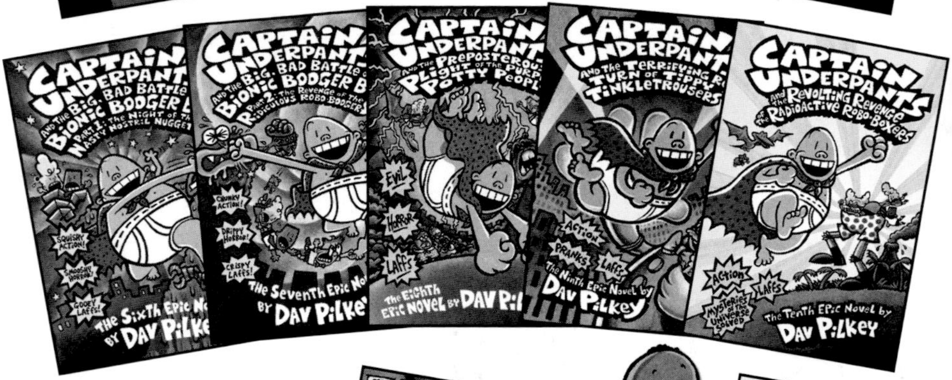
Captain Underpants and the Big, Bad Battle of the Bionic Booger Boy Part 1: The Night of the Nasty Nostril Nuggets
The Sixth Epic Novel by Dav Pilkey
Captain Underpants and the Big, Bad Battle of the Bionic Booger Boy Part 2: The Revenge of the Ridiculous Robo-Boogers
The Seventh Epic Novel by Dav Pilkey
Captain Underpants and the Preposterous Plight of the Purple Potty People
The Eighth Epic Novel by Dav Pilkey
Captain Underpants and the Terrifying Return of Tippy Tinkletrousers
The Ninth Epic Novel by Dav Pilkey
Captain Underpants and the Revolting Revenge of the Radioactive Robo-Boxers
The Tenth Epic Novel by Dav Pilkey

Check out THE ADVENTURES OF CAPTAIN UNDERPANTS APP!

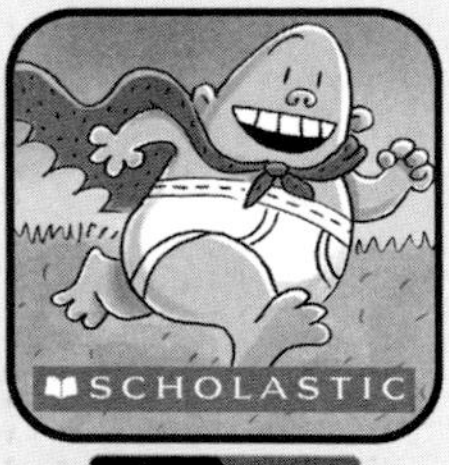
SCHOLASTIC

Available on the App Store

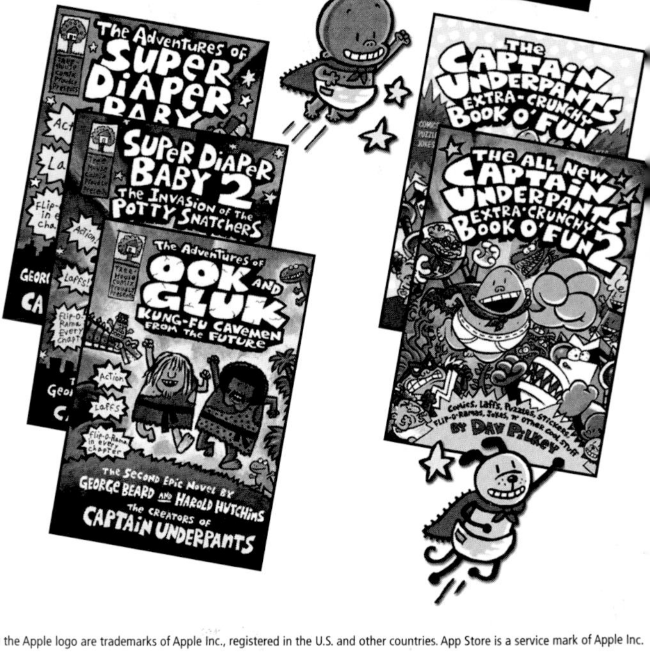
The Adventures of Super Diaper Baby
Super Diaper Baby 2 The Invasion of the Potty Snatchers
The Adventures of Ook and Gluk Kung-Fu Cavemen from the Future
The Second Epic Novel by George Beard and Harold Hutchins
The Creators of Captain Underpants
The Captain Underpants Extra-Crunchy Book o' Fun
The All New Captain Underpants Extra-Crunchy Book o' Fun 2
By Dav Pilkey